The LOST and FOUND NECKLACE

LOUISA LEAMAN

sourcebooks
landmark

Published by Sourcebooks Landmark, an imprint of Sourcebooks
P.O. Box 4410, Naperville, Illinois 60567-4410
(630) 961-3900
sourcebooks.com

Library of Congress Cataloging-in-Publication Data

Names: Leaman, Louisa, author.
Title: The lost and found necklace : a novel / Louisa Leaman.
Description: Naperville, Illinois : Sourcebooks Landmark, [2021]
Identifiers: LCCN 2020058173 (print) | LCCN 2020058174 (ebook) |
    (trade paperback) | (epub)
Classification: LCC PR6112.E245 L67 2021 (print) | LCC PR6112.E245
    (ebook) | DDC 823/.92--dc23
LC record available at https://lccn.loc.gov/2020058173
LC ebook record available at https://lccn.loc.gov/2020058174

Printed and bound in Canada.
MBP 10 9 8 7 6 5 4 3 2 1

To Danae & Thom

Chapter One

BEHIND THE HEAVY OAK DOORS OF HUTCHINS AUCTIONEERS LIES A necklace in a glass cabinet, waiting for the touch of warm skin and the eyes that will admire it in its next cycle of life. Like all good heirloom jewelry, this art nouveau beauty holds more energy than its small, exquisite form would suggest. Jess Taylor, nearing thirty and frequently fearful of her expanding quarter-life crisis, has little idea what the necklace might do for her, but nevertheless feels rather sentimental as she stares at the glossy auction catalog photo and its accompanying description:

> An emblematic art nouveau design comprising a silver neck chain with a central butterfly pendant and moonstone. The wings are a fine example of the "plique-à-jour" enameling technique, embellished with mother-of-pearl and set within a delicate silver frame. A combination of twentieth-century craftsmanship and the allure of one of nature's most enchanting creatures make this a perfect addition to any collection or an ideal gift for a loved one.

She spins back to the one childhood memory in which the necklace features: herself in her mother's bedroom, maybe five years old; the pine dressing table with its tantalizing three-way mirror, hair straighteners, a bottle of CK One, that hardened pool of spilled nail polish in the corner. Then, in the drawers, the lipsticks, the hairspray cans, the homemade Mother's Day card from Jess and her sister, Aggie—and best of all, the velvet jewelry box.

This, Jess remembers vividly: the allure of the box, a magnet for her magpie soul; her pudgy hands hovering over the lid, her anticipation as it lifts. That tang of metal, silver chain links running cold and loose through her fingers; the candy-like beads and glass gems. And then the butterfly necklace, the iridescent wonder of its plump, pluckable moonstone; the enamel of its wings glowing like a miniature cathedral window, emerald green.

Jess remembers her mother warning her not to touch the wings, saying "very old" and "art nouveau" with a smile and a faux French accent. Jess looks once more at the catalog photo, imagines the actual necklace in her hand; how it will feel to have it resting in her palm again, so light and delicate, as though it could flutter away at any moment—rather like her mother did.

"Is it usually this rowdy?" Aggie asks, snatching Jess back to the moment. "Feels more like a sweaty boxing ring than an antiques auction."

The room is hot, made worse by the number of people spilling in, coughing, fidgeting, swapping seats, checking their phones, flapping their catalogs, talking loudly.

"Just wait," says Jess. "Some dealers play dirty. I've seen fistfights before."

Aggie eyes her.

"Not me. There's an unspoken etiquette if you're into it. When someone else clearly wants an item, don't deliberately bid it up to make them pay more than they need to and *definitely* don't cut in at the last moment."

Aggie fans herself with the bidding card, then nods at the catalog photo.

"It's pretty, but I'd struggle to find something to wear it with."

Of course Aggie would struggle, thinks Jess. She's a functional dresser. She only has three colors of clothing in her wardrobe: black, white, and navy. Today, it's the crisp white blouse and jeans. She wears the same every Friday, almost as though it's her getting-ready-for-the-weekend uniform, a conscious effort to dial it down. Except there's no dialing down involved. That shirt, not a mark on it, has been starched and pressed to perfection, probably at 5:00 a.m., which is Aggie's "me time." Her jewelry item of choice, aside from her wedding band, is a watch. Very occasionally she'll wear a set of pearl earrings, but always removes them halfway through an evening, because they "irritate" her. Jess, by contrast, plans her clothing around jewelry, sometimes plans her days around it. Life lesson: When wearing long pendants, avoid activities that involve leaning over gas cooktops.

"It's too stylized—"

"It's typical art nouveau, Aggie, which is all about flowing, sensuous lines and whiplash curves."

"Okay, expert, so what exactly is the art nouveau?"

"A short-lived but influential design movement," Jess explains.

Having trained as an art teacher, then built a small online jewelry business, she knows her way around Victorian diamond cuts, Edwardian filigree, and art deco geometry; but it is this, art nouveau, that she loves most of all.

"It lasted from around 1898 to the start of World War I. Essentially it was about good design and craftsmanship, an attempt to backpedal away from the growing taste for mass-produced, machine-made goods."

"Bulgari versus Primark?"

"Something like that. In the simplest terms, think of it as a reaction to the industrial revolution of the nineteenth century—"

"Smelting and slums? Little Victorian kiddies getting their hands trapped in weaving looms?"

"You've watched too many costume dramas, Aggie."

"Why a butterfly?"

"Nature was a hot theme, lots of flowers, insects, and birds. And women. Women seem to feature a lot, either as sexy, naked nymphs or…something scarier."

"Very Freudian. Designed by men, no doubt."

"Well, here's the thing," says Jess, eyes glinting. "Not our necklace. Apparently this one was designed and made by our great-great-grandmother, Minnie Philomene Taylor. Cool, huh? I mean, back then, female jewelry designers were a rarity."

"Very cool," says Aggie, somewhat unconvinced, "but that dangly moonstone will break off in seconds."

She tenses her shoulders, furrows her brow.

"Really, Jess? Are we really going through with this? A thousand pounds for something you'll never dare wear because it's too flimsy?"

"It's survived a century so far," Jess argues, knowing she'll pay five thousand if she has to. "I have faith." She shuts the catalog. "Besides, it's not for me, is it? We're doing this for Nancy."

"Oh yes, dear, sweet grandma Nancy."

"Whatever you think of her," says Jess, eyeing her sister, "she's our only remaining family on Mum's side. When she goes, all our history goes with her. This necklace means something to her. If getting it back into her hands is the one thing I can do, then I'll know I've done my duty."

"Okay, but just so we're clear about the limit—"

Jess feels her eyes roll up in their sockets, her eyelids flicker. How is it, she wonders, that she and Aggie always slip so readily into their little and big sister contours?

"Since the necklace has a reserve price of one thousand, we go no further than that, agreed? Ed wants a skiing trip next February. Steph's broken her phone screen for the millionth time, and Marcus is demanding every game console under the sun. If I blow the contents of my rainy-day jar on a piece of unwearable costume jewelry—"

"Heirloom jewelry."

"Yes, that."

"A piece of heirloom jewelry that represents our family's heritage, Aggie. These things matter."

"Not as much as my desire for the new-range Mercedes S-Class."

"You are so shallow."

"And you are so…"

Aggie exhales, clenches her fists.

"Can't think of anything, can you?"

"You're so…"

"Well?"

"Nostalgic!"

"Is that all you've got?"

The man in the row behind them leans forward and berates the sisters with a sharp *Shh!*, causing them to fall together and giggle like schoolgirls. When they've recovered, they realize the auction team—the caller and the lead men—are gathering at the front.

"I need the toilet!" says Jess, a rush of nerves aggravating her bladder.

She rises, spies the exit to the lobby at the other end of the hall. "I'll be back in a second."

"But—"

"Save my seat."

"Well, hurry, or we'll miss everything and dearest Nancy will never be reunited with her long-lost bloody necklace!"

Jess shrugs and starts to move off, but as her left leg trails, she is reminded that the journey to the lobby and back will not be as speedy as she'd like, as it used to be. A quick "pop to the loo" is no longer in her body's vocabulary. With big sister sovereignty, Aggie passes Jess her walking cane, watching protectively as Jess leans heavily into the pole, wincing with pain.

The bidders in the front row take care to clear the path of bags and coffee cups. They smile as Jess passes—and out of politeness she smiles back, but inside, she would rather not play the game of pity tennis. Sympathy, she's discovered, has a way of feeling oppressive. She knows people mean well, but concerned looks are a painful reminder of her how her life has changed. Because before that *dreadful* day, she'd had no need for help or pain medication or rest breaks. She'd been independent, self-assured, full of spirit and curiosity.

The lobby, like the auction room itself, has a certain classical elegance. Its mint-green walls are adorned with stucco plasterwork and gilt-framed oil paintings. Jess makes her way to the toilets, but once she's done, with that same nostalgia Aggie has just critiqued her for, she dials her grandmother Nancy on FaceTime. She knows the connection might not happen quickly, that she needs to allow for those eighty-two-year-old fingers to fumble around the device, but after a minute Nancy is there, looming into the screen with her thin, white hair and papery skin.

"Hello, you," says Jess warmly.

"Jessy!"

"How are you feeling?"

"Oh, you know, so-so. Went in the gardens, did some digging. Damn foxes have been soiling the lawn again."

"Those foxes! Listen, Grandma, I'm here to get your necklace."

"You are?"

Her eyes brighten, the "Nancy twinkle."

"I'm at the auction. Aggie is here too. Front row. Don't worry. We'll get it for you. I caught a glimpse of it in the catalog. It's so beautiful! And you really think it was made by my great—what is it?—great-great-grandmother?"

"Minnie Philomene Taylor. A trailblazer, Jessy, just like you."

"I'm no trailblazer, Grandma."

"Well, you were."

"I've had to calm down."

"Never calm down."

Jess smiles.

"We all have to calm down at some point," she says. "I'd like to hear more about Minnie though."

"I have a photo of her in my bureau. I'll show you when you next visit. There's lots I want to tell you, Jessy. Minnie's necklace binds us all. If it wasn't for"—she sighs, half closes her eyes—"for all those years we were without it."

"Yes, I've been dying to ask, what happened to it, Grandma? Why did it leave the Taylor family?"

Jess ponders the possibilities. Was it stolen? Was it lost? Was her mother somehow responsible? Did she take it out of the velvet jewelry box one day, then lose it at a party? So many questions, but before she can get them out, Nancy shuts her down.

"Never mind the why," she says sharply. "The important thing is *you're* now bringing it home. And how are you feeling? How are your legs?"

Jess nods, realizing she'll have to pick her moment if she's to unearth the family gossip. Nancy has always been prickly around talk of the past. In her spritely days, she had a few anecdotes: her brag about being "born in Hollywood," her travels as a punk rock fan, and her pride in the fact that following convention had never been the "Taylor way." There'd been the occasional reminiscence from Jess's estranged father, Richard, but he'd never welcomed questions. In fact, he'd never really welcomed the Taylors, period. In recent years, he'd pretty much washed his hands of them. So Jess learned not to probe but to live, instead, with a certain thinness of heritage.

"I saw a specialist last week," she explains, indulging Nancy's change of subject, "who thinks he can get rid of the worst of my back pain. With an epidural, like they give to women in childbirth."

The phone crackles.

"Childbirth?"

"Sorry, Grandma. Signal's terrible."

"Are you telling me you're pregnant? With that Tim?"

"No, Grandma. No babies. Not yet. Tim and I are happy as we are, one step at a time. I'll bring him to meet you, so you can see for yourself. Anyway, I better go because they're about to start the auction. Wish me luck. I promise I'll make it happen. Love you."

"You too, Jessy."

As Jess hobbles back to the action, she is shocked to see the room is now full. Standing room only and even this is in short supply. The wide oak doorway is crowded with hawk-eyes, arms folded, acting casual. She knows the sort: the Rolex-wearing old guard, a club of retired men in their sixties who do this for sport. They study the catalogs, home in on a particular item or lot. They always arrive late, then stand at the back, hiding their intentions from the rest of the room and, more importantly, from each other. There's banter to begin with, but when the bidding opens, the camaraderie drops. It's every silver fox for himself.

Jess moves past them uneasily, praying their interests lie in the array of Victorian hair brooches and model trains that precede item twenty-two, the necklace. She doesn't want to go up against them, have a bidding war or, worse, have them win her item. Unease, however, is not a good mix with a dodgy back and a walking aid. She places the tip of her cane awkwardly, feels her leg buckle as she stumbles into the person in front of her.

"Sorry…so sorry!"

The person, a man, unexpectedly youthful for this auction room, helps her steady herself. Their eyes meet fleetingly. His dark sparkle, beneath hooded lids and a mop of chestnut curls, startles her. Immediately she is drawn to the rest of his face, to his arched nose and full lips. There is something endearingly boyish about his mouth, but those eyes, they hint of an old soul. She goes for a smile, but then she spots it, the emergence of that spark-killing pity gaze as he glances at her walking cane. She can practically feel the question surfacing in his mind: What's with the stick?

Then, smooth as silk, he leans toward her, whispers in her ear. "That's one accessory I could make use of right now."

She blinks.

"To help me fend off these tyrants," he says, nodding toward the hawk-eyes. "Lend it to me. So I can pin their thieving arms to their bodies, and stop them from doing their usual trick of bidding up everyone else's items."

He grins, eyes ablaze, and immediately Jess realizes she had him wrong. He hasn't been blindsided by her frailty. He's not a pity person at all. He's a life force. A sudden and unexpected thrill rushes through her limbs.

"Certainly it has its uses," she says, matching the glint in his eye with her own before plowing a path back to the front.

Aggie seems anxious. She doesn't care for the necklace, of course, but she likes a win.

"Game plan?" she urges, as Jess slides into her chair.

"The most important thing is to get the auctioneer's attention."

"Like this—?"

Aggie delivers a round of melodramatic nods and winks.

"No, Aggie, that's just how it happens in movies. No real-life auctioneer is going to notice that. And if they do, they'll probably assume you've got pink eye. It has to be something more emphatic."

Jess flicks her bidding card.

"Higher," says Aggie, pushing up her elbow.

"Not too high," says Jess, pushing back down. "We don't want to give our game away."

"Honestly, this is becoming more convoluted than Ed and Tim playing chess. And that's—"

"Convoluted."

"If you want the necklace that badly—"

"We," Jess corrects.

"Then I think we should catch the auctioneer's eye, flirt a bit.

Although in a place like this, such lascivious behavior might be dicey. We're bringing the average age down by half, you realize. All old codgers. I can practically smell the beta-blockers."

Jess turns back to the crowd.

"Not all of them are old," she says, looking out for the curly haired, sparkly eyed man, wondering if she imagined him among the sea of white comb-overs, salmon-pink yachting chinos, and plaid shirts.

"Quick. They're about to start."

"Good afternoon," says the auctioneer. "We have a packed event for you all, a veritable cornucopia of items big and small. Bids at the ready. Starting with lot number one…"

The sisters sit back and exhale in unison. A set of mother-of-pearl cuff links is paraded around the stage by a stern lead man, who looks as though he'd snap the display box shut on the fingers of anyone who so much as pointed at them. The room is slow to get going, which Jess takes as an encouraging sign. They sit through a complete model railway, a crystal decanter, two rare watches, and a variety of Clarice Cliff ceramics. But the waiting is hard. Each time the hammer falls, they are one item closer.

Half an hour in, the necklace is next. Jess's palms start to sweat. Aggie fusses over the bidding card.

"You know our rule," she hisses. "Stick to the limit. Don't go mad."

"Yes, yes," Jess replies, eyes wide, fixed on the auctioneer, waiting, watching.

"Item twenty-two," the auctioneer bellows, "this exquisite art nouveau butterfly necklace, constructed with enamel, silver, and moonstone. Thought to have been made around 1906, its exact origins are unknown, but our experts have suggested it bears some resemblance to the work of French designer René Lalique. A first glance charms. A second impresses the mind. And the third… Well, that's the magic, ladies and gentlemen. A third glance has the onlooker beguiled, awed by something he cannot quite fathom. Pleasure in the art nouveau aesthetic, perhaps? An interest in lepidoptera? Or…something else? A must for fans of twentieth-century jewelry design, or how about a gift for that special person in your life? With a reserve of one thousand pounds, I open the floor at six hundred. Any advance on six hundred?"

Her breath held tight, Jess's hand shoots up.

"That's six fifty. I have six fifty… Any advance on six fifty? Thank you, sir, seven hundred."

The sisters spin around to see who has dared bid against them, but the bids come so fast the auctioneer's call bounces around the room like a ping-pong ball. There is no way to see where it has landed or where it will go next.

"Seven fifty…eight hundred…eight fifty…to the gentleman in the green hat, eight fifty. Do I see nine?"

"I wish he'd stop doing that," Aggie hisses. "He's putting ideas in their heads."

"That's the point," scolds Jess.

She thrusts her bidding card out again, desperate to catch the wave.

"Nine hundred, to the brunette lady in the front."

She grins, triumphant that she has reclaimed control, only to have it snatched away immediately. Her hands, at first sweaty, are now trembling.

"Nine fifty…one thousand…one thousand fifty…one thousand one hundred…that's one thousand one fifty. Remember, ladies and gentlemen, this is a very special item. Do I have one two?"

Jess lifts her card again, her teeth clenched so tight her jaw aches.

"Back here at the front, one thousand two hundred… How about one two fifty?"

"We said no more than one thousand," Aggie warns.

"But we can't stop here. It's only just cooling down. We need to keep control of the bidding until it slows completely, then make sure we get the last—"

"One thousand," Aggie asserts. "That was the limit."

"One thousand three…one three fifty…can we go to one four?"

Jess bites down on her thumbnail, then shoots the card up. Aggie clamps it back down. They glare at each other.

"It's just a silly bit of costume jewelry, Jess."

"It's Nancy's. Don't you care?"

"Jess, she's barely with it these days. You'll get it for her and she won't remember what it is."

"That's not true. Sometimes she is with it. She certainly was just now."

The bids continue to bounce around the room. One four fifty. One five. One five fifty. Jess's heart thuds. Aggie bows her head despairingly.

"Not with my money," she presses.

"Fine," says Jess. "Then I'll do this alone."

She thrusts the card out one more time, holding the auctioneer's gaze.

"One six, right here," he says, smiling. "Excellent choice. Any advance on one six?"

The auctioneer takes his attention to the rest of the crowd, but the room is silent. A whirl of emotions fill Jess's body. The necklace is about to become hers, back in Taylor hands for ever, where it should be. But six hundred pounds more than she said she would spend! Her thoughts fling from one side of reason to the other. She sickens at the thought of the money.

"Last time," says the auctioneer, "or it goes for one six to the brunette lady at the front."

Jess glances at Aggie, so stiff, so sensible. Perhaps she should be more like Aggie. But then there's Nancy. She loves Nancy. She gets Nancy. Nancy gets her. She screws her eyes shut, waits for the hammer to fall, fingers crossed, brow furrowed…

Another bid slips past.

"One six fifty," the auctioneer calls, a touch of surprise in his voice. "I now have one six fifty. Madam, can you advance on one six fifty?"

Lost in her torment, Jess doesn't hear, doesn't open her eyes, doesn't respond. What was it Nancy said? *Minnie's necklace binds us all.* It has to come back. It needs to come back, where it belongs.

"Once…twice… Okay," says the auctioneer. The hammer falls hard, the sound reverberating like a shotgun. "One six fifty to the gentleman at the back."

"Wha—?"

Jess's eyes ping open. The gentleman at the back?

The room relaxes into a chorus of chatter and coughing.

"How? Who?" says Jess in outrage. "*What* gentleman at the back?"

"The gentleman that's just been your savior," says Aggie, arms folded. "Honestly, Jess, that was ridiculous."

Jess blinks, shakes her head.

"Why didn't you tell me? Some asshole bid over me, and you just let him get away with it! You knew I hadn't noticed, didn't you? You could have nudged me, given me the chance to bid against him! Now it's gone! Our chance has gone! Our necklace…"

The shock and disappointment cascade over her.

"It should be ours," she says, disbelieving. "That necklace is meant to be ours. It was loved by our family forever. It's not for some random stranger who doesn't care."

Aggie rearranges the collar of her shirt.

"Once again, Jess, you're totally over-romanticizing things. Clearly it hasn't been loved by our family forever, because…why would it be here, being sold for a frankly ridiculous amount of money in some musty auction room?"

Jess just stares into nothing, incredulous that the Taylor necklace has been snatched away, right under her nose. With a groan she hunches over, then galvanizes herself to make sense of it.

"Who got it?" she pesters. "Did you see?"

"Behind you," says Aggie, the intensity of her sister's disappointment prompting remorse. "Mister Smug Face over there. He's still holding up his card. No, wait… He's getting up… He's going to collect the necklace!"

Half covering her eyes, Jess turns to look. As she focuses on the distant figure working its way up the side aisle, she gasps.

"Oh my god, no! It's him! It's…the curly, sparkly cane guy!"

"The who?"

"Oh, never mind. Just…what a scoundrel! He implied he plays fair, said he wanted to stop the hawk-eyes from nicking other people's bids. And now he's done the exact same thing to me. It was obvious I wanted the necklace more than anyone else in this room. I kept my bids in line. Ugh, how dare he!"

She stares in fury as the curly haired, sparkly eyed man strides up the steps, shakes hands with one of the auction assistants, and is handed a purple box, presumably with the necklace inside. Her heart feels as though it's tearing in two, made worse by the fact that the man casually tucks the box under one arm.

"Like it means nothing to him," she snarls, "shoving it under his sweaty armpit."

"He looks too coolheaded to have a sweaty armpit," says Aggie sullenly.

"That's beside the point. He's stolen from us, in a roundabout kind of way, therefore—"

"Therefore?"

"He's going to hear my wrath."

"Jess—"

"It's wrong and I'm going to—"

"Jess! He bid on it fair and square. Besides, the price was out of your league and you know it. Let's call it a day, go drink a bottle of merlot or something. I'll break the news to Nancy if you can't."

Jess crumbles, buries her head in her hands.

"Oh, Nancy." She sniffs. "No. I'll tell her. This was our thing."

As Jess sulks, Aggie reapplies her lipstick, digs for her car keys, and checks her phone for messages.

"Three voicemails," she moans, clamping the handset to her ear. "Scratch the wine," she says, teeth gritted as she listens. "It's Steph's school. She's been skipping class with the Vegan again. Why? *Why* does she do this to me?"

"Because she's sixteen," says Jess. "And you're her mother."

"I have to go," says Aggie. "The high school wants a meeting. Honestly, I never skipped class when I was her age. You did. But I was always on point. My daughter should take after me. Not her rogue aunt. Are you coming?"

Jess pauses, distracted by the memory of Nancy's telling-off voice; how she'd audibly berate Jess for her subpar school reports, but all the while be hiding a smile, the Nancy twinkle in her eyes. One teen rebel to another. Jess sighs, the disappointment of the necklace feeling like the most enormous fail ever.

"You go," she says. "Get Steph sorted out. I might hang about for a bit, see if I can waste my money on some other silly piece of costume jewelry. I'll see you later."

"But how will you—?"

"Aggie, please. I'm not completely incapable. I can handle an hour on public transport."

"All right, all right. I'll see you at home."

"Good luck. And…don't be too hard on Steph."

Chapter Two

JESS SITS OUT THE REST OF THE AUCTION, BARELY AWARE OF THE LOTS that come and go. She doesn't lift her card again, but sits shredding it, venting her wrath on its flat, passive form. As the auction comes to a close and the hall starts to empty, the compulsion—and perhaps her true motive for staying behind—comes to the fore. Curly-Sparkle is one of the last to leave, having spent time chatting with other dealers.

As he makes for the door, Jess staggers after. By the time she catches up with him, he's in the street hailing a taxi cab, the boxed necklace still tucked under his arm. The air is warm, summer in Knightsbridge. The high street is busy with afternoon shoppers. As a cab pulls up, she knows it's her only chance—now or never.

"Wait!" she cries.

He doesn't hear but climbs into the back of the cab and starts giving the driver instructions. Jess slams herself forward, ignoring the pain, then blocks the door with her stick. Now he looks up.

"Oh, hello again."

"We need to talk."

"We do?"

"Yes." She eyes the purple box. "About that."

"You mean my necklace?"

"My necklace," Jess corrects.

"Er?"

Jess leans into the doorframe. Curly-Sparkle gives her a puzzled smile.

"Something tells me—could it be the way that you're staring at me with a slightly demonic look in your eyes—that you're annoyed I won the bid."

"That necklace," says Jess, brow furrowed into a deep V, "is my family's heirloom. I came here to get it back for my eighty-two-year-old grandmother. I had my handle on the auction the entire time, and then just as the hammer was about to drop on my final bid, *someone* decided to throw out a chippy little one-six-fifty offer. Literally as the hammer was about to drop."

Curly-Sparkle shrugs.

"Some you win, some you lose."

"Oh, come on. I deserved that bid and you know it."

The cab driver coughs. "Do you want this ride, mate?"

"Yes," says Curly-Sparkle. "Just…give me a moment."

He turns back to Jess.

"Look, I'm sorry how things turned out, but ultimately my bid won. I appreciate you feel the necklace has something of personal value to you, but you took your eye off the ball. What can I say?"

Their gazes lock together. Jess tries her best to glare him into submission, but his confidence doesn't waver. He is utterly self-assured. Why…why does this have to be a trait she finds alluring?

She stares into the darks of his eyes, wills that beguiling sparkle to go cloudy. He is not. Never. No way.

"Perhaps I could give you a lift somewhere?" he suggests. "And on the way maybe we can resolve the matter. Or you could just scold me some more, whatever helps. Either way, can we come to some kind of peace? I like to sleep easy at night and"—he grins—"you're strangely endearing."

Jess snorts her outrage.

"No, thank you," she asserts.

He smiles, unfazed.

"It's a hot walk to the Tube."

"I'll be fine," says Jess.

"Suit yourself."

He shuts the door. Jess hobbles on, purposefully pounding the concrete with her cane, holding her nerve, masking her emotions with a fixed frown. Smart-talking cavaliers? Oh no, she's been down that road already and look where it got her! A shattered body and a shattered heart. As if to reinforce the point, her hip joint twinges, stopping her in her tracks. She stiffens, winces, waits for the pain to pass. In her periphery she sees the cab move off. Good riddance. Another unnecessary, unhelpful and, no doubt, messy flirtation averted.

As she walks on, however, a small torment bores into her soul; the thought that Nancy's necklace, there on the back seat, is about to disappear once more. She'd come so close, but now…no tears. There will not be tears. Oh god! There *are* tears! They stream down her cheeks, blur her eyes. She increases the pace, determined to bury her frustration. *It's just a necklace*, she tells herself. There are bigger things to worry about. But then…

The cab slows beside her. The passenger window comes down. Curly-Sparkle leans out.

"Are you sure?" he says. "I'm heading for Portobello. I can drop you where you like…"

He holds out the purple box as though trying to tempt her with it. She takes a breath, clenches her fists. The moment spirals inside her. He's trouble, of that she's certain, but the necklace…its history, its beauty. She *can't* let it go. With a resolute shiver, she stops walking, turns to face him.

"Are you open to deals?"

"I might be."

The door opens. Jess climbs in.

"Well, here we are. I'm Guy, by the way, and you are?"

"Jess."

"Nice to meet you, Jess. First, where are you headed?"

"The Central line would be good. Queensway or Lancaster Gate."

"Hear that, driver? A drop-off at Queensway Tube. Thanks."

He turns back to Jess, brushes a hand through his curls. Immediately she notices a large and unusual gold leopard's-head ring on his middle finger. She always notices people's jewelry, her way of reading the world. Most people have little idea that every time they place an item on their body, thinking they're merely accessorizing an outfit, they're actually sending out a message, leaking some inner truth about their personality.

Bold, she thinks, staring at the leopard ring; someone who's not afraid of standing out, who knows their own mind, dares to take risks. Someone who lives to be happy. A thought catches in her mind, one she dare not examine. Her gaze drops to the purple box. The urge to lift the lid tingles through her fingertips, but Guy has it right beside him, his ringed hand resting protectively near. He watches her watching it. He isn't going to give it up easily, she senses, not now it's a prize pawn.

"So, what of this necklace?" he says, still watching her, drumming the lid with his forefinger. "You say it's a family heirloom. What else can you tell me?"

"If I tell you, will you sell it to me?"

He shakes his head.

"Will you at least let me look at it?"

"But I don't want to tease you, give you hope then let you down."

"Which is a roundabout way of saying you've got no intention of selling it to me. I'm wasting my time?"

Guy sighs.

"If I could sell it to you, I would. In fact, I'd give it to you if I could. But I have my reasons for wanting it too. I have…a responsibility. Anyway, how can you be sure it's your family's exact necklace?"

"I'd know it anywhere. I used to play with it when I was little, in my mother's jewelry box. It disappeared after she died."

Guy lowers his eyes.

"Sorry about that."

"It's okay," says Jess, racing through the sentiment. "All a long time ago. The thing is, recently my grandmother's started asking for it. I've been keeping an eye on auction sites for her, not thinking I'd ever find it. And then, well, it turned up, didn't it? Almost as though…it was meant to. But then you came along and ruined it."

Outside, the traffic slows to a standstill. The warm evening descends into the streets, bathing the Georgian mansion blocks of Knightsbridge with its mellow light. Long shadows of smartly dressed pedestrians pattern the pavements, the bags at their sides bearing high-end labels: Harrods, Selfridges, Fortnum & Mason. And then, smashing this sedate backdrop, a trio of drag queens march out of a side street, followed by a pair of stilt walkers, whose primary attire seems to be body glitter. They weave between the motionless vehicles, dancing their way to the opposite pavement.

"Overspill from Pride," says the cab driver. "Half the streets in central London are gridlocked."

"Looks like we're going nowhere fast," says Guy, sinking into his seat, the sun on his face. "So you're stuck with me a little longer. If you can bear it."

Jess gives a noncommittal nod, hiding the fact that she feels curiously glad, a little nervous, a little exhilarated—and very disconcerted by the prospect. To calm herself, she winds down the window, sits back.

"Is that Versace, circa 1976?" says Guy, leaning over to share her view of the drag queens and their incredible assortment of costume jewelry. The colors are kaleidoscopic: plum, turquoise, peridot green, citrine.

"I love those paste brooches," he says, as the queens strut past. "It's like they're telling the world: you think we're super frivolous, but we're epic enough to rock vintage Versace."

Jess throws him a side glance.

"But it's what they're saying, isn't it?" He shrugs. "I mean, they're hardly dropping under the radar with Thomas Sabo eternity rings. They like a spectacle. Yet they also want us to know they take their art seriously."

"That's how I think," she says, surprised.

"You take drag seriously too?"

"Yes. I mean no… I mean…that's how I think about people, through their jewelry. No one *has* to wear jewelry. Earrings, brooches, bracelets—none of it's necessary, not in the way clothing and foot-wear are."

"The ultimate extra," says Guy, smiling, "its only purpose to reflect some intangible quality that we believe is our essence, or that might make us distinctive or attractive to other people."

Jess grins, intrigued.

"It sounds like you think about jewelry as much as I do!"

Guy laughs. "Okay, I admit I have a fascination with small, spar-kly things. I collect huge amounts of crap and generally like anything that shines."

Tickled, Jess momentarily shuts her eyes, a warm, melting sensa-tion filling her stomach. When she looks again, her attention returns to the gold leopard ring on Guy's left hand. He twists it, revealing the ring's emerald eyes.

"It's a favorite," he explains. "It's sacred to me."

"Your own family heirloom?"

"Kind of."

"And what does a golden leopard head say about Guy…?"

"Van der Meer. The full hit is Guy Arlo van der Meer."

"That's quite a name."

"My ancestors were big in the Dutch diamond industry. Old school."

Jess nods, cautiously impressed. She has always preferred the unpretentious allure of semiprecious gemstones, but she'll take diamonds if she must.

"Okay, Guy Arlo van der Meer, what does your choice of finger adornment say about you?"

"I think *you* should answer that question," says Guy teasingly, "since we both know that the optimal way to appreciate jewelry is to see it on another person's body."

He lifts his ringed hand, offers it to her for closer inspection. She takes it, thrilled to touch his warm skin, to feel the sinews of his tapered fingers in hers. She looks up from the shadow of her brow, holds his gaze.

"Very playful," she says, unable to resist flirtation, "but I can see that it's fine. Good gold, carefully worked. Are they real emeralds?"

"Of course."

"My favorite precious stone," she says, scrutinizing the tiny verdant leopard eyes.

"Mine too."

"Beautiful but innately flawed," they say together.

"My next thought," Jess continues, "is how does a fine but quirky statement ring chime with the rest of your image? I'm seeing expertly ruffled hair, a T-shirt, jeans, and linen jacket—trying to look casual, but all very carefully put together. You want people to think you're relaxed about your appearance, but really you're right on it, carefully managing the way the world sees you, creating a smoke screen, covering up the truth of your dirty laundry. Perhaps you're something of a con artist?"

"Ouch."

"You asked for it."

"And I certainly got it. But hang on a minute…you talked about my general appearance—what specifically about my ring?"

"An heirloom, you say?"

"That's right."

"Then I'm going to assume you're not entirely shallow. And that you're desperate to tell me your life story, something about your grandmother's great-aunt who smuggled the ring on a cruise liner, tucked in her corset, so it wouldn't get pinched by the riffraff."

He laughs. "How did you guess?"

"There's always a cruise liner and a corset involved," she replies, relishing the banter, taking in his face with a surreptitious flick of her eyelids. Those chestnut curls, ruffled but not shaggy… They are—she feels it in her core—so tempting to touch. What would he do, she wonders, if she gave in to that urge and went for it, drew her hands to his forehead, swept those luscious loops from his face, leaned forward, brought her lips to his…and…

Oh, Jess! she berates herself sharply. *No!*

She folds her arms, presses the small of her back into her seat, and thinks about office furniture—her go-to solution when besieged by unhelpfully seductive thoughts. Just because he looks like her type and acts like her type doesn't make him her type. If life—and Aggie—have taught her anything, the lesson is definitely: stay away from "her type." Besides, she has Tim. She has matured and found Tim, who is lovely and gorgeous and, best of all, a fully functional human being.

"Look," she says, dropping Guy's hand, matter-of-fact, returning to the purple box, "you outbid me and won. I accept your victory. I just need you to understand that this necklace means more to my grandmother than you could begin to imagine. I told her I was getting it for her. I made a promise."

"Never promise."

"Too late. The bottom line is, I'd do anything—"

"Anything?" says Guy, his left eyebrow scaling his forehead in a way that can only be interpreted as roguish.

"I'll give you the sum of money that you paid the auction house. In cash."

Guy shrugs. "Actually, I was thinking more along the lines of dinner?"

Jess shuts her eyes. Never mind hardwired flashes of physical attraction or the delight of their common interest in jewelry. He's one of those, can't help himself. She could say no a hundred times and he'll still believe that, deep down, she really wants a date with him. And that he'll get one. Until he's distracted by the next blond/brunette/redhead that he fancies, and then suddenly he'll drop off the face of her earth. Standard.

"No, thank you," she replies. "I'm spoken for."

"Spoken for?"

"I have a boyfriend."

Guy shrugs, the rejection ricocheting off him. "So?"

"So I don't intend to go to dinner with a stranger."

"But we're no longer strangers. We're cab sharers. Inextricably linked by an art nouveau butterfly necklace. Obviously dinner is the next step."

Jess sighs, throws her head back. *Just stop*, she thinks. All this attention, making out that a dinner date is their destiny. She knows exactly what Aggie would say. Hallmark behavior: the charming deceiver. Been there. Done it. Over it.

"So who exactly is this boyfriend who speaks for you," Guy asks. "The love of your life?"

"Quite possibly," says Jess, as she fixes her thoughts on Tim.

Tim, who is so utterly handsome with his solid, square jaw and sweet brown eyes. A proper grown-up with a steady soul, who makes her head fill with calm whenever he's near.

"I'm here for the necklace, that's all," she asserts. "If you'll sell me the necklace, then we can go our separate ways."

"And if I don't?"

Silence bulges as the cab moves forward, crawling to the next set of traffic lights. She could get out and walk. Even with her cane, she'd probably reach the Tube station quicker, but…the necklace. As though reading her mind, Guy pulls the purple box even closer to him. On the pavement ahead, a crowd has gathered in front of a shop window.

"What are they looking at?" says Jess, hoping a more neutral conversation will defeat the tension.

"I'm not sure," says Guy. "Some kind of sale or giveaway. Let's see—"

Before she can react, he opens the door of the cab.

"I'll be right back!" he calls, dashing toward the heart of the crowd.

Jess blinks. Curiosity has fueled her since childhood, often mistaken as waywardness or disobedience. The places she's never been, the things she's never done, the people she's never met—they shimmer in her thoughts like unopened gifts. Indeed, she's also been known for rash decisions and fits of impulse, but she has never joined a random crowd just to see what the fuss is about. She looks at her watch, makes brief eye contact with the cab driver, then realizes the purple box, the necklace inside, is now there on the seat unguarded.

Her heart thuds. What to do?

The necklace. No barriers. At least have a look at it.

She creeps her fingers toward the lid. Why should she feel guilty? After all, it's what she climbed into the cab for. She opens the box, peeps inside.

"Oh!" she gasps, drawing a hand to her mouth.

It is more beautiful in real life than she'd remembered. Immediately, it speaks to her, its little, fat moonstone glinting in the sun. She lifts it out of the box, cradles it in her palm—the impossible delicacy of the wings, the way the light blooms through the emerald enamel, every line and curve, such free-flowing grace. Here in her hands, the essence of what it is to be a Taylor woman, her mother, her mother's mother,

her mother's mother's mother, and beyond, now here, caught forever in the luster. She turns the main pendant over and there, on its base, carved in shaky lettering, is one simple word: "*OUI.*"

She looks up, feels a lightning strike of emotion in her soul.

With no sign of Guy, she knows she has her chance, right now, to take the necklace. She could tuck it in her pocket, exit through the passenger door, walk away. Tomorrow she could deliver it to Nancy, who'd never need to know the tussle involved. And that would be the end of the journey. But…she hesitates. She can't quite find it in her conscience. She places the necklace back in its box, snaps it shut, sniffs, and blinks.

"Doughnuts!"

Guy is at the window, holding a tray of sugary, chocolaty doughnuts.

"They were selling doughnuts. That's what the crowd was for. I bought us some. You okay? You look a little…startled?"

"I'm good," she squeaks, smiling through it. "Look at those bad boys!"

"Have one."

He shoves the tray in front of her, grins like a schoolboy.

"Oh, I'm not hungry."

"Go on. You only live once."

"True," says Jess, caught by the word: *OUI.*

She accepts one of the smallest on the tray, which nevertheless has an entire Mars Bar chopped on top. They eat in silence, licking the sugar from their lips. The traffic opens up, and a few minutes later, the cab pulls in front of Queensway Tube station.

"Well," says Guy. "This has been a pleasure."

"Thank you for the doughnut," says Jess. "And…if you should change your mind about selling the necklace—"

"I'll stalk you on Instagram."

"Promise."

"Never promise. But for the record, yes, you'll be the first person I go to…if I change my mind, that is. By the way, the dinner invitation is still very much open."

"Right. Thanks. In that case, I'll be sure to stalk you too…if I change *my* mind, that is."

"Oh, you'll change your mind," he says, holding her gaze, an infuriatingly cocky fix in his sparkling dark eyes.

She half smiles, opens her door, takes longer than necessary to back away. Then finally they part, the necklace between them—craftily, quietly playing its part.

Chapter Three

THE AROMAS OF SUNDAY LUNCH—SUCCULENT MEAT, CRISPY potatoes, buttery carrots—fill the airy kitchen-diner extension. Every weekend since its installation, the John Lewis marble-topped island unit has hosted occasions big and small: cocktails with school mums, wine with book group, cupcakes for the neighbors, and dinners of various origins, from Malay to French to Cajun, all prepared and presented with Aggie's signature precision. But this joint of beef, thinks Jess, as she places dish after dish on the dining table, is her sister's culinary trump card—not to mention a thinly veiled attempt to persuade her daughter, Steph, that a traditional meat feast is a worthy alternative to textured soy and pinto beans.

"Open-plan living, lesson number one," says Aggie, fanning the oven, "the smells get everywhere. Fine when you're baking sourdough. Not fine when you're roasting half a cow."

She then turns to her husband, Ed, flaps her hands, and is bemused when he doesn't immediately understand that the gesture means "Open the bifolds." Eventually, he shuffles to the aluminum doors and heaves them apart. A bolt of cool, fresh air blows in.

Everyone seats themselves, and the dishes are shared and served to the tuneful chink of cutlery on china.

"Wine?"

"Yes, please," says Jess.

"Me too," says Steph, eyeing the bottle of Picpoul, crisp and cold, fresh from the built-in wine fridge.

"I think not," says Aggie, snatching her daughter's glass away. "And don't start with the 'All my friends' parents let them' nonsense, because I know your friends' parents and they all feel the same way I do."

Steph scowls, while Marcus, her younger brother, smirks at her from behind his floppy bangs. The exchange isn't lost on Jess, who, having lived at her sister's for the past eleven months, has grown close to her niece and nephew—and the intricacies of their ceaseless rivalry. She prods Marcus under the table, gives Steph a bolstering wink, tries to diffuse the dynamite. She then casts her eyes to Tim, hopes he's ready for this hefty slice of domestic life. But, of course, he's easy with it, complimenting Aggie on her crispy potatoes, chatting bikes with Ed, giving the Hoppit children no reason to think he's a total dork.

Once the plates are loaded and the glasses—apart from Steph's—are poured, he gives a little cough, the educator in him that likes a captive audience.

"So," he says. "I got short-listed. I'm in contention for the deputy head post."

Ed cheers. "Great news, mate!"

"Excellent," says Aggie. "That school is lucky to have you."

"Well," says Tim modestly, "the post's not mine yet, but—"

"He'll get it," says Jess, with a rush of pride.

She remembers the first time she saw him in action at school; how he commanded the corridors with such authority, yet was liked by the students. From her own wayward school days, she knew that took something special.

"When's the interview?"

"Next week."

"Good money?"

"It's a jump, but the main thing is, it's where I want to be. I'm thinking three years, then I might start looking for a headship…"

He glances at Jess and it gratifies her that he looks for her approval, that it matters to him what she thinks of his future plans. She can see Aggie from the corner of her eye, also looking pleased, her boyfriend-with-prospects gauge swinging high. Although Aggie has never admitted it, Jess knows it was her who set them up, asking Ed to pinpoint the most eligible man in his cycling club, then somehow have him "drop in" one Friday evening just as Jess and Aggie were mixing rhubarb gin and tonics in the sun-filled back garden.

That evening—firepit ablaze, drinks aloft—everything changed. Truth be told, Jess was initially lured by the muscular bulge of his cyclist's thighs, but then she became aware of his lovely, calm demeanor. The way he presented himself, so solid, so sorted out. Not showy or arrogant. Just…in control. They talked all evening, with Aggie and Ed in the wings, whispering and tittering like a Shakespearean fairy chorus.

The next morning he phoned—not a text—to say he'd had a lovely evening and would she like to have dinner sometime? He took her to a steak house, and they swapped stories about families and books and the challenges of working with young people. She noticed he wore a good-quality watch and a single copper bracelet, which, when quizzed, was apparently to ward off arthritis.

"But you're still the good side of forty?" said Jess.

"It's preventive," he explained. "I'm shoring myself up for the future."

Honest from the start, he explained he'd been married before. It had shattered him, but now he was over it and excited for what was next. He loved his job, loved school life. Also loved the idea of being a hands-on dad. Right there, right then. He just dropped that in. So used to the company of men who visibly panicked at the mention of parental accountability, Jess was thrown by this candor. Thrown and charmed.

When the first date led to a second, then a third and fourth, Jess had to check herself: an attentive, grounded boyfriend with a steady job! What was happening to her? All her exes had been passionate, live-for-the-moment types. But really, who needed romance so intense it hurt? All that pain for nothing.

Yes, Tim is the antidote. Love with pace. Not overblown, not the passionate extreme. And actually, she's starting to see how a predictable life can be liberating; knowing what's coming next, knowing the path ahead, kind of takes the fear away.

Oui, she thinks, the engraving on the necklace suddenly surfacing in her thoughts, its dainty lettering belying its bursting sentiment.

Just one word, but what a word! So who put it there? And why? Her curiosity ticks as a gravy boat is passed around the table.

"What about you, Jess?" says Ed, a forkful of mashed potatoes wavering in his hand. "Had any more thoughts about what you'd like to do next? More teaching? I know you've got your jewelry business, but that's just a sideline, right?"

Here we go. The "what are you going to do with your life?" interrogation. Jess is used to it, has crafted a thousand different phrases to deflect it. There's little point in saying the truth—that she's happy with her "sideline" jewelry business—because they won't believe it. The Ed/Aggie manual contains an exacting five-point plan: earn money, spend money, earn more money, spend more money—and if it doesn't have Farrow & Ball on the label, throw it away.

But she'll let them off, because for all of their materialism, the Hoppits have been so kind—and she has needed their kindness this last year; the cajoling "right, let's this sort out" brusqueness of her big sister, the lurking calmness of her brother-in-law.

"I've told Jess she should go part-time at Baxter Academy," says Tim, emptying the last of the gravy on his plate. "In fact, the Creative Department is looking for another teacher right now. She'd be great." He looks at Jess. "*You'd* be great."

"Hmm," says Jess, quietly dissenting, "there's only so much teen action I can handle."

"But you're very good with them," says Aggie. "I mean, Steph tells *you* things she never tells me—"

"Because Aunty Jess is the only sane person in this family," growls Steph.

Silence ensues, and in the gap, little brother Marcus spots an opportunity:

"Callum Arnold says he saw Steph and Vegan Jared kissing behind the cricket pavilion, when they were supposed to be in study group. He says they were all over each other. And did you hear that Jared got arrested for smoking—?"

"Oh, shut up!" Steph hisses, flinging the head of a Yorkshire pudding at her brother. "No one gets arrested for smoking."

"No," says Aggie, cheeks sucked tight, "they just die of lung cancer."

Ed sighs, catches Tim's eye.

"Another Sunday, another Hoppit family lunch. Fancy a pint later, Tim?"

"Would love to, mate, but Jess and I have got plans—"

Jess blinks.

"We have?"

This is news. She'd planned a night of chocolate eating and crime dramas, because in the nine months they've been dating, Tim has shown a consistent preference for spending Sunday evenings preparing for the school week. She catches his eye.

"So…what are we doing?"

"You'll find out," he says teasingly.

She smiles and wonders, digs into her beef, the tang of horseradish spiking her tongue as her thoughts turn inward. What's happening? She's grown used to Tim's predictability, *likes* his predictability, and now he's throwing the habit in the air, planning a mystery Sunday evening for her. As she chews and swallows,

the twin sensations of excitement and apprehension grip her—
the possibility of a ring in a box. Surely not. They're not *there*
yet. They've discussed it. Marriage, kids, maybe definitely in the
future, but not yet.

"So," says Ed, refilling everyone's wine. "I hear you ladies had
fun and games at the auction on Friday."

"Stress, more like," says Aggie, cutting Jess a frown. "But all's
well that ends well. We haven't, thankfully, blown one and a half
grand on a necklace—"

Steph's eyes widen. Marcus gasps.

"One and a half grand? I could buy a top-of-the-line virtual reality kit for that," he rails.

"Yeah, but why would you?" says Steph, baiting.

"What would you spend it on then? Rizla rolling papers for your
boyfriend?"

"Oh, go away!"

"No, you go away!"

"No, you—"

Aggie hammers the table with her fists.

"Steph! Marcus! Just *stop*!"

Jess and Tim wink across the dinner plates, share smiles of solidarity. Is he thinking what she's thinking, that this could be them
in a decade or so, clinging to the sorry scraps of family life that
their precocious offspring throw at them? Tim dabs his lips with
his napkin. *So well-mannered*, thinks Jess. He'd never talk with his
mouth full, flick peas, or throw the heads of Yorkshires. Yet thankfully he doesn't seem fazed by the tabletop warfare, not offended,

not put off. No doubt he's seen enough teenage drama in the school corridors that he's inured to it. He'll make a great dad. A wave of contentment washes over her, and she likes the feeling. Finally, is it starting to happen? The maternal instinct, the urge to settle down, make roots, start a family.

"My mum used to have an heirloom sapphire brooch," Tim muses, clearly for her benefit, "given to her by her great-aunt Maeve. She lost it at a party on St. Patrick's Day. She was devastated, pined for it ever since."

"There you go," says Jess, catching his eye. "Some people care about their family heirlooms."

"It's not that I don't care," argues Aggie, "but it was such a vast amount of money. How did Nancy take the news, by the way?"

Jess bows her head, stares into her plate.

"You haven't told her yet?"

"I just…didn't want to do it over the phone. I'll go and see her. I thought I'd take the train one day next week."

"Well, I'm sure she'll appreciate it," says Aggie. "I'd join you, but—"

"You're working."

"I'll go," chimes Steph. "I haven't seen Great Granny in ages."

"You, young lady, will be in school," Aggie chides. "I'll take you one weekend"—she glances at Ed—"when there isn't cycling."

Steph sneers. "There's always cycling."

Ed looks to the ceiling, wishes there was cycling right now.

"What's for dessert?" Marcus demands.

"Trifle!" exclaim Jess and Aggie, clapping their hands in synchrony—the shared knowledge that, at the climax of every fragmented Sunday lunch, cold custard pulls the loose ends together. Indeed, the announcement triggers a unified cheer.

"You two," says Tim, nodding between the sisters, "you're so different and yet…you're peas in a pod."

Jess catches Aggie's eye, feels a strange, fierce rush of love for the sister who, in one moment, can rile her with her snippy, patronizing remarks, and in the next, make her feel like there's no one in the world she'd fight harder for.

"Jess has always been the jaunty one," Aggie elaborates. "I'm the dry one. While I did the chores, she used to dress up in our mother's jewelry and flounce around in fairy-tale land. All the fun for her, while I had to be sensible."

"Oh, poor Cinderella," says Jess. "As I remember it, you were bossy and boring and never wanted to play anything unless it involved being in charge. No chores involved. I played dress-up simply to keep myself entertained."

Jess remembers again her mother's jewelry box, the temptation inside, the sheen and luster—amber rings, a coral-pink cameo brooch, a tangle of necklace chains, the occasional unpaired clip-on earring. They were portals into a happier, lovelier land, the joy exploding out of their tiny forms. They were the one thing—especially when the joy became absent in day-to-day life, after her mother died—the one thing that remained beautiful. She shuts her eyes and sighs for Nancy's lost butterfly necklace.

After lunch, Aggie is excused to go and drink restorative fennel tea, while Ed and Tim help Marcus make a set of Roman armor out of tinfoil, and Jess and Steph clear the table. As they rinse and stack Aggie's prize earthenware plates, Steph is thoughtful.

"Mum says that before you met Tim, you always went for bad boys—"

Jess throws her head back and laughs.

"Mavericks," she corrects. "I like to say 'mavericks.' And what your mum doesn't realize is that while, yes, some of them were a little flaky, they were also lots of fun to hang out with."

"Tell me more."

"I'm not sure your mum would approve of my kind of relationship advice."

"Well, it's got to be better than hers. She's never even *met* Jared, and all she can say is vegan this, vegan that, like, really, what's the big deal about being vegan? We should all be vegan, save our frickin' planet. She heard one bad story about him trying to buy marijuana, and now she's all over it—"

"Um, I think she's heard a few stories actually. The skipping class, the smoking roll-ups, the snogs behind the cricket pavilion?"

"But he's not *bad*. He's good. He stands for good. He cares about stuff. I could do a lot worse, you know? There are kids in my school who spend their life threatening to cut each other, setting fire to bus stops, taking photos of girls in their gym uniforms, generally not giving a shit and—"

"I get you," says Jess. "I really do. But your mum, she…she just wants the best for you."

"Best for *her*," Steph whispers, shaking the drips from a pair of stemless wineglasses. "So who were they then," she pesters, "the maverick exes?"

"Okay," says Jess. "First of all there was Brian the artist—although, really, he was just a high school senior with a big ego and paint on his trousers. Then there was Andrew, who was six years older than me and ran his own music night. Ah, Andrew, he made me feel like a grown-up while all my mates were dating silly boys. He had his own car, which was a massive deal back then. He used to pick me up from school, drive into central London, and we'd go to gigs. Such a buzz! But then he turned out to be a total control freak and I had to bail. Then there was a thing with a musician from Ireland, who played bass in a ska band. They were nearly famous, but unfortunately he had some, um, bad habits. After that…well, then I went international and dated a professional rock climber from Canada, who was pretty married to his favorite rock. And then…I fell in love with a skydiver from South Africa—"

"He was a choice pick, wasn't he?" says Aggie, sweeping in. "Second problem with open-plan living: no such thing as a private conversation. Steph, don't believe anything Aunty Jess tells you. They were bad boys. But now—hallelujah—now there is Tim Dukas. Which means there is hope. *Jess.*" She spins to face her sister. "He's getting ready to leave, and he wants to take you with him. Go get your coat."

She has a slight smile on her face. Jess senses her sister knows something.

"What?" she quizzes. "What's going on?"

"Go!" says Aggie, fluttering her fingers. "Go follow your Prince Charming."

Then as Jess turns to leave, Steph grabs her hand.

"For what it's worth, Aunty, I wish you *had* bought that necklace. Despite bitching about it, Mum told me it was really amazing."

Chapter Four

"Any ideas?" Tim asks as he leads Jess across the trimmed lawn.

He is brimming with excitement, that feeling of giving a much-wanted gift, making another's wish come true. He looks across at her and smiles. It's like a second life. When things first fell apart with his ex-wife, Cassidy, he was in a spiral. It wasn't just the rug. It was the floorboards, the joists, the foundations—*everything* pulled out from underneath him. Everything he thought he'd have at that point in his life—a happy marriage, young kids, a home, and a career he was proud of—suddenly whipped out of his grasp. Those first months were bleak. He'd cried like a baby to his parents, which had been hideously uncomfortable for all concerned. And then, of course, he'd had his brothers to field, with their got-it-made IT jobs, one in Florida, one in Hong Kong, both too busy to offer little more than a pseudo-sympathetic plenty-more-fish email exchange.

All he'd wanted to understand was what he'd done wrong.

Up until the day Cassidy had told him she was leaving, his life's mission had been to make her happy. Everything she'd asked for: a new car, a NutriBullet, a five-star all-inclusive adults-only fortnight in the Canaries, ballroom-dance classes, a pottery wheel (never used), a garden plot (also never used), and an enormous pile of decorative cushions. But with the divorce now done and dusted, he realizes his mistake. He should never have married, and given his soul to, someone as needy and self-centered as Cassidy.

He sighs, shakes her off.

Because now he has Jess.

The two women couldn't be more different. They've never met, never will, but he's pretty certain they'd repel each other on sight. Jess is everything Cassidy wasn't. She is thoughtful, fun, imaginative, and curiously independent. She doesn't seem to want much from him, yet she brings everything. Will she love what he's done for her? He hopes so.

He is baggy-eyed from all the lunchtime wine, but his eagerness to unveil the Sunday surprise propels him. He can see in her eyes she is intrigued, wondering what they're doing in the environs of Stratford's Queen Elizabeth Park. They've walked in the area several times before and even have a favorite picnic spot beside the water fountains, but this is a whole other stage.

"Any idea?" he teases.

"Not a clue," she says.

"Oh, come on, you must have an idea."

"Honestly, I don't know."

Her eyes scan his shirt pockets. Is she looking for a ring-box-shaped bulge? He hooks one hand over her eyes and the other around her walking cane, gently guides her forward.

"Don't look, don't look!"

"Where are you taking me?"

"Through here—"

He leads her toward the newest of the rows of apartment blocks, the expanse of sleek glass and wooden cladding towering over them, the top half still covered in scaffolding. He leans against the entrance door, types in a key code, and ushers Jess into the atrium. Her eyes still covered, she waves her hands into the space, then he presses a small, hard object into her right palm.

"Open your eyes," he says.

Before she can fully comprehend what she's seeing, he turns her toward an orange door bearing a number three. She looks at the door, then at the object in her palm. It's a key.

"Is this—?"

"Our new front door," he says, the smile bursting out of his face.

Stunned, Jess inserts the key in the lock and twists: a brand-new apartment, open-plan, real hardwood floors, fully furnished. Dazzled by the shapes and surfaces that now surround her, Jess steps forward. It's ready to live in, ready-designed—a corner sofa, designer dining chairs, one of those kitchens where all the appliances are hidden behind dark-gray door panels, and a balcony with city views. There are even a few carefully positioned vases and picture frames to add interest and color.

"This is just the show flat," says Tim, "but you get the idea. We can choose a different kitchen, whatever colors we want on the walls."

"For real?"

He nods.

"I've paid a deposit. Obviously the block's still being finished, but one of these units is ours. In the very near future."

"Ours?"

"My house is under offer. Your flat can be rented out. But this place… *This* can be ours. Come see."

He leads her across the room.

"Oh, Tim!"

She sways and blinks, the enormity of the idea overwhelming her. It's a happy enormity, of that she is certain, but an enormity nonetheless. Not a ring—but a huge step toward a ring.

"It's carbon neutral," says Tim, distracted by the data. "Triple-glazed. Even has an air-filtration system to remove all the dust and pollen. My hay fever, it'll be a thing of the past. And look—you can see the park from the balcony, and there's Stratford station and Westfield shopping center and… Well, what do you think?"

"I think it's amazing. You're… This… It's just…*amazing.*"

He smiles, relieved, then opens his arms. With bewildered exaltation, Jess falls into them.

"I know it's a big deal," he whispers, "but you'll struggle going back to your old flat. And it's pretty claustrophobic at your sister's. This is the answer, right? Our own place."

The thought of the old flat gives Jess a twinge. Her first grown-up purchase, the deposit paid when she was still in full-time teaching, it had been her home up until last year. The third floor of a yellow-brick Victorian terrace in Leytonstone with high ceilings and cast-iron fireplaces, original tiles in the hallway, mottled but charming, so much history in those walls. But Tim is right—there's no way she'll be able to negotiate the three flights of steep, narrow stairs. It will never be home again. A rental income will at least cover the mortgage.

"You've…you've totally surprised me," she says.

"You have your sister to thank for that. I asked her advice, and she told me to keep you on your toes."

"Did she now?"

"She was just trying to help," says Tim. "All to the good. Personally, I wasn't sure if you'd go for this, if you were ready. I mean, sometimes you're, you know…"

"What?"

"A bit…faraway. I can't always tell what's going on in your head. Your cues confuse me."

Jess frowns. "Sorry."

"Don't be. Honestly. It's fine. I'm in. You're in. It's celebration time!"

Tim goes to the pristine kitchen and starts opening a bottle of champagne. Two flutes rest expectantly on the countertop.

"I arranged this with the woman at the property office. She suggested the champagne. Sweet, huh?"

"Very sweet," says Jess, accepting her glass, still absorbing the shock of it all.

❦

They sip their champagne on the balcony and admire the view—the urban patchwork of Stratford, East London's hub of hipsters and young professionals; the cranes and apartment blocks and, in the distance in miniature, the pulse of the city center, its landmarks gleaming in the evening sun.

"I'm sure you don't want to live in a flat forever," says Tim, taking Jess's hand in his, "but this is a start. There's a great little play park down there and shops, cafés, bars…everything we need. It's ground floor, but if you want to go higher, the lifts are amazing."

"Can we afford it? What's the cost?"

"Don't worry about that. My salary will more than cover it. And if I get the deputy headship, we'll be sweet."

"But we'll go halves, right?"

"If you really want—"

Yes, I want, thinks Jess, instinctively urged to keep things equal. She's never relied on a man before, has no intention to start now. The walking aid, it's a physical hindrance, but it doesn't mean she has to be "looked after." She takes a deep breath, hopes he sees it, the independence in her, the need to be free. If he sees it, and he can accept it, then they'll be good.

"No pressure," he says, topping up her glass. "Take a few days to think it through, but this is me telling you that I'm buying this flat and I want you to live here with me. I love you, Jessica Taylor."

He pulls her toward him, kisses the top of her head. She shuts her eyes, safe in his circle, feels the warmth of his mouth, his arms enveloping her.

"You're a diamond," she whispers.

How lucky has she been? When they first met that summer evening, she was only just starting to emerge from the lowest place she'd ever been. She'd lost her job, her physical freedom, her confidence, and her hope. She'd pretty much sworn herself off men, had no faith in her ability to pick a decent one. She'd never imagined that, in less than a year, she'd be standing on the threshold of a healthy new relationship, with a man who not only said the right things but *did* them too.

She looks around and reimagines the apartment filled with her own furniture, her flea market finds and timeworn trinkets. In truth, she's never considered living in a new building before—housing in its infancy, not a trace of history in it, other than the chemical smell of the plastic film covering the fixtures. But maybe it's up to her and Tim to embed the history? The first couple to tread its floors and flick its switches, give it life. Every home starts somewhere.

Suddenly they are disturbed by the pip of Jess's phone. It's Aggie.

"Well? Do you love it?"

Jess can picture the grin on her sister's face.

"So I gather you knew about this?"

"Obviously. I helped it happen. It'll be ideal for you guys. You'll only be down the road. You can come for Sunday lunch every week. That's if you can bear the arseholes that are my children."

"I can always bear them," Jess says, laughing.

"Well, congratulations from all of us. Can't wait for the house-warming. I'll make mojitos."

"Thanks."

As Jess says goodbye, Tim puts his arm around her, clinks his flute against hers.

"Cheers."

"Cheers indeed."

"Jess," he says with utter sincerity. "You make me so happy. I can see it all ahead of us, the loveliest life. Kids…maybe two, three? A dog?"

"And cats?"

"I can do cats. And bikes. We'll all get bikes. A tandem for you and me, and a trailer for the juniors—"

"Sounds perfect," says Jess, pressing her head to Tim's chest, drinking in the serene scent of his body.

Then her eyes spring wide.

"Tim," she says, peculiarly alert, gripped by impulse. "Before all of this comes together, you need to meet my grandmother—"

"Your grandmother…Nancy? The one with the necklace?"

"Yes. Come with me this week. It would mean a lot to me."

"Consider it done."

Chapter Five

Wednesday, a bright, clear day, Jess and Tim take the train to Sydenham. Tim has cleared the afternoon for interview prep, but dutifully agrees to squeeze in the requested grandmother visit. And although his attention is meshed to the conundrum of possible interview questions, the tightness with which he grips Jess's hand makes him feel very much present.

Nancy's care home is a 1960s monolith on a hill. It's the nicest they could find in the area—and Nancy was particular about the area, despite it being the other side of London. She'd insisted on being in the shadow of the Crystal Palace, even though there is little of the palace left, save for the overgrown garden colonnades and a few tired stone sphinxes.

"Brace yourself," says Jess, as they push through the double doors. "Her lucid moments are rare now and she's prone to the odd sweary outburst, so don't expect instant approval."

Tim grins.

"I need her *approval*?"

"Don't worry. It's not a deal breaker. To be honest, you could be the Lord Jesus and still not get her approval. Anyhow, Aggie has most definitely given you the thumbs-up, so—"

"I'm going in the right direction."

"You totally are."

They catch each other's gaze, then holding hands, they smile and walk down the corridor together. After signing in at reception, they proceed to Nancy's room. The sterility of the beige walls and rubber floor saddens Jess. It is hardly the realm of a woman who, in her sixties, moved to a plot of woodland in the wilds of Snowdonia, where she built her own log cabin, with only a little help from a local tree surgeon and some slow-witted donkeys. Now she has a list of ailments and medications and requires round-the-clock care, but...she is Nancy still. Every now and then that twinkle in her eyes resurfaces. As soon as she sees Jess, she sits up.

"Jessy!" she croaks.

Her skin is yellowing, showing signs of a tired liver. One by one, those hard-worked body parts are slowing down.

"Hello, Grandma," says Jess tenderly, kissing her cheek. "Look, I've brought someone to meet you. This is Tim—"

Nancy takes her time, scanning Tim's features with her small, sharp eyes.

"Hi," says Tim, offering his hand.

When the effort is ignored, he grins, not sure where to put himself.

"Good news," says Jess in an attempt to bolster the introductions. "We're moving in together."

Nancy tips her head back.

"Why do that?" she sneers.

"*Grandma—*"

"You used to be a true Taylor, Jessy. Doing your own thing, always going off to new places with your backpack. What's happened? Lost your spirit?"

Jess winces.

"I'm *fine*. Sure, I've had to slow down a bit"—she waves her cane—"but I'm still me. And I haven't lost my spirit. I've just… matured."

Jess glances at Tim, gives him an eye roll of solidarity.

"It's not maturing," Nancy mutters. "It's shrinking. Did you see those foxes have been tearing up my lawn again?"

Always the foxes. Except Nancy hasn't been near her lawn in a year.

"Okay, Grandma," says Jess, resigned. "Let's get you comfy."

She fluffs Nancy's cushions, then turns back to Tim.

"At least she hasn't sworn at you," she whispers. "That's good. Have a seat. And…sorry."

Tim squeaks into a plastic-coated armchair, while Jess arranges her gift of bananas and puzzle magazines, but she can see Nancy twitching, her pupils flitting from one side to another, looking… looking for the necklace.

"Where is it, Jessy?"

Jess sighs, shakes her head.

"I'm sorry, Grandma. It went to someone else. I tried. I tried so hard, but there was this guy—called Guy, as it goes—and he swooped in at the end of the bidding and cinched it. I did everything I could.

I even chased him down Kensington High Street, hijacked his cab, sat and pleaded with him for an hour while we waited in traffic—"

She sees Tim flinch.

"He must have thought I was bonkers, but, well, I kind of hoped I could win him around. I told him how much the necklace meant to you, thinking he might then have the heart to sell it on to me, but"— she pauses, sighs—"unfortunately, Grandma, he wouldn't play ball."

"Bastard!"

"He really was—"

"Find the bastard, get it back off him."

Jess laughs.

"Oh, Grandma. The moment's passed. I was wasting my time. He was one of those...cocksure...full of himself...despite the fact that he was—"

Jess stalls, catches a dreamlike vision of Guy's sparkly eyes, the thrill of their chat, the verve and vitality that sizzled between them. She takes a breath, chases the memory out.

"Anyway," she blusters, "I won't go there again."

But suddenly Nancy grips Jess's hand, digs in her nails, and speaks with utter authority, as though it's the clearest thought she's had in weeks.

"*Find him*," she insists. "Get the necklace."

And then she is silent.

Jess and Tim exchange glances. The wall clock ticks. Tim picks up a puzzle book, pretends to read it.

"You didn't tell me you got in a cab with that *Guy* person," he says, a crease in his brow.

Jess squeezes her fingertips together. How to explain? After all, it was hardly the situation she imagined she'd be in at the end of the auction.

"I–I didn't think it was relevant." She shrugs. "I mean, the man nicked my bid, wasted my time, then refused to sell. That's that. Effing annoying, but what can I do?"

"You should be more careful, Jess, especially with your—"

He gestures at her walking cane. Immediately she bristles.

"Just...be more careful is all I'm saying. Getting into cabs with random strangers is foolish by anyone's standards."

"Then I'm a fool," she mutters, wishing she'd never mentioned it.

She pulls out the latest copy of *TV Weekly*, tries to distract Nancy—and herself—from the sour air. *TV Weekly* is snubbed, so Jess then offers a sip of water, pressing the tip of the straw to Nancy's lips. Nancy just shuts her eyes, spits it away.

"What about a walk then, Grandma? It's beautiful out. We could go to your favorite place, like always."

"Not today," says Nancy.

The clock ticks on. Jess sighs, twiddles her thumbs. She knew the news of the necklace's loss would cause upset, but the intensity of Nancy's despondence is bruising. That this art nouveau treasure should be so emotionally resonant to an eighty-two-year-old woman with a soul of steel makes it even harder. She's always been pragmatic, never sentimental about anything, so to see her so sullen makes Jess ache with remorse. She straightens the bedsheets, then adjusts the curtains, remembering the day her grandmother left for Snowdonia. She and Aggie were still teenagers. One autumn afternoon, among packed boxes and shimmering blue IKEA bags, Nancy waved good-bye to the brick and plaster of her urban street, gave each of her granddaughters a brisk hug, then took off in her tatty red car. The decision to leave happened suddenly—that Taylor tendency to act on impulse—and was the trigger for a large quota of domestic chaos.

"But the girls need you here," Jess's father, Richard, had complained, having been unhappily reliant on Nancy since their mother's death.

"Don't be ridiculous," Nancy had countered. "They're all grown up now. What they need is life, not some old sack like me getting in the way."

In packing she'd been ruthless, throwing or giving away anything she didn't need. She'd confided to Jess, after two pints of stout, that she had no regrets about going "minimal," because she'd already lost two of the things most precious to her. One of those was her daughter. She never said what the other one was.

After five minutes of silence, Tim is restless.

"Perhaps we should let her sleep," he suggests. "Get a coffee or something? Come back later?"

Just then, as though a switch has been flicked, Nancy opens her eyes, sits up, pushes off her blanket, and brightens.

"Oh yes," she exclaims. "Could you take me out? I would dearly like a turn around the Great Shalimar—"

"The what?" says Tim.

"The Palace," Jess explains, amused by her grandma's timely change of heart. "It's her name for the Crystal Palace. Every time I visit, that's where she asks to go. We wheel around the concrete, read the graffiti, check out the stone sphinxes, and then she asks for a cup of tea and we come back. It's sweet, if a little repetitive."

"You know the glass is really something," says Nancy—another of her stuck-record remarks.

"Was," says Jess, kindly but firmly. "The palace isn't there anymore, Grandma. It burned down in 1936. It's just a ruin now, but we can go and take a look, can't we?"

She smiles and squeezes Nancy's hand, relieved that if she can't deliver the necklace, or an acceptable life plan, she can at least do this for her grandma, take her for a walk. Tim helps Jess fetch a wheelchair from the nurses' station. She signs the relevant release forms, then ushers Nancy into a wool coat and sheepskin boots. Nancy giggles, her spirits no doubt buoyed by the prospect of exiting this small, plain room.

The sun shines, dispersing the few clouds that dare to intrude on the June afternoon. Up on the hill, however, there is a breeze. Tim strides into it, while Jess follows behind, pushing Nancy's chair. The chair helps her balance. *What a pair we are*, Jess thinks. *Walking canes and wheels.* Ten months ago, she was in a wheelchair herself, completely reliant on Aggie and Ed. The thought of this throbs, but she quashes it with a dose of gratitude. At least now she can put one foot in front of the other, albeit with some discomfort.

And she has Tim. She sees him ahead and feels at ease, warmed by the prospect of their Stratford home, the idea that they will soon be nesting together, cooking breakfast on Sundays, snuggling on the sofa with takeout and Netflix. Tim is glued to his phone, searching for facts about the Crystal Palace. She loves how he relishes encyclopedic detail—an inquiring mind, always interested in understanding how the world really is rather than accepting it at face value.

But still, Nancy's scolding critique pesters her conscience: *Lost your spirit?*

A year ago she'd had plenty, and look where it got her. There were days when it seemed like she'd never walk again, never be independent. There were also days—many—when she feared she'd never be able to trust another human. So whatever Nancy's judgment may be, Jess has conviction: it's time to embrace the grounded life, to be a mature, cohabiting person who no longer needs rescuing from remote parts of Mexico.

And as for the "You're a Taylor!" assertion, what does that even mean? To be a Taylor? Like it's a badge of honor. Jess sighs, thinks back. As a child she was constantly restless. Aggie was always looking straight ahead, while Restless Jess wanted to know what was off to the side or around the corner or just beyond, where the eye couldn't reach. Always looking for the next adventure. Is *that* down to Taylor genes?

They approach the first of the stone sphinxes, which flank a tattered staircase and a vista of nettle-filled scrubland. Such grandiose entrance guards with nothing to announce. They are, thinks Jess, like an unfinished breath, inhaling, pausing, forever waiting for their palace to return.

"Built for the Great Exhibition of 1851," says Nancy, mechanically recounting as she always does. "First in Hyde Park, then moved here. I never saw this happening, of course."

"No." Jess laughs gently. "You weren't born."

"Nor was your mother, Carmen. Nor was my mother, Anna. And nor was Minnie."

"Oh yes, tell me about Minnie—"

"Minnie Philomene Taylor, born in 1881. She was your great-great-grandmother. She made a necklace."

Jess winces. "Yes, *the* necklace."

"A butterfly necklace. Jessy, you were going to get it for me—"

"And I failed, Nancy. Once again, I'm massively sorry."

Nancy bows her head, then brightens again.

"My mother once called it the True Love Necklace. She gave it to me when I was seventeen. Oh, I'd so like it back."

"I know," says Jess regretfully.

Then as the wind blows, Nancy's focus recycles itself.

"The Crystal Palace," she repeats, "built for the Great Exhibition of 1851, first in Hyde Park, then moved here, where it still stands."

"Or at least its remains do," Jess corrects.

What a shame, she thinks, that something so magnificent, that transformed so many people's view of the world, is now a mere concrete slab, the sparkle of its aisles gone to dust.

"Ah, time," says Nancy, staring down at her wizened hands. "It does have a habit of degrading things. Can we see it? Can we go?"

"We're here, Grandma," says Jess affirmatively, realizing the conversation is going in circles.

"So we are."

Jess turns Nancy's chair toward where the palace entrance would have been. Nancy's eyes widen, as though she is seeing the crystalline marvel as it was—the cast-iron structure towering above, the sheen of the glass, the trees, the towers, the fountains, the elegant Italianate gardens, people everywhere. The past in the present, the dead resurrected for just one transformative instant to delight an ailing imagination.

"It was the world's first theme park," Tim reads from his phone, "known as 'The Palace of the People.' Apparently it housed sports matches, festivals, and concerts. Even had a roller coaster. *And* it featured the first public toilets, for which guests were charged a penny. And—oh, Jess, you'll like this—exhibits included a single nugget of Chilean gold weighing fifty kilograms and the world's rarest pale-pink diamond from India."

"How does *he* know?" says Nancy scathingly.

"Wikipedia," whispers Jess. "He likes looking up facts on his phone."

Nancy snorts.

"Our Minnie," she says, with an imperious air, "didn't need the Wikipedia. She saw the Great Shalimar in all its glory. It was her playground."

"It was?"

"In her teens she would go for walks, which would turn into three-hour meanders of wanderlust, often to here."

Jess's curiosity accelerates. Behind her, Tim rambles on, quoting more dates and details, but she is distracted instead by Nancy's remark—the impact the palace would have had on a local girl like Minnie, with its ever-changing program of events and entertainments. In the late 1800s, presumably Minnie's most exotic experience of nature would have been the primroses in her front garden. Yet in the palace she could stand among great palms from the tropics, observe creatures from the sea, bird shows, water fountains and, according to Tim, a stuffed elephant dressed in a full rajah's howdah and trappings.

"Apparently Minnie loved to sit at the foot of the stone sphinx," Nancy continues, "near the entrance, where she could admire the ladies. She liked to look at their finery—their bustles and shawls and brooches."

Jess smiles.

"The whole place must have made such an impression on her," she says.

"Yes," says Nancy, "but what really opened her eyes was Paris—"

"Paris?" Jess blinks, intrigued to swim deeper into the heart of her history. "When did she go to *Paris*?"

"Enough now," says Nancy, suddenly prickly. "I've had enough. I want to go back."

"Sure," says Jess, flustered, frustrated by Nancy's half-dangled snippet. "We can do that. Of course."

Back at the care home, a quietness engulfs them. Tim sets to work on one of the puzzle books, periodically checking his watch, too considerate to make bolder overtures toward wanting to leave. Nancy remains agitated. She rocks in her chair, rubbing her arms.

"Grandma, what's the matter?" says Jess.

Nancy scrunches her eyes shut.

"I want to show you something," she says.

She nods to the top of the bureau, to a folder that looks like it hasn't been touched since the seventies. Jess fetches it, remembering Nancy being particular about it coming with her when she left Wales. Jess had assumed it was full of bills and bank statements. With trembling hands, Nancy fumbles in the file, then pulls out a pair of photographs and presses them to her chest. She then straightens the first photograph and hands it over: a Victorian family portrait. Within the crumpled sepia, Jess sees a woman in a dark dress with mutton-chop sleeves standing beside a mustached man. On their laps are a young boy in a sailor suit and a baby in a lace gown and bonnet. Dark eyes, faces stern—the formal stiffness of the nineteenth century.

"These are my ancestors?" says Jess, wide-eyed.

"Yes. This is Minnie with her parents."

"She's the baby?"

"Yes."

"And the boy...her brother?"

"Died young," says Nancy as though it's no big deal. "Burst appendix."

"Oh."

Jess holds the photo close, awed by her connection with these long-dead figures, her forebears. Here is Minnie Philomene Taylor, serious-faced infant who, according to Nancy, grew up to be a trailblazer. A handwritten date on the back says 1882. Jess briefly offers the photo to Tim, but he doesn't notice, eyes down, shoulders hunched over a sudoku.

"How do you know all this?" asks Jess, turning back to Nancy, intrigued to understand how, after more than a century and with so little airing, these distant family details still *live*.

Nancy looks thoughtful.

"My mother told me stories," she says.

"You mean Anna?"

Jess processes the name. Anna Taylor—a woman she never met, yet owes her life to. Suddenly it sinks in, that as well as being Nancy's mother and her great grandmother, Anna Taylor was also Minnie's daughter.

"Yes," says Nancy, smiling to herself. "Anna told me stories, about her life, about Minnie's life. Stories kept her going. We lived in such squalor when we left Hollywood, but Anna's sparkling stories elevated her. Everyone needs sparkle from time to time, Jessy."

"Yes," says Jess. "They really do."

"She was highly prone to hyperbole, my mother. Some of what she said was pure exaggeration. But I did enjoy hearing about Minnie's life."

"Tell me," says Jess, leaning forward.

"Her parents—your great-great-*great*-grandparents—were upright people from Sydenham," Nancy explains, her voice slow and precise. "He did accounts, earned enough to afford a house on Hammond Road with two servants. She was an accomplished viola player, very musical."

"Musical?" says Jess, recalling her own appalling efforts with a clarinet. "I guess that genome skipped a few generations. Was Minnie musical too?"

"I believe not. She had a governess and was given lessons in everything from pianoforte to watercolor painting, but showed a lack of application. Never badly behaved, just easily distracted. Rambunctious, one might say."

Jess smiles. "Now *that* I can relate to."

"Her instinct for jewelry began in childhood. She took an interest in the trades on the high street, wanted to understand how things were made, how craftsmen worked. On one occasion she went 'missing' for hours, until her uncle found her, filthy and sweaty, down at the local blacksmiths', watching them firing up their furnaces. Her parents were horrified. Their hopes for their daughter had never included the 'masculine' chaos of ironmongery. Their antidote was to find a suitor. In 1899, after some stiff warnings about the tragedy that might befall her should she fail to secure her social status, our Minnie was persuaded to marry Robert Belsing, a junior accounts clerk at her father's firm, whose parents had some standing among the London livery companies."

"You say 'persuaded'?"

"Well, it wasn't for love—not on Minnie's part—but in her parents' view, it was a good match. That's how marriages were in those days, Jessy. After the wedding, Robert Belsing applied for an overseas office. In 1900, he and Minnie relocated to Paris."

"Aha, Paris."

"Yes. They arrived just in time for the Exposition Universelle."

"1900! France's world fair! I know of it," says Jess, delightedly plumbing her knowledge of art and design history. "It's where art nouveau came to prominence. Did Minnie go?"

"I believe Robert agreed to take her after some coaxing. And a good job, too, because it was here that she found her purpose: all she wanted was to make jewelry. You see, out of all of the wonders at the Exposition, what enchanted Minnie most was the Palace of Decorative Arts and, in particular, the jewelry boutique of René Lalique."

"Yes!" Jess beams, eyes bright, immediately wondering if this explains the stylistic references she'd seen in the butterfly necklace— the auctioneer had even mentioned them—the use of semiprecious stones and plique-à-jour, the interpretation of the natural form. Lalique, famous for his art nouveau jewelry and, later, his glassware in the art deco style, was one of the most influential designers of the period. If Minnie had seen his boutique at the fair, she would have seen some of the finest creations imaginable.

"So Lalique's jewelry inspired Minnie to make our necklace?"

"No, Jessy. Lalique's designs gave her the visual language, but her inspiration—the true *heart* of her intent—was her discovery of true love."

"How sweet. With her husband, Robert?"

Nancy stiffens.

"Absolutely not."

"Oh."

"After the Exposition, Minnie began keeping a sketchbook of ideas," Nancy explains. "In secret. She'd sit listening to gossip in Paris salons, quietly watching the women, studying their earrings and brooches, then she'd hurry home to draw and make notes. She dreamed that one day she might take her sketchbook to Lalique himself, to be praised and handed a set of metalwork tools. She begged

Robert to let her inquire about training at Lalique's workshop in Paris, but he wouldn't allow it, couldn't accept such a modern ambition for his wife. Back then, jewelry—both its craft and its business—was very much 'man's work.'"

"So how did she manage to make the butterfly necklace?"

"According to Anna, when Robert discovered the sketchbook, stuffed down the side of Minnie's daybed, he flew into a rage. He locked her in their apartment, feeding her little more than bread and water. And when she tried to escape, the fool used his fist. Paris was spoiling her, he said. She needed to learn proper conduct."

Jess shudders, looks to Tim, nose buried in a puzzle book, whose twenty-first-century temperament poses no threat, no patriarchal clipping of her wings, and feels very grateful.

"Quickly, Minnie realized that if she was to survive she would have to play along. As Robert's ire faded and he allowed her some basic freedoms again, she squeezed herself into his vision: the modest, decorative, obedient wife. But then—"

Nancy sighs, shuts her eyes, clearly starting to tire.

"What?" begs Jess, wide-eyed and anxious, knowing Nancy's focus will only hold for so long before confusion consumes it. "What then?"

"She ran away," whispers Nancy, resting before she continues. "With the little money she'd managed to sneak from Robert's desk, the dress she was wearing, and a hunk of dry bread, she ran from him. She knew the consequences, that there was no going back, that if Robert ever found her, he'd destroy her, that her parents, as soon as they heard, would disown her. But still, Minnie ran."

"Where did she go?"

"Be patient," Nancy snaps. "I'll show you."

With a shaky hand, she holds the second photograph toward Jess.

It's a portrait of Minnie as a young woman.

"Oh my goodness!" Jess exclaims. "She's wearing the necklace! There it is!"

The butterfly shines like an emblem above Minnie's chest, plique-à-jour wings ready to fly. Minnie, meanwhile, sits upon a garden wall, the natural light suggesting a summer afternoon. Jess can see the family likeness, her DNA—that same round face, bow lips, and the short, sturdy Taylor physique, made all the more elegant by the flattering cut of 1900s clothing. Bizarrely, Minnie holds a peacock on her lap, its distinctive patterned tail feathers draping down her leg.

"She was on the trail of the suffragettes," Nancy croaks. "Never take for granted your independence, Jessy."

"No," says Jess. "I never will."

"She was a one," says Nancy, tapping Minnie's face with her fingernail.

Jess smiles, having heard the same said of Nancy over and over again. She then notices the pronounced split in Minnie's skirt; it is, in fact, a pair of wide-legged trousers.

"She must have been bold to wear trousers back then. Is that in Paris?"

"No," says Nancy. "After. That photograph was taken at Pel Tawr."

"Pel Tawr?"

The name resonates, the pine-forested estate in Snowdonia

where Nancy's log cabin stands. Jess sits back, scours her memory. She recalls the big, old arts-and-crafts house on the top of the hill above the cabin, the sign at the gateposts: Pel Tawr.

"Grandma," she presses, fearing Nancy's return to those painfully circular conversations about the Great Shalimar and that Minnie's story—the origins of her family's necklace—will be forever silenced, locked away in Nancy's dying mind. "Is that the same Pel Tawr where your cabin is? Why did Minnie go there?"

"To *be*," Nancy whispers. "You see, just before she ran away from Robert, she found an article in an English newspaper, left by one of Robert's cousins, about an artistic community in the Welsh mountains. The owners, the Floyd family, had made their wealth in copper and were avid followers of the late William Morris and his Kelmscott Press. They were liberals, full of grand ideas about how to make the world a better place. They'd thrown open the doors of their arts-and-crafts house to *all* who shared their values of design and community—amateur, experienced, young, old, male, female. When she read about this, Minnie realized her time in Paris had ignited her artistic ambition, but Robert had trapped her soul. Pel Tawr could save her. She had to find her strength. She had to find her strength, Jessy, and *go*—"

"To live her best life," Jess concurs, suddenly tearful, caught by the fleeting thought that her own "best life" might be behind her, body broken, unable to do what it used to do. Stealing herself, she blinks away the self-pity, cups Nancy's hand with her own.

"So did Minnie make the necklace there at Pel Tawr?" she asks.

"Yes," says Nancy. "With Emery—"

"Emery?"

"Emery Floyd."

Nancy then squeezes Jess's hand, pulls it tight to her chest.

"We called it the True Love Necklace," she strains, barely audible. "Because everyone who wore it found their soul mate. First Minnie. Then Anna. Then me. Then your mother."

"So who'll be next?" says Jess, half-joking, before realizing the significance of the answer. "Oh, Grandma," she says, scorched with emotion, "I'm so sorry I didn't get your necklace."

She goes to stroke Nancy's face, but Nancy pulls away. Maybe sleepy from exhaustion, or just pretending—her way to shut out the world she's grown tired of—she closes her papery lids over her gray eyes. After minutes of silent stillness, Jess pulls away.

"Well," she says quietly, to herself more than anyone, "I may not have the necklace, but I certainly have my soul mate."

She glances at Tim. He looks up and smiles, eyes full of warmth.

"You okay?" he says.

"Yes," she says.

Jess kisses Nancy goodbye, then picks up her bag and goes to him: her savior, who makes her feel loved, who says he's there for her and means it, who'll never hurt her, or tell her she can't enjoy jewelry, or make her feel like his property. She thinks of the day they move into their Stratford flat, their first sleep in their new bed—the sweet relief of waking up each morning with a kind, trustable human. She reaches into her bag, finds her painkillers, pops one into her mouth, then as Tim rises from his chair, it's the least she can do to kiss his cheek and tell him how lucky she feels.

Chapter Six

IN THEIR LOCAL RESTAURANT THAT EVENING, JESS FEELS CLOSER TO Tim than ever and is distracted by the pleasure of his broad shoulders and neat jaw as they eat sticky ribs and sweet potato fries. She smiles to herself, sips her gin and tonic, then surveys her fellow diners: sets of couples in their thirties and forties, chatting about work, whether or not to tip the babysitter, whether to drunk cycle home or call an Uber. It's a decent life: some pleasure, some security, some purpose. Perhaps not seat-of-your-pants stuff, but decent nonetheless.

She could be like them. She *is* like them.

"The glass weight was minimal," says Tim, still recounting facts about the Crystal Palace, between mouthfuls of charred corn, "so it needed no heavy masonry or foundations. You know, she wasn't as scary as I thought, your grandmother—"

"Ah, she's mellowed with age, but she used to be a spitfire. She enrages my sister. And my dad can't be in the same room as her. She just…had her own way of doing things, single-minded. Always lived alone, managed for herself. It's strange to see her dependent on nurses and carers. Sometimes I wonder if she'd have been happier if we'd left her to it—"

Jess shuts her eyes, recalls Nancy's cabin in Wales—the smoky smell of the wood burner, the rough-cut beams, the dust on the floor, and the extraordinarily loud birdcall at dawn. Then her mind wanders to the house on the hill, to Pel Tawr, to Minnie Taylor and her necklace, the "*OUI*" engraved on the back. Why is it there? What does it mean? She knows it translates as "yes," but yes to what? To life? To love?

"I should go there again," she says, eyes wide, jolted, "to check on the place."

"Wha—?"

"To the cabin. I should go to Nancy's cabin."

Tim nods, having not quite followed Jess's train of thought.

"Right. Sure."

"This week?" she suggests, a sense of urgency rising in her—sensitive to her grandmother's decline and with a growing compulsion to find out all she can about her family and their necklace before it's too late.

"You could come with me?"

Tim twitches.

"Um…work. It might be tricky. School term. I can't just—"

"Of course. Don't worry. I'll go by myself. Maybe I'll get a train down and—"

"Really?" Tim stares at her. "On your own?"

Jess tenses. The thought corkscrews through her mind. True, she hasn't done anything of significant independence—no long journeys, no heavy-duty days out—since her accident, and certainly not since Tim has known her. In the early days, she wasn't even able to bathe or move from room to room without help. A trip to Wales all by herself would be a big step, but she feels a little lift in her heart as she thinks of it—that Taylor spirit perhaps? The "*OUT*" effect? Maybe her adventurous soul can start to be revived, even if her wrecked limbs can't.

Tim shakes his head, his brow furrowed with concern.

"I'm not sure, Jess. How will you cope? I'd be worried. Why not wait until we can go together, so I can be on hand to—"

"To what?" says Jess, remembering the awkward insinuation back at the care home, that she should "be more careful," given her physical challenges. Oversensitive perhaps, but the sting is still there. She stares at him from the rim of her glass. She can tell he's wincing, knows he's on the spot.

"It's just, with your back and hip, you're…more vulnerable than most."

"*Vulnerable?*"

Under the table, Jess kicks her walking cane away.

"I don't mean… Uh, I'm not explaining this very well. It sounds bad, whatever. You're not vulnerable. What I'm trying to say is if you go on a trip, you might need help at some point. But if I'm there, I can give you that help. I can carry your bags, help you on the stairs. And if your back starts to throb in that horrible way that makes you yelp, I can massage it for you. Hell, if it comes to it, Jess, and you're not able to walk at all, I can carry you."

Jess knows he's referring to the epic piggyback, when her hip seized from too much sitting on low grass at a friend's picnic, and he had to carry her all the way from Victoria Park to Hackney station. How she kept saying "sorry," but he gleefully, insistently went whole hog.

"I love helping you, Jess," he says brightly. "I mean, my mum always told me I was the nurturing type—"

Jess stiffens.

"That's like you're saying you're with me just because you can *nurture* me."

"No, Jess, I'm with you because I love you, because you make me happy…because…because having both had our ups and downs with relationships, we now want the same things. We're ready to settle and grow together. Our lives can grow. That's it. We can grow, move in, get married, have a family, have everything."

Jess knocks back the rest of her drink, crunches an ice cube between her teeth.

"Thank goodness for my heroic boyfriend, helping me grow, saving me from my wretched self."

"Sorry," says Tim. "I sound like a dick."

"It's okay," she says, softening. "I kind of know what you mean. We've met each other at the right time. I had my wild days. You had your PhD and your evil first wife. We've got the kinks out of our systems, and now we're both in a place where we're ready to—"

"Grow."

"If you must use that word."

They both laugh, then grab hands across the table.

"And you know what?" says Jess, holding his gaze. "I actually love that you're a nurturer and that you're honest and thoughtful. Hell, I've had my share of bad boys."

"I *know*. When I asked your sister if she thought it would be a good idea to invite you to move in with me, I got the talk of doom, about how you're prone to rash decisions, and that because of this, you've picked some wrong 'uns. She actually recounted a list of your exes and their failings—"

"The joker, the philanderer, the man-child, the man-child philanderer, and the escape artist?"

"Those."

"She believes I made poor choices. I say I had a blast."

"The escape artist wasn't so fun, though, was he?"

Jess looks down.

"No, he wasn't."

"Your type?"

"Not anymore," she says, with an emphatic smile.

"We're a good team."

"We so are."

On Aggie's doorstep, like prom-dating teenagers, they kiss farewell. Jess has an inkling she would like more than a quick makeout session, but Tim has already stated his intention to head back to his own house for an early night, so he can wake up fresh and prepare for his interview. She playfully runs her hand up his inner thigh, curious to see if he can be persuaded, but he grins and pushes away.

"Not tonight," he says. "You know I've got to be sharp this week."

She flickers her lashes, pouts her lips, but it's just a performance. He's too sensible to cave. She sighs, steps back.

"I'll make it up to you once I've got the job, I promise," he says, then kisses her one more time and strides into the night.

As Jess enters the darkened Hoppit household, she hears sniffling. She wanders through the hallway to the kitchen-diner, where a single dimmed spotlight is illuminating the forlorn shape of Steph, hunched over the kitchen island, dripping tears onto her smartphone.

"Hey!" says Jess, concerned. "What's wrong with my favorite niece?"

Steph looks up, wipes her sleeve across her nose.

"My mum is such a cow!" she wails.

"Uh-oh. What's happened now?"

Jess pulls up a seat beside her.

"I was out with Jared. We weren't doing anything wrong. He'd planned a picnic for me, down at the clearing. Then she turned up, raging…literally *raging*. She totally humiliated me, then made me get in the car and go home. He went to soooo much trouble. He even made his own pesto."

She bursts into tears. Jess pats her arm.

"Was there alcohol?"

"No."

"Cigarettes?"

"*No*. I keep telling Mum, he's straight edge now. He's stopped all that. She just hates him because…he's more clued in about the world than she is."

"Hmm." Jess ponders this statement, while using the instant-boil tap to fix them both a mug of chamomile tea. She passes one to Steph, then lifts the other to her chin, inhaling its soothing vapors.

She has watched Aggie and Steph fight and fight, in the way that only a mother and daughter can, cracking down on each other, cracking up, the fuel of their ire as close to love as it is to anger. All said and done, they'll always be mother and daughter.

"Woolly," Jess says eventually, being careful not to betray her own sisterly bonds. "I think she perceives him as woolly."

"Woolly?"

"The environmental activist thing, the gender-free thing, the drugs should be legalized thing. Plus that whole 'I don't believe in money' conversation you had last week—"

"So? No one should believe in money. Rabid consumerism is killing society."

"True, I know that. You know that. Jared clearly knows that. But your mother, what she cares about most is the tiny details of your life within the bigger picture. Here she is, having created this comfortable, secure home for you all"—Jess gestures around the kitchen at the Smeg appliances, the sleek countertop, and the Boden apron—"this is the stuff that matters to her. Don't ask me why, but it's her idea of a life well lived."

"What's this got to do with Jared?"

"She thinks Jared, with his—shall we call them 'liberal' views—won't be able to offer you a John Lewis kitchen...and it scares her."

"But I'm *sixteen*. I don't want a John Lewis kitchen. I want to eat Doritos and stuff that comes out of microwaves. I might never want a John Lewis kitchen. And even if I did"—she suddenly rallies—"I'll buy it myself."

"I've no doubt you will," says Jess.

"She just wants to control me," Steph rails on. "She interferes in everything I do. Always telling me what to eat, how to revise, how to do my hair, how much screen time I can have, who I should be seeing. You know she's obsessed with me hanging out with that moronic Charlie Fitzwilliam kid because his dad's some big-time property lawyer and she thinks it'll make her look good. She's literally a conversation away from arranging a marriage for us—"

"She's not trying to control you, Steph. She just wants to...guide you."

"But I don't need guiding. I do fine and I've got my own mind."

"That you have," says Jess, feeling all of Steph's torment threefold. They both sip their tea.

"Where've you been anyway?"

"Out with Tim. I took him to meet Grandma Nancy, then we had supper." Jess pauses, smiles. "You know he's asked me to move in with him. What do you think about that?"

"It'll please Mum," says Steph with a shrug. "She'll buy you a cookie set to match hers."

"Huh?"

"Matching cookie-cutting lifestyles. See what I mean? She wants to control you as well, get you to fit in with her idea of how women should be."

"Listen, I'm moving in with Tim because I want to. It's my choice."

"Really?"

"A hundred percent. I'm well past the age when I should be

asking anyone's permission to do anything, let alone move in with the man I love."

Steph shrugs again in that passive-aggressive teenage way that says everything and nothing.

"What? Don't you like Tim? I thought you two got on well—"

"Yeah, he's nice."

"*And?*"

"'Nice' isn't fireworks."

"No…but eventually a woman learns to value dependability over quick thrills. One day you'll understand. Hopefully, one day soon."

"I don't think so, Aunty. I'll never depend on anyone but myself, but thanks for the chat." She yawns. "I'm off to bed. Don't tell Mum we spoke, will you? Love you."

Jess sighs, smiles, throws her head back in mock despair, realizing she'll never outsmart the self-possessed guile of youth. She kisses her niece good night and watches her sylphlike form tiptoeing down the hall, long, skinny legs in boxer shorts, young enough not to care which parts of her flesh she exposes and to whom, fiercely idealistic, recklessly sure. Please, Jess thinks, let this fire lead somewhere wonderful for Steph; let all the Jareds of the world become crown princes instead of toads.

Chapter Seven

THERE'S A SALE COMING, THINKS GUY. HE CAN FEEL IT. AS STELLA gazes at the sea-green butterfly wings, her expression says it all. She'd make an appalling poker player. No game.

"It's luscious," she says, stroking the opalescent moonstone. "Oh, Guy, it's just what I've been looking for. I adore things with insects. How old is it?"

"It's art nouveau, early 1900s, so you're looking at well over a century."

"Ooo, let me write that down. You know what I'm like with the facts and figures. But hooray for this… *This* will get the vintage crowd in a flap."

"So you're interested?"

"Assuming there'll be a nice friend's discount?"

"For my best client, of course. I bought it for one six, but I reckon it'll be worth way more in a few years. Art nouveau jewelry is due a resurgence."

"Then I'll have to lead the way. Will you put it on me?"

She turns, lifts her hair, revealing the gently tanned nape of her neck—holiday leftover from a week in Saint-Tropez. He removes the necklace from its box and places it around her shoulders, then turns her toward the mirror.

"Love it," she says.

Guy nods. As long as Stella's happy, the world is at peace. But then he pauses, puzzled. With its exquisite butterfly form and luster, the necklace is such a vivacious piece, yet somehow on Stella, it looks dead. He daren't say this, of course; he needs Stella to love it. Every time she's photographed wearing one of his finds, his business gets a boost. Like the day she wore that oversize pot-metal and paste 1940s dress clip... He gained five new clients and a two-page spread in *Harper's Bazaar*. With something as Instagrammable as the art nouveau necklace, a single Stella Weston power pose could be a game-changer. If this necklace gets the likes and shares it deserves, interest in Guy van der Meer Jewelry will surely proliferate.

He blinks, flashbacks of childhood briefly zipping to the surface: all those years of disappointment, no one present in his life long enough to notice his quick mind and artistic eye. So many empty days, wasted and broke. In the circles he'd grown up in, it hadn't been cool or "manly" to be creative. No one gave a damn about jewelry, unless they were nicking it out of other people's bedside drawers. And school hadn't added much to the proceedings. That troublemaker label had followed him everywhere—four expulsions and an addiction to smart-arse remarks had meant his teachers had known of his reputation before they'd even met him, then dismissed him as "destined to fail."

Here in Stella Weston's high-ceilinged Chelsea hallway, fears for what his life might have been start to loom. But then Guy catches his bright reflection in the mirror, a sentinel next to Stella—the fashion media superstar who utterly trusts his opinion and knows nothing of his frowzy past—and is reminded that he has built this incredible life for himself, relying on little more than his natural affability and eye for design. He has done it, succeeded; proved the ghosts of his boyhood wrong. Okay, so he's told a few fibs along the way, but the high-end jewelry trade is a closed group. He's had to hustle, had to have a reason for them to let him into their tribe. A good name is everything. With a sigh, he compresses the shame and focuses on the gains.

A prize antique necklace for Stella. It's a dream deal.

Yet as he gazes at those tiny plique-à-jour cells, the discomfort of the pairing grates. The bare fact is it doesn't look right on Stella. To his expert eye, the length of the chain is wrong, the shape of the butterfly clashes with her pointed face, and the color has a dulling effect on her skin. Good jewelry should enhance its wearer's appearance, not sully it; but there is something else too, an awkwardness, a *resistance*, almost as though the necklace doesn't want to be there.

A thought strikes his soul. The woman who accosted him in his taxi—Jess—she'd laid claim to this butterfly with such fire. Maybe it would look different on her? All that stuff about it being her family's heirloom… At first he'd shrugged it off, fixated on how much profit he could make selling the necklace to Stella, but what if the necklace knows better? Like Cinderella's slipper, what if it's only meant for one person? What, then, would that make him…*Prince Charming*? He grins, sweeps a hand through his curls.

All said and done, he appreciates the fact that heirlooms aren't showpieces. They're personal, the material remnants of family identity when all the ancestors have gone to dust. He looks down at his emerald-eyed leopard ring. If he ever lost the leopard, he'd be devastated. So he understands. He understands why Jess was mad at him.

The question is, will he ever see her again?

Sure, he'd flirted. He'd asked her for a date, standard behavior for the world he lives in. A dozen flirty rich girls come by, talking about shopping trips to New York and parties in LA, and they expect him to flirt. They'd be *insulted* if he didn't. So...he plays the game.

But this wasn't flirting. *This* was something else. Chemistry, perhaps? Is that even a thing anymore? He glances at Stella, who is now distracted from the necklace and is busy inspecting her eyelids for crow's-feet. Stella, he suspects, has no clue about chemistry—either the romantic or the scientific sort—unless the equation involves super yachts.

Jess—maybe Jessica—with her cupid lips, bright eyes, and short-girl feistiness, the rightful bearer of the art nouveau butterfly. Looking back, he realizes he had a sense about her the moment she fell into him in the auction room, nearly taking him out with her walking cane. The fact that they ended up going after the same piece of jewelry, well, that was just a freak coincidence. Wasn't it? He smiles again, eyes sparkling.

"What are you so merry about?" Stella probes.

"Nothing," he says, pushing the smile back inside.

Jealousy doesn't rub well between him and Stella. He knows the deal. Stella shares the spoils of her lifestyle, introduces him to useful people. In return, he decorates her with the best of his treasure and gives her his undivided attention.

Meanwhile, on the other side of London, Jess sips the rest of her tea in the dim light of the Hoppit kitchen and thinks about Steph and Aggie and their fractious understanding of each other. Aggie, she recalls, was always a perfectionist at school, on time, hard-working, worrying about exam grades. These days her happiness seems to be intrinsically bound to other people's admiration of her things: her big house, her glossy hair, her clever and talented children. So the idea of her mini-me daughter going rogue with a vegan pansexual hippie whose career plans mostly consist of international fruit pick-ing is a big leap.

But, really, who is Jess to judge, in the wake of her extended quarter-life crisis? A pang of guilt rises inside at memories of how Aggie took care of her, how she negotiated with doctors, chased the arsehole insurance company, paid a bunch of medical bills and never asked for the money back. But before that, even, how she picked up the pieces whenever Jess had a new broken heart, after the phi-landerer, the man-child, and the man-child philanderer had done their worst. And before *that*, when they were children, growing up motherless, with a disinterested father and a difficult grandmother, how Aggie had been the surrogate parent, taking care, making things right, ever patient whenever Jess was in trouble at school.

A twinge in Jess's hip forces her to stand, and with searing sharp-ness, the memory comes back to her: that moment at the airport, waving goodbye to the Hoppits. *Just a quick trip*, she'd said, promis-ing Aggie she'd be back in time to see Marcus get his next grading in karate. A knot of regret fills her chest. *Why* did she do it? What the hell motivated her to quit her job in teaching and buy a one-way ticket to Mexico City?

Why didn't she see it then? The infamous Taylor "spirit" reconfigured as a load of old nonsense. How about a simple, straightforward life like everyone else, with a good man and a sound job and a nice home and maybe...maybe a child? *Why* didn't she see it then, that a normal life could be just as rewarding as a wild one?

Those nights in hospital. The sensation of Aggie's hand on her forehead, gently stroking the hair from her eyes.

"Maybe it's time to stay in the quiet lane, Jessy," she'd whispered.

And in that soft light, unable to move, unable to speak, machines beeping all around her, Jess had made a silent pledge. From now on, she would make better choices. She would stay in one country, live one life, get one job and stick to it. She would avoid all men owning more than one mobile phone. And make a conscious effort to replace the words *spontaneous*, *thrill-seeking*, and *adventurous* with *erratic*, *unreliable*, and *fraud*. She would rebuild her life, step by aching step, and in healing, and in time, she would make her sister proud.

Mission refreshed, Jess empties the dregs of her tea and goes to turn out the light, hopeful she'll reap the benefits of an earlyish night come morning. Just then, however, she hears her phone buzz. Out of habit, she checks it, then stalls and blinks. It's a friend request from Guy Arlo van der Meer. A booty call? She checks out his account and sees what she thought she'd see: a photographic carnival of glamorous parties, gallery openings, and film premieres, supported by a cast of art collectors, fashionistas, and super-wealthy Instagram influencers.

And in his profile he describes himself as a treasure hunter. She laughs heartily.

"What kind of overblown job title is that? What a nob!"

She laughs some more, then clipped by annoyance that he wouldn't sell her the necklace, she denies the request and shuts off her phone.

Chapter Eight

WITH HER LAPTOP, HER JEWELRY STOCK, AND A BOX OF PACKING materials spread across the Hoppit kitchen countertop, Jess spends a productive Friday afternoon sorting and preparing shipments for customers. A quirky 1950s rhinestone brooch in the shape of retro sunglasses is going to Kent; a Deco revival bracelet with pearlized frog clasp is destined for Inverness; and a 1980s statement necklace with coral cabochons is traveling all the way to Japan. Carefully, she wraps the coral necklace in three layers of turquoise tissue paper, ties the package with a magenta ribbon, and adds one of her gold stickers: Miss Taylor's Retro and Vintage Costume Jewelry.

Jess's one-stop online shop—specializing in vintage jewelry from the forties to the eighties, with the occasional early twentieth-century treasure thrown in—is starting to grow. She hand-selects every piece, sourcing them from auctions, estate sales, and flea markets. She never buys in bulk, only sells items she would wear herself, and always looks for quality, distinctiveness, and the possibility of a signature or known designer. It's not as stable as teaching snarling fifteen-year-olds to gouge linoleum, but it feels a lot more joyous.

She deals in the orphans of the jewelry world, all those

once-loved, now-forgotten pinnacles of female glamour, lost to the shadows of dingy attic shoeboxes and flea-market cabinets. She finds them, revives them, gives them another lease of life. There's some great old jewelry circulating, she thinks, as she admires her next offering: a chunky 1960s bangle with a mound of prong-set agate. She slips the bangle over her wrist and considers the possibility of its original owner, imagines it paired with a crepe maxi dress, and swung through Carnaby Street, among the rebel music, street art, and fashion boutiques. Who saw it there, dangling from its wearer's arm? Whose attention did it attract?

There are so many untold stories: a hidden myriad of birthday parties, balls, restaurants, theater trips, job interviews, anniversaries, and first dates. Her regular customers understand this. They love the magic of heritage, the way that jewelry can tell stories and connect people. There are those who ask her to find specifics things. One of her clients loves anything themed around ladybugs; another only wants amethysts. Occasionally she gets inquiries from people looking for their misplaced favorites, hoping she's some kind of lost-and-found service. The idea of reuniting some longed-for family brooch with its owner... That's *true* treasure hunting. The chances are slim, but, well, it worked for the Taylor butterfly necklace. Almost.

Jess sighs, places the bangle into a gift box. At least this piece will get to have more fun. She writes the recipient's address on an envelope, seals the box inside, then clears away the evidence of the day's work. Aggie gets stressed when, after a long day of insurance brokering, she finds the bowels of Jess's "hobby business" spread across her kitchen countertop. Not long now, however, and Jess will have a kitchen countertop of her own from which to run her empire. Right on cue, her phone buzzes. Tim's number flashes up on the screen. She grabs it, eager to hear the news.

"So?"

"So…I got it!"

"You did? Woo-hoo! Does this mean I'm officially moving in with a deputy head teacher? I mean…how did that even *happen*? Honestly, Tim, if you knew what I'd been like at school, you'd see the irony—"

"I can only imagine."

"We should celebrate—"

"Got it covered. My workmates have organized drinks for this evening. The Star Tavern. Eight o'clock. And…maybe we should announce we're moving in together as well. Make the night extra special."

"That's a lovely idea. Although shouldn't we go somewhere more exciting than the Star? Change it up a bit? It's not every day you get a promotion and a new flatmate."

"You're more than a flatmate, Jessica Taylor!"

"Exactly. This requires somewhere fancy."

"Nah. It's got to be the Star. Friday night tradition. We'll have fun, promise. Right, I better get back to work. Love you. See you tonight."

"Love you too. And…well done."

Jess sits back, smiles, and sighs. Her horizon is changing. This time last year, the view was very different. She'd only just gotten back to London and was in constant pain. But the aches in her body were at least something concrete, something she could understand—smashed bones, fixed back together, making measurable and ongoing improvement thanks to a regimen of physical therapy, painkillers, and rest. She'd never wanted for kindness and support. Everyone had rallied around. Aggie, Ed, all her friends… They'd been there for her. They could see the damage. Aggie had even seen the X-rays. And then, of course, there were those big, loud injured-body claxons: the wheelchair followed by the walking cane. What her family and friends hadn't seen, however, was the damage to her mind.

That's where it really hurt.

But now…now she has Tim, the archangel of men to keep, and the horizon is changing. Aggie and her Cupid's dart had scored a direct hit. And this, if anything, has been the medicine for the emotional damage.

Step after clunky step, Jess climbs the stairs to her bedroom—formerly the Hoppits' expansive guest suite—and starts plundering her wardrobe. A denim shirt-dress to match her favorite chunky brooch, with a pair of Tatty Devine rainbow earrings. Then she switches the dress to a more dainty chiffon number, then swaps the brooch for an enamel choker. Rings? Bracelets? More? Less? The balance between amount and style of jewelry has to be right, and there should be no conflict between clothing and adornment—all of it coming together in a beautiful homogenous whole. Although sometimes it's difficult to resist wearing everything at once.

She wonders what Tim's teaching colleagues think of her, always dressed in some big, fancy statement thing. Their physical embellishments are mostly restricted to smart watches and wedding bands, practical people with schedules to keep. Except for Tim's closest ally, Duff, the IT teacher, who wears a wolf pendant on a leather thong and a replica Starfleet combadge. The women of the group, mostly science and math teachers, are silver chain wearers—understated femininity, modest manners. Jess smiles to herself, imagines shaking them up a bit, getting them going with a bunch of old-school hip-hop bling.

"How about this then?" she ponders, picking a black sundress, then pairing it with her turquoise scarab-beetle bib necklace. She checks the combination in the mirror. The simple dress allows the artistry of the necklace to stand out. The necklace itself is historical, a classic example of twentieth-century Egyptian revival, when the world went crazy for all things ancient, inspired by the discovery of Tutankhamen's tomb in 1922.

"Bingo!" she says, pleased with her choice.

The scarabs will be a talking point, helping her handle a pub full of supersmart high school teachers. She jumps in the shower, belts out three verses of the Bangles' "Walk Like an Egyptian," brushes her teeth, then starts drying her hair. Through the noise of the dryer she doesn't hear the door when Aggie comes home, doesn't hear her calling, doesn't immediately notice her in the doorway. Finally, she shuts of the dryer and grins.

"Hey, Aggie, how was your day? Help me get my hair right, will you? We're celebrating. Tim got the job."

"Jess—"

"I'm now officially the girlfriend of a deputy head teacher! Can you believe it?"

"Jess—"

"You can come out with us, if you like. It's just the usual school crowd over at the Star—"

"*Jess*. It's Nancy." Aggie pauses to breathe and frown. "The care home, they called on my way home from work—"

"What? What's happened?"

"I'm sorry, Jess. They think she's really deteriorated."

Jess shudders, a cold shroud descending over her.

"But I only saw her a few days ago—"

"Her stats are all over the place. Her heart rate keeps slowing. They said days, weeks maybe, if we're lucky."

Jess sinks to the floor, swamped with sorrow. Aggie goes over and pulls her into an embrace. She brushes Jess's semidamp hair from her eyes and whispers.

"It's the natural and orderly way of things. She's had a long life, Jess. Eighty-two. That's really something. I know how much she means to you, but…it has to happen."

Jess can barely hear her sister's platitudes. All she can think of is the sadness on Nancy's face when she told her she'd failed to reclaim the necklace. Through her tears, staring over her sister's shoulder, she catches her reflection in the mirror and thinks of Nancy's words:

We called it the True Love Necklace.

Where is it now? The thought of it being driven away in the back of Guy van der Meer's taxi is crushing. Why did she let it go? Four generations of Taylor women had owned it, cared for it, and worn it. They had also—according to Nancy, perhaps with a touch of Anna Taylor hyperbole—found their soul mate because of it.

Quite a legacy for one small pendant. Her thoughts sweeping into a sudden and all-commanding sense of purpose, Jess releases herself from Aggie's grip.

"I—I have to go," she says. "There's something I have to do—"

She checks her watch. There is time—just about.

"Do what you have to," says Aggie, kissing Jess on the cheek. "And it's great news about Tim's job. Really it is. Nancy would be thrilled to know you've finally sorted yourself out and bagged a good one."

"Uh…yeah," says Jess, sniffing, wiping her tears, a little less convinced of this than Aggie.

When Aggie has gone, Jess picks up her phone and scrolls through her feed to find Guy van der Meer's friend request. She clicks Accept, then without thought or fear, starts typing:

> Please. I need the necklace. Buy/borrow. It's urgent. Can we meet in an hour? Will explain then. From one "treasure hunter" to another, thanks in advance. Jess (of the doughnuts)

If he will meet her, central London somewhere, and if it's a quick transaction, she can get the necklace and still be back in time to toast with Tim. She stares at the handset, wills Guy to reply. What if he's one of those people who never checks his messages? Surely not. His show-off profile hints of an ego that's far too interested in social status to risk being out of the loop. She drums her fingers on the dressing table, contemplates the multiple journeys she'll have to make, a normal day suddenly made crazy. But then she thinks of poor Nancy, alone in that room. Yes, she's lived a long life, always on her terms, and, yes, at eighty-two, it has to happen. But…there is still so much to talk about.

Her phone buzzes. Two minutes. That's all it took. She grabs it and reads his reply.

> Jess (of the doughnuts). How you intrigue me. Heavy schedule, but I'll make you priority. Meet me in the jewelry galleries of the Victoria and Albert Museum. In front of the best stuff. One hour. Guy

She smiles. The best stuff? What would that be? And how is it that he's chosen her favorite place in London—the jewelry galleries, the most intimate gathering of history's finest sparkles. Why does he have to…*get it right*? She can hop on the Central Line, change at Mile End, take the District Line all the way to South Kensington, hobble through the tunnel, and be there in fifty minutes. She downs a painkiller, stretches her leg, pummels some life into her left thigh, then sets to work on the rest of her body. She ruffles her hair, draws on a pair of eyebrows, adds a dab of color to cheeks and lips, then dons the black dress and scarab necklace. Finally, she checks herself in the mirror and is surprised to see something like exhilaration gazing back at her.

"Only for the necklace," she tells herself. "For Nancy. Get the necklace and go. That's all."

Then with a faster pace than she's been used to, she is out of the house, race-hobbling into the bright, fresh day.

The Victoria and Albert Museum in South Kensington, the grandfather of London's museum quarter, houses five thousand years of human creativity. Jess knows her way through the grand entrance, down the marble stairs, along the corridor, to the two-tiered cavern of the jewelry gallery. The black walls are like the interior of a gift box, their velvety depths punctuated by rows of illuminated glass cases, all focus on the exhibits themselves, which range from Celtic breastplates to plastic punk chokers to the tsavorite ring of a well-known pop star.

He is not here.

Yet.

The gallery is quiet, save for a few fashion students sketching medieval torques. It is a place for peace. The darkness is contemplative. The best stuff? She scans her eyes across the rows of cabinets, all eras and movements represented. Instinctively she is drawn to the twentieth-century cabinet, where she seeks out her long-time favorites: an unerringly sexual art nouveau hair ornament in the shape of an orchid and a Lalique pendant in the form of a female head with snaky tentacles curling out of the hair, beautiful and terrifying at the same time. And certainly a world away from the dainty floral motifs that preceded them and the stark geometry that came after.

Jess's attention is then drawn to a nearby screen, where black-and-white images flicker. The inscription reads: *Original footage from the Exposition Universelle, Paris, 1900.* She gasps. Here, in moving glory are the very things necklace creator Minnie Philomene Taylor would have been inspired by: the foreign pavilions, the Eiffel Tower painted bright golden-yellow, the palace of electricity, the Ferris wheel, the moving walkway—the sheer wonder of what humans can make and do. Through these distant, grainy, silent scenes, magnificence blooms. Minnie, she can only imagine, would have been in a constant state of visual seduction, the art nouveau aesthetic of fluid, whiplash curves appearing almost everywhere in every form: from posters, with their languorous females stretching in sultry sleepiness, to glass, to ceramics, to the buildings themselves.

Then there in front of her, captured on camera, is René Lalique's jewelry boutique, surrounded by crowds of onlookers. *Is Minnie among them?* she wonders, her nose pressed to the window, awed by the dark fantastical beauty of the objects displayed: large pins in the form of hummingbirds, combs in the shape of bats, nymphs entangled in fauna, picked out in pearls and opals. Eerie, beautiful, and impossible to forget…

Suddenly she hears a voice behind her.

"You chose well."

Guy is reflected in the glass, eyes glinting, framed by those telltale curls. As he steps toward her, a nervous flutter fills her stomach, which she suppresses with a tight, reasoned smile.

"So the art nouveau is your best stuff too?" she asks.

"Close but not quite."

He takes a seat beside her and points to the glowing case of

Queen Victoria's sapphire and diamond coronet, its intricate formal gem work glinting in the light.

"*That*," he says emphatically, "is the best stuff."

"Hmm. Impressive for its sparkle," says Jess thoughtfully, "and its enormous market value, but too stuffy for me."

"Never mind the value," says Guy. "The point is, you don't wear a headpiece like that and get ignored. You rule an empire. You make history."

They face each other. Jess feels her pulse quickening, her lips moistening. She breathes slow, desperate to dissolve the no-good temptation to meet his gaze.

"Thanks for coming," she says. *Stick to business.*

"No problem. You had me at treasure hunting. So what's the deal?"

"Do you have it?"

"Have what?"

"The necklace," she says, exasperated by his casualness. "I *need* the necklace. This wasn't just a ruse to get you to hang out with me again—"

But her plea glides over him.

"No?" he says. "You've made an effort with the Cleopatra affair though. Definitely a notice-me piece."

Jess reaches her hand to her chest, to the shield of turquoise beetles.

"Scarabs were a symbol for good luck in ancient Egypt," she shrugs. "Soldiers wore them into battle."

"Ah, so you've come to do battle?"

"I've *come* for the necklace."

Guy laughs, flicks his hair.

"I'm serious," Jess urges, huge sails of emotion sweeping through her. "My grandmother… Her health is bad. We had a call from her care home, and it's not great news. I just want her to see the necklace before…before she…"

She tenses, shuts her eyes, squeezes back the sorrow, but tears brim anyway. They trickle down her cheeks. Then her composure crumples entirely and the tears turn into sobs.

"*Oh*," says Guy, mouth open, sparkle shadowing.

Tentatively he wraps an arm around her, pulls her toward him.

"I get it," he whispers softly. "You want the necklace for her. For family. Family is everything, right?"

But Jess, obliterated by her sorrow, barely hears his words. She sobs into his shoulder, simply grateful that it's a shoulder, never mind the fact that it belongs to Guy van der Meer. Her tears and snot dampen the fabric of his navy shirt, while thoughts of Nancy tangle themselves up with thoughts of her long-deceased mother, Carmen, and all of it is overwhelming.

After a minute, however, the purging magic of a good cry sets in. Deep calm replaces the pain. Jess sits up, wipes her cheeks, blinks and winces and apologizes for her outburst.

"It's fine," says Guy. "Happens all the time."

"Does it?"

"Well, no, but—"

He smiles and she can't help but smile back. And it occurs to her that, beneath the bravado, he at least has the compassion to give a stranger a hug when they need one. Guy meanwhile stares into the depths of the glass display case in front of them.

"Mad, isn't it, to think that humans have worn jewelry through the ages, that the instinct to decorate ourselves came way before our civility. Obviously we're no longer adorning our bodies with animal teeth and bones in the hope that they'll make the sun rise and terrify our enemies, but how much have we really changed? The basic tenet is the same: put on a big, badass bunch of rings, look like a boss. So…you're a treasure hunter too?"

Jess sniggers.

"Why is that funny?"

"Because I saw it on your profile. It's the most ridiculous and overblown job title I've ever heard."

"It was good enough for Long John Silver."

"Who was a fictional character—"

"A fun one though."

"Well, yes, but—"

"I wouldn't take it too seriously, Jess. Job titles aren't my thing. But in a roundabout way, I'd say treasure hunting describes what I do. I deal in antique jewelry. My clients come to me looking for something a little bit special."

Jess's insides somersault. He deals in antique jewelry. Of course he does! Why does it feel like the universe is making him more and more attractive to her, when all she needs is the necklace? His arm is still resting on her shoulders, and it's a thrill. She jiggles her toes, leans out of his embrace, and with the post-cry breeziness still blowing through her, she allows herself to explore her intrigue. Just a little.

"So who are these clients?" she quizzes.

"London's wealthy, money to burn, the sort who don't want what everyone else has got."

"They want everyone to want what *they've* got."

"Exactly."

"Any famous names?"

"Oh, I'm exceedingly discreet"—his eyes shimmer—"but yes, I get some interesting jobs. Last month I had to find a gothic ring with a big, pink ruby for an international rock star. Before that, I sourced a nineteenth-century pearl-and-diamond tiara for a well-known social-ite's wedding day. And yesterday I reunited a war veteran with his beloved art-deco fob watch. That's what I really like doing, helping people find items they've lost."

"So you like a quest?"

"I do. I've had clients fly me to far-flung corners of the world in the hopes I'll unearth their engagement ring from the depths of whatever souk/sea bed/nightclub floor they dropped it in. You'd be amazed the lengths people will go to in order to be reunited with something they treasure—"

"Not at all amazed," she says pointedly.

"I tell you one thing; it beats pushing paper clips around an office desktop."

"Agreed. I've always avoided the paper-clip/office thing too."

He smiles.

"So you understand me?"

"Maybe," she says, folding her arms and fighting to contain the push-pull of her feelings.

He leans forward, inspects a shiny, gold dress clip on a black mount.

"Are those fire opals?" he mutters, more to himself than to Jess, who cannot quite fathom that she has met someone more knowledgeable and committed to the world of jewelry than she is.

"And how do you find these clients of yours?" she presses. "I guess it helps that you're from a well-established diamond family?"

"I guess it does."

"They trust you."

"Yes."

"So you're trustworthy?"

He looks at her.

"Of course."

His phone buzzes, a pester in the quiet space. He shuts it off.

"I'd love to tell you more about it," he says, "and hear more about *your* treasure hunting—"

"Oh, my business is small time. I don't have wealthy clients who fly me to exotic locales in search of engagement rings. I work from my sister's kitchen."

"But you love what you do?"

"Totally."

"Then we should talk about this much more. How about that dinner, later?"

Jess lowers her eyelids, thinks of Tim, their big night.

"Not today," she says.

"Well, that's an improvement on outright no. A cup of tea then? You could surely do with a cup of tea. The café's just down the corridor."

One cup of tea. One small cup of tea. Would a cup of tea do any harm? She checks her watch, nerves churning.

"Okay," she says, dropping her shoulders. "But please, I'm on borrowed time. A quick cup of tea, just so we can sort out the necklace, then I *have* to go."

"But, but, but," says Guy, gently mocking her as he rises.

In the resplendent café, among the bottle-green Victorian tiles, the stained-glass windows, and the twinkly contemporary space-ball light fixtures, Guy nudges Jess to a table next to the grand piano, then goes to order. It is raining outside—another summer downpour—and the sound gives the space a cosseting, snug feel. Jess takes a seat and prays Aggie isn't watching over her with some undisclosed crystal ball. Even though nothing has "happened" between her and Guy, his presence feels like a deceit. In his company—she can't help it—she just seems to *glow*. What if other people can see this? What if they can tell she's having tea with someone who isn't her boyfriend? She swallows her guilt. She shouldn't—mustn't—go down that path. Just get the necklace and go.

Guy returns with a tray of tea and mounds of cake, including pecan pie, lemon drizzle, and scones with clotted cream. So much for a quick cuppa. The sight of this indulgence shocks Jess.

"Wow, you have a sweet tooth!" she exclaims, remembering how he'd chased down the doughnuts that day in the cab.

"One of many weaknesses," he confesses, "but life's too short for alfalfa."

He hands Jess a spoon, then dives into the fruity, creamy, cakey jumble. Jess eyes him, the way he eats with gusto. At over six feet, with coat-hanger shoulders, he's somehow managed to stay slim, although she notices, at his waist, a certain bulge around his belt—a cake paunch. It's infuriatingly endearing, a hint that he is perhaps not as vain as she took him for.

"So you're just a down-to-earth dude who happens to be mixed up with the top 1 percent?" she asks, scooping a piece of pie into her mouth.

"I'd say 'mixed up' is a little strong. I merely hang on to their Gucci coattails."

"Hah! So you're a wannabe?"

He laughs, unfazed by her repeated attempts to topple his crown.

"I'm just canny, Jess."

"Why do I get the feeling there's something slightly scoundrel-like about you?"

He shrugs, eyes twinkling. A glimpse of his leopard-head ring reminds her of her initial instinct about his character. That magnetic charm spell he seems to cast... No doubt it gets cast quite regularly. She lays down her spoon and sits back, arms folded. He copies, all the while holding her gaze.

"Are you always this suspicious?" he asks.

"One can never be too careful about the company one keeps," she replies.

"True. One must never hang out with boring people."

Jess suppresses a giggle. "That's not what one meant."

"So tell me more about your jewelry business," says Guy, holding her focus, leaning forward as though keen to know every detail.

"It's called Miss Taylor's Vintage and Retro Jewelry. I find great pieces, then give them a second home. My mission," she says, smiling smartly, "is to smash the throwaway culture that has us reaching for two-for-one mass-produced supermarket charm bracelets sooner than we'd buy something preloved."

"Quality, design, fine craftsmanship, and the magic of past adventures captured within," adds Guy.

Jess's eyes widen with glee. How he *gets* her! She hands him her business card.

"I'd like to grow it," she says, "reach more people."

"Of course," he says, giving the card a little flex. "You know, if you need any contacts—"

"Thanks, but to be honest, I'm thinking of going back to teaching this September. Design and technology for rogue fifteen-year-olds. There's a post available. Apparently their last teacher quit suddenly after an incident with a jigsaw blade—"

"Yikes! Are you sure about this?"

"It's a grown-up job," she says with a shrug. "And I'm trying to be grown-up."

"A grown-up?"

"Uh, I owe it to a few people to make more sensible choices in life. Besides, the soon-to-be deputy head is my, um, boyfriend."

"Oh yes, the boyfriend who speaks for you. How's that working out?"

"Great, actually."

"And now you're thinking of working together. How commendable."

"It's a good opportunity. It'll give me some stability. We've got plans together and—"

Their eyes meet, fervently absorbing each other's meta-signals.

"What jewelry does he wear?"

"A smart watch and a copper band for warding off arthritis."

"That's not jewelry. That's…artless timekeeping and quack medicine."

Jess bristles, her gaze catching on Guy's emerald-eyed leopard ring.

"We can't all be diamond magnates," she says. "So tell me about your jewelry business and your family, the van der Meers? Are you close? Did they inspire you?"

"Something like that," he says evasively.

The way he brushes his hand through his curls, jiggles his knee, and looks everywhere but at Jess, she senses he'd prefer to avoid the topic. But still she presses on, determined that if her life choices can be interrogated, so can his.

"Are you a fine or costume person?" she asks.

"All of it, but if I had to choose, I'd say costume. Less snobbery. More playfulness. You?"

"Costume always." She lowers her eyelids, thinks back to her mother's dressing table. "My mum had this jewelry box, and when I was little, I used to go through it and play with everything. I had this idea that she was *extraordinarily* rich because she owned so many rubies and sapphires. I didn't realize they were cheap colored crystals and plated brass."

Guy laughs. The rain drums hard on the window above them. They both take mouthfuls of unctuous lemon drizzle.

"So, with all this cake in your life, do you ever go to the gym?" Jess asks.

"God no! *Bor*ing! I probably don't do as much exercise as I should, but I like walking in the city. And dancing—that's exercise, right? And I've also been known to do a bit of waterskiing in my day. And I once tried horse riding, but that was a big mistake. You?"

"I used to do all sorts," say Jess ruefully.

Guy casts his gaze to her walking cane.

"So what happened?" he says.

She shuts her eyes at the question she dreads. At least he's blunt about it, and there hasn't been a single pity smile. So she takes a breath, readies herself to dive into the past.

"A year ago…I fell out of an airplane."

"*What?*"

"It wasn't intentional. I did a skydive in Mexico. My parachute failed to open."

His eyes widen.

"*Whoa!*"

"Well, it sort of opened, but not enough. I hit a tree branch, then a bush, then a field full of alpacas. The flora damaged me, but at the same time it broke my fall and saved my life. If I'd hit the ground directly, I'd have been jam."

Guy blinks, openmouthed.

"That…that wasn't what I was expecting to hear. Do you…do you remember it?"

Jess lowers her eyelids and smiles. That he would ask such a probing, personal question intrigues her, tells her something of his nature.

"You mean you want to know what it's like," she says, leaning close, "at six thousand feet in the air, to have your mortality rush to meet you?"

"I so do," he says, leaning closer.

"The din of white sky, the loom of the green, green, green fields, and the eerie serenity that engulfs you when you realize…death is real and it's coming. And all you can think is: Have I done it right? Have I lived my life the way I was meant to?"

Guy blinks.

"Jesus. It's not often *I* get stunned into silence."

He leans closer still, the tip of his nose just inches from Jess's. She can sense the warmth of his face, the musky smell of his aftershave.

"If it's not impertinent of me to ask," he says, holding her gaze with fierce intensity, "have you? *Have* you lived the way you were meant to?"

Jess dips her gaze, tunes into the ache in her back.

"I thought I had," she says. "I used to be very carefree, not one for settling, but…my outlook is changing. I'm *growing*. Like, I can see myself as a mother, sort of. Or, at least, as someone who gets married and goes on one holiday a year rather than ten. Just, you know, normal stuff."

"Rrrright. Good luck with that."

"Do I detect sarcasm?"

Guy shrugs.

"Leopards," he says, flashing his ring. "Some say the spots never change."

"Are you saying you don't believe I want to be normal?"

"I'm saying it sounds like motivational self-talk."

Jess shakes her head.

"Nah. Trust me. I've had my fingers burned and learned the lesson. No more high jinks. From now on I want a calm, simple, sorted life."

"So what were your injuries?"

"I fractured my spine and smashed my pelvis. I was airlifted to Mexico City in a helicopter, but by then I'd lost consciousness. I woke up in hospital a week later. Four operations and seven titanium plates to piece me back together. After that, I spent two months in a rehab center, where I healed and found a new way to walk. And then I flew home to the UK"—she takes a breath—"and now I'm trying to find a new way to live."

"But you *do* live. And you *can* walk."

"And it's getting better every day," says Jess, brightening, drawing hard on those inner reserves, positive all the way.

"What were you doing in Mexico?"

"Looking for silver."

"There we go, treasure hunting!"

"It was to help start my jewelry business," she explains. "Before I went to Mexico, I was a struggling trainee teacher. I mean, I liked the idea of it, but my head of faculty kept telling me I needed to write this report and that report and set targets, which then had to be SMART targets, and that I had to follow a specific curriculum and use certain kinds of vocabulary and, in the end, I don't think I taught anything interesting. Anyway, I was fed up and wanted a change and someone told me the silver in Taxco was good and then I saw a cheap flight and…went for it."

"So where did it go wrong?"

"I made the mistake of falling in love."

"That old chestnut?"

"He was blond, actually. Matteus from South Africa. We had a great time. For six months we lived out of each other's pockets. I kept posting my Taxco silver back to London, storing it up for the future, and we carried on living the backpacker dream. We hiked through rain forests, lazed in hammocks, ran along deserted white-sand beaches, explored secret Mayan temples and azure waterfalls. Lots of quesadillas and *lots* of tequila."

"Was Matteus into silver too?"

"Nope." Jess sucks her breath. "He was an extreme sports instructor. He took jobs around Central America, teaching zip-lining, rappelling, canyoning, and"—she pauses, feels the anxiety ripping through her—"skydiving."

"*Oh*—"

"That day…he packed my parachute."

Guy blinks, half-horrified, half-captivated.

"He packed your parachute? *Your boyfriend packed your parachute, and it failed to open?*" His voice is so loud and animated that other guests in the café turn to look. "Jeez! I mean…did the boy not like you or something? Was he *trying* to bump you off? Was he after your silver?"

Jess forces a laugh. "He'd packed a thousand parachutes before. He was fully qualified. The authorities investigated, said the issue was technical. No foul play, just a snagged string. One of those things."

"But *still*, he's got to be blamed for something?"

Jess hangs her head.

"It's complicated. I don't blame him for my accident, but… after…"

She shuts her eyes, exhales, feels the sting anew.

"At first he really cared for me. He was there every day at the hospital. My sister flew out and he helped her, too, made sure she had a decent hotel, assisted with the Spanish. There were issues with travel insurance and medical bills and what have you, but he helped out with all of that. And while I was trapped in that hospital bed, in shock and utterly immobile, he told me everything I needed to hear. We made plans, mapped out the rest of our lives. It was the thing that got me through, the thought of getting back to London with Matteus and making a life together.

"He made me feel like everything was going to be fine, better than fine…*great*. And then, just as I was coming around from my fourth surgery, completely out of the blue, he sent a text saying he was very sorry, but he just 'couldn't do it anymore.' Said he was going fly-fishing in Guatemala or something. Although judging by his Instagram account, it was pretty clear he'd met someone else. I don't know. We've lost touch."

"Oh, Jess! Good lord! You need to improve your taste in men!"

"Noted. And I have. I mean, Tim is lovely. He's nothing like Matteus. Total opposite."

"Glad to hear it."

Jess sits back, relieved to have shared the story. She has rarely felt comfortable talking about it, yet now that it's out there, a wall has come down. It has also, she realizes, provided a cautioning of sorts: don't mess me around; I've had more than my fill of it. In the following silence, she takes a mouthful of pecans, pastry, and cream.

"So where are you now?" asks Guy. "Where are you with your recovery?"

"My extreme sports days are numbered, but I'm good. I've been well looked after, staying with my sister and her family. And now I'm ready to get my independence back. In fact—"

She pauses, feels suddenly self-conscious about revealing the news that she and Tim are moving in together. A nearby phone alarm beeps, reminding her of time passing, time she hasn't got. Aggie's comment flits through her mind: *They said days, weeks if we're lucky.*

"Anyway, about my necklace," she urges, steering back to purpose.

Guy stretches, scratches his belly, releases a slow exhale.

"I assume," she asserts, "that it has no real meaning to you, not in the way it does for me, so if we can make a deal right now—"

Guy winces.

"It would mean so much to me," she persists. "And obviously it would mean the world to my grandmother."

"I get that, Jess, but—"

"*Please.* At least, if you won't sell it to me, maybe I could borrow it for a day? That's all I ask. One day. Lend it to me for just one day."

Guy shakes his head.

"I'm sorry, Jess. If I could, I would, but—"

"But what?"

He shuts his eyes.

"It's no longer mine to lend. It's in the hands of my client now."

"Your *client*?" Jess cringes at the word. "Who…who is this client?"

"That's confidential."

"Oh, please."

"Stella Weston."

"The supermodel?"

"Ex-supermodel turned influencer. She has a thing about butterflies. She's planning to wear the necklace to the Capital Gala. She's been negotiating with dress designers all week. That necklace is hopefully going to get her hashtag trending for days. Fashion cred, it's what she lives for."

Jess glowers, pained at the idea of her necklace—the potency of its Taylor past, the rhythm of its Taylor heart—now reduced to a mere fashion accessory for an Instagram post.

"But would it hurt to swap it for something else?" she pleads. "I mean, I could find her an equally lovely butterfly necklace, for free."

"Ah, Jess, there's no way she'll pass it up now. She's consulting with her media team as we speak. In fact, that was her phoning. I expect she wants me to take her to her favorite sushi place and feed her seaweed."

"How romantic. Well, enjoy that, won't you?"

"Jess, I'm not her boyfriend. I'm just—"

"Her bitch?"

"That's not the word I use."

"But you run around after her, do whatever she tells you?"

"We're good friends."

Jess huffs.

"It's a red carpet event," he says optimistically. "She'll be in all the papers. Who knows? Your necklace might be the star—"

"So you concede it's *my* necklace?"

"Ach. You got me."

His phone buzzes again and his head drops. Suddenly he looks exhausted, as though being "good friends" with Stella Weston is more an effort than a joy. He checks the screen, shuts his eyes.

"She wants me now."

"Oh, does she? Well, off you trot, then—"

"But it feels like we've only just sat down. I don't *want* to rush off. I don't want a time limit."

Jess is unmoved.

"Time limits? I'll tell you about time limits: how about my dying grandmother." She throws her hands up in despair. "My god! I need to be with her, not squandering precious minutes with you staring at cake crumbs—"

"Yes, of course you do," says Guy. "I'm sorry."

Jess gets up to leave.

"Wait—" he says.

He grasps her hand. His touch makes her shiver.

"The gala is coming up. Once she's worn the necklace, it'll go in the closet, and after that she won't look at it again. Won't even miss it. If your grandma can hang on, once Stella's had her moment, I'll get it for you."

"*If* she hangs on—"

"I'll do what I can," says Guy. "Don't worry. I'm a pro at these sorts of shenanigans."

"I bet you are," says Jess, sweeping her raincoat as she walks away.

In the main vestibule, where the walls are lit, the ceilings are high, and naked marble torsos mingle with loud-shirted patrons, a sense of a dream comes over her—did this hour with Guy really just happen? As she shoves herself through the revolving doors, the street sounds assaulting her senses, a kernel of panic rises. No necklace for Nancy, and now she's running late for Tim—his big night, *their* big night. She checks her watch, tugs her coat around her shoulders, and hobbles headlong through the rain to the Tube station.

Through the cozy light of the bar, she sees him. He is in the Baxter Academy huddle, the trestle table at the window—the same one as always. She can see in his face that he's a little forlorn. And she knows, arriving an hour later than promised, that she has done this to him. She steels herself, smiles, and waves.

"Jess—"

"I'm *so* sorry," she says, diving to kiss him, breathless with guilt. "I–I just got…*caught up*."

Tim makes room for her on the bench.

"Hey, everyone," she says, extending a wave around the group.

They all smile, say hi, take a moment to ogle the scarab necklace, then return to their conversations. *Luck in battle*, she thinks. She might need it.

"I messaged you twice," says Tim, mildly accusatory.

"I know. I'm so sorry. I was on the Tube."

"The Tube? Why were you on the Tube?"

Jess hesitates, Guy with his sparkly eyes close in her thoughts. What to say? What not to say?

"I–I wanted to look at some sparkles," she says, instinct ordering her to go easy with the truth, "so I went to Kensington, to the Victoria and Albert Museum, just to browse."

Why ignite a prickly conversation on their big night?

She holds her breath, straightens her scarabs, knees twitching. Tim stares at her as though trying to read the thoughts in her head—only for a second, but it feels like a minute.

"You and your sparkles," he says eventually. "You're here now. That's the main thing."

He kisses her softly and everything shifts back into position, warmth and unity restored. Relieved, Jess steals a sip of his pint and snuggles into him.

"Have you told them?"

"About the promotion—yes, of course."

"No, I mean, about us moving in together."

"I was waiting for you."

"Ah, yes." Jess looks at her lap. "Sorry again."

"Oh, come on," says Tim, jostling her. "Shall we?"

He clears his throat, tings his door key on his beer glass.

"People. We have an announcement."

They stop immediately, look toward him.

"Don't tell us," crows Duff, "they've already demoted you!"

The quip is greeted with jeering and laughter. Tim beats it down with an affable grin.

"Watch yourself," he jokes. "As of September I'm your line manager, remember? But no, this is personal. We just wanted to tell you all…Jess and I…we're moving in together."

"Oh wow!"

"Aw. You two are perfect for each other."

"About bloody time!"

"This calls for another round," says Duff. "You getting them, Tim?"

"Yeah, yeah," says Tim, relishing the moment of being "the one," as everyone jumps in with man-hugs, fist bumps, and handshakes.

Colette, one of the silver-chain-wearing math teachers, who tonight has branched out with ear studs in the shape of treble clefs, leans forward and kisses Jess on the cheek.

"Congratulations. I was hoping things would move on between you two. I've known Tim for years. He had a rough time with his ex, but…you make him happy."

"Thanks," says Jess. "He makes me happy too."

"Good," Colette says, nodding profusely, grin fixed, giving Jess the distinct feeling she's being second-guessed.

Are the silver chains on to her? Do they know? About what exactly? About Jess meeting Guy again and allowing herself, for just an hour, to enjoy his company? *Get a grip*, she tells herself, chasing out the paranoia. No crime has been committed, apart from the half-truth she told Tim about where she'd been. But that was only to protect him, to avoid an unnecessary niggle on a nice occasion. Oh, who is she trying to kid? She tenses, makes her excuses, and escapes to the toilet.

The cubicles are quiet and Jess is grateful for the peace. She runs a tap to rinse her hands, despairing at her ability to throw the pieces up in the air, just when everything seemed like it was falling into place.

"Oh, Jessy," she sighs, pulling her hands down her cheeks, dragging the flesh of her lips with them. "What are you *doing*?"

Disloyalty is not her style.

And Guy is not her type.

Guy van der Meer is one hundred percent definitely not her type.

Anymore.

She's grown up, moved on.

Because any man can look good on the spot, say the right things, make a girl feel special. Hell, she's fallen for it before. All those blue-eyed boyfriends who seemed too good to be true—they were! Matteus being a prime example. But kudos to Tim, who'll soon be helping her box up her things, carrying her forward into a future that works. Happiness secured: new home, good jobs, nice life, start saving for a John Lewis kitchen extension with a built-in wine cooler and make damn good trifle.

But—she shudders—is this really what she wants?

The woman who once rowed five miles down a river in the Belizian rain forest in the hope of finding a fabled bejeweled cave. The woman who spent a year teaching art and English to children in a remote village in Cambodia. The woman who said "yes" to every extreme activity going, from caving to kitesurfing to the ill-fated skydiving. The woman who gave two years of her life to sixth-form college, only to give it up on a whim when she heard there were full-moon raves in Thailand that would change your life forever.

Is the conventional life really for her?

Oblivious to the comings and goings of a group of drunk women, one word plays over in her head: *OUI*. She thinks of Nancy with her cabin in the woods. Of Minnie, fleeing marriage when her yearning for creativity took hold. And Anna, the Hollywood dreamer with the exaggerated imagination. What would *they* do? In their own ways they were all risk takers, but were there happy endings for each of them? Were the risks worth it? And what, then, of Carmen, Jess's own mother, who never had the chance to take risks, her story cut too short?

Suddenly she wishes she'd known her mother better, known *all* of them better. If she had, maybe she would know herself better. She ponders Nancy's proclamation: *We called it the True Love Necklace*. The sweet but unlikely notion that the translucent wings and shimmering moonstone could fast-track the necklace's owner to her soul mate—a Taylor talisman. Oh, if only! Jess throws her head back, stares at the strip lights on the ceiling. Cupid in a jewel, helping her make good choices in love. What a lot of heartache that would spare, especially when the people who are good for her and the people who thrill her seem to be very different creatures.

She shuts her eyes, breathes slow, and makes a silent pledge to find out all she can about the lives and loves of the women who made her, hoping that somehow their stories, their journeys, will lead her to clarity.

⊂─⧈─⧉

Early the next day, Jess goes to the care home. As she pushes the double doors, she is engulfed by the possibility that this might be one of the last times she makes this journey. She pads down the corridor through the disinfected air and enters Nancy's room. Nancy is asleep, thinner than ever, barely making a mound in the sheets, the ridges of her skull clearly visible beneath her wispy hair. She looks as small as a child. *How strange*, thinks Jess, *that at the end of our life we almost return to the beginning.*

"Hi, Grandma," she whispers.

Nancy opens her eyes, takes in the light but doesn't speak, so Jess fills the silence with questions.

"Are you comfortable? Is there anything you need?"

Nancy just smiles and stares, as though the beige wall in front of her is a point of impelling interest. *She is fading*, thinks Jess, having always found her conversational. A nurse bustles in.

"Oh, hello," she says. "Don't mind me. I'm just checking her charts."

"She's not talking," says Jess. "Is it—?"

She doesn't quite know what she means to ask.

"Her focus is coming and going," says the nurse kindly. "Last night I got a very crisp commentary about life in Hollywood, of all things."

Jess laughs. "Oh, that one. She claims she was born there, you see."

"So she told me. She said something about a house, a fantastic house, that she had to leave—"

"Hmm," says Jess ruefully. "To be honest, I don't know much about her early life. I dearly wish I did, but she was always very secretive. There's a family rumor that she and her mother lived in Hollywood, but I'm not sure how much of it is true."

If only Nancy had told the stories while she still could! The comfort of knowing where you come from—your traits, your talents, your strengths, your weaknesses, your inherited genes, all helping you make sense of yourself, giving credence to your fleeting existence in time.

"Who knows?" says the nurse, placing a check mark on the clipboard hooked to the end of the bed. "Maybe you should watch that TV program—*Who Do You Think You Are?*—where the celebrities trace their ancestry. I love a bit of genealogy."

As the nurse chats, Jess notices a tarnished Victorian locket peeping out from her collar. She smiles, wonders if a pair of nursing ancestors are tucked inside, always carried with her, making her feel just a little more connected to her past, to her history.

"I like your necklace," she says.

"Thanks," says the nurse. "Actually, you've just reminded me… Last night your grandma talked about a necklace. She kept repeating it. I got the impression it was really bothering her."

"Ah yes," says Jess, flooding with guilt. "Yes, that's something I *do* know about. Thanks."

"No problem. She's a sweetheart," says the nurse. "A really sweet lady."

Ha, thinks Jess, *if you only knew.*

Chapter Nine

THE NORTH WELSH COUNTRYSIDE IS GREEN UPON GREEN: LOW PAS-tures, little rivers with stone humped bridges, a backdrop of heather-clad mountains, and the jagged outline of pine trees. As the taxi pulls up to the entrance of the Pel Tawr estate, Jess leans out, takes a gasp of air, and smiles. She has one night booked in a nearby guesthouse. Aggie couldn't—wouldn't—join her. Tim couldn't get the time off work at the last minute. But maybe time alone is what she needs right now; time to think. She pays the taxi driver, and with a wince and wrench—all that time sitting on the train has stiffened her spine—she clambers out of the cab.

The pollution of London is well behind her. There is not a single traffic noise, just the bleat of sheep and the trickle of waterways. No wonder Nancy loved it here, Jess thinks, in her cabin in the glade, sun glinting on the dewy grass. It must have felt like heaven, to be peaceful among the birds and trees, which never once complained or told her how she should live.

Remembering the route from her previous visits, years before, Jess makes her way down the hill, through the trees. The fresh, resin-ous scent of conifer catches in her nostrils, while at her feet, the ground is a crunchy brown blanket of last year's needle drop. There ahead, in a shaft of sunlight, is Nancy's cabin. Jess stops to absorb the full, albeit dilapidated, chocolate-box nostalgia of it—and pay her respects to the sheer feat of its existence. The logs in its walls came from the woods. The windows were retrieved from a nearby scrapyard. And although Nancy had help with the heavy work, the details had all been down to her and her handsaw.

Building it, living in it, had given her peace and solitude, but since she took ill, it has been standing empty. Jess can immediately see evidence of its neglect. The overhanging roof is rotting, and the porch is threatening collapse. Possibly it isn't structurally sound. Possibly it never was, not that Nancy would have cared.

The door shudders open. There was never a lock, typical Nancy. Inside, the air is dank, but the single-celled interior still has its hobbit-hole charm—so different, thinks Jess, from the sheen of her and Tim's future Stratford City new-build. She wanders inside, straightening chairs, wiping the dust off surfaces. Wood pigeons have built a nest on the shelf above the bed. There are feathers everywhere. The bed itself is strewn with a hand-knit patchwork throw, just as Nancy left it.

With a sigh, realizing her grandmother will never sleep here again, Jess straightens the blanket and plumps the pillow. She then goes to the drawing desk beneath the window, still cluttered with paper, ink pots, pencil sharpenings, and sketches of oak leaves and acorns—the remnants of Nancy's final artistic musing before being carted off to institutional perdition. She'd been an illustrator, special-ized in natural forms.

Curious to see what other artwork might be around, Jess sifts through the desk, opens the drawers. They are filled with piles of used cartridge paper, a menagerie of squirrel, flower, and beetle sketches. One of the drawers is locked. She spies a key on the window ledge and tries it. The lock releases. Inside, there is a calculator, a bag of loose change, a string of paper clips, and beneath all of this, a large yellowed envelope. She tugs the envelope free, intrigued to know why it merits a lock. She dips a hand in: thick glossy paper, like photographs. She empties them onto the desk and her mouth drops open.

The photos, at least a dozen, are all images of young Nancy, a teenager perhaps, not much older than Steph, posing against a brick wall. At Nancy's neck, the distinctive butterfly necklace dangles like a beacon. Jess is drawn to it immediately. Its sinuous, stylized fin-de-siècle form looks incongruous against Nancy's sturdy circle dress; that full skirt and stiffened petticoats, hallmarks of fifties fashion. In some of the images Nancy is posing beside a street sign: Denmark Street. The name resonates, a known London landmark, the UK's answer to Tin Pan Alley. It was the center of the music industry in the fifties and sixties, housing numerous song publishers and recording studios and La Giaconda, a café where the likes of David Bowie and Jimi Hendrix hung out.

All of the photos are beautifully shot. Not the snaps of an amateur, but someone who knows what they're doing. Jess turns one of them over and sees a small gold sticker in the corner: *Paul Angel Photography, 1954.*

She searches her memory. Paul Angel? It doesn't catch.

"Oh, Nancy," she whispers, "look at you!"

Apart from the born-in-Hollywood brag, she knew that Nancy had traveled, that she'd spent a year in Berlin being "punk," that she loved a protest, that she'd first trained as a furniture restorer, then an illustrator. But there was never any mention of her modeling. Jess laughs, delighted that even in her twilight, Nancy still has the capacity to surprise.

Satisfied the cabin is at peace, Jess tucks the envelope of photos into her bag, then goes outside and looks up to the big house on the hill. Pel Tawr. Fueled by curiosity, she stamps her walking cane into the dusty ground and plows forward. With the sun still high in the sky, it wouldn't hurt, surely, to have a discreet little peek? She picks her way through the woods, follows the remnants of a path, ever conscious of Nancy's photographs in her bag.

Eventually, she reaches the tree boundary, and there ahead, over-looking a large sweeping lawn, is the house itself. It is huge, at least seven bedrooms, and unmistakably arts and crafts with its notional medieval beams, Gothic turrets, leaded windows of all shapes and sizes, multiple chimneys, and carved stone. It's skirted by clusters of well-shaped topiary bushes, their neat appearance suggesting it is still a living home. Suddenly Jess is aware of a rustling in the undergrowth behind her. Before she can move, a knee-high mound of golden fur comes bowling into her, jumping at her legs, sniffing her pockets.

"Oh! Who are you? Where did you come from?"

The fur mound—a lively but genial golden retriever—is then overshadowed by its owner, a tall, elderly man in a wax jacket.

"Are you lost?" he says with relieving kindness.

"Um, not exactly," she says. "I was just—"

As the man steps into her sight line, he stares at her, a flash of white teeth brightening his face.

"Well, I never! If I didn't know better, I'd say you were a Taylor."

Jess blinks, nods.

"You…you know me?"

"I know that look. Those round cheeks, those huge green eyes. So you *are* a Taylor?"

"I am. My name is Jess. I'm—"

"Nancy's granddaughter."

"Yes!"

"She told me all about you. How's she doing, old girl? We've missed her terribly, Rufus and I." He ruffles the collar of the dog, which Jess assumes to be Rufus. "We used to trek down to her cabin every week, have a cup of tea with her, make sure she was okay. It was me that found her in that terrible state—"

"Oh, of course."

"I spoke to someone…not you?"

"That would have been my sister, Aggie. She's everyone's emergency contact, very solid in a crisis. But thank you for making that call. If you hadn't checked, who knows how long she'd have been that way."

"Well, I never liked to interfere too much. Nancy liked her space. She made that clear when she approached us to buy the land."

"She approached you?"

"Yes. All her idea. We hadn't considered selling any of our land before, but when she inquired, well, we realized it would be an ideal way to raise funds for the upkeep of the house and grounds."

Jess nods, intrigued. She'd always been puzzled by Nancy's random relocation to Snowdonia, but now she sees that it wasn't random at all. Maybe it was because of Minnie.

"How is she now?"

"Not so well, I'm afraid. She's being well looked after, but—" A prickle of emotion catches in Jess's throat. "I don't think she'll ever be coming back to her cabin."

The man nods sadly. Then as the wind shushes the trees, Rufus whines and brushes between his legs.

"Introductions," he says, snapping up. "I'm Bevan. Bevan Floyd."

Floyd? Jess recalls Nancy's description of how Minnie had "made the necklace there with Emery *Floyd*." Her stomach flutters, but before she can say anything, Bevan starts ushering her across the lawn.

"Grand old girl," he says, gesticulating to the house, proud to show it off. "She's been in the family for generations. Used as a communications base during World War II, then my sisters briefly ran her as a girl's boarding school in the seventies. A year of neglect, then my wife and I took her over in the late eighties. But originally she was built as a country retreat at the turn of the century, overrun by deep thinkers and artists. Toward the end of the Victorian era, she was one of Wales's most thriving creative hubs. We had furniture makers, weavers, potters, calligraphers, and all the dramatics of the socialists. It was the Arts and Crafts movement—"

Jess laughs, delighted.

"This interests you?"

"So much."

"Then perhaps you'd care for a tour?"

Jess grins. "I would *love* a tour."

❦

The smell of oiled oak hangs in the air. *It is the smell of age*, thinks Jess, as she steps inside the semipaneled main vestibule, picturing all the artists and thinkers who have passed through this space, their laughter and conversation absorbed into the wood grain. The interior is immaculately kept. Even the wallpapers are original, their colored botanical designs swirling across the walls.

"Are they William Morris?" asks Jess, awed.

"They are. A little faded in parts, but we won't be replacing them. They're the character of the house."

The vestibule opens into a large double-height space, surrounded by nooks and fireplaces, doors leading into other rooms, corridors into rooms, corridors into corridors. Like a burrow, so much more exciting than the average three-bed semi. What a place to grow up!

"The maintenance is getting a little much for my wife and me," says Bevan solemnly. "So we're working on plans to pass the old girl to the community. We have no children, you see. And one fears selling outside the family, only to have her knocked down and turned into an all-seasons spa and holiday village. We feel she should be a museum. This is history as much as it's a home."

"Absolutely," says Jess.

"And we rather like the idea of converting the barns back into art studios. Restore some of the creative glory. After all, it was what she was first known for."

Jess nods.

"So I'm dying to ask," she ventures, "but are you any relation to Emery Floyd?"

"Why yes, he was my great-uncle. He had the run of the place in the early 1900s. Quite a well-known cabinetmaker in his day—very inspired by the happenings of William Morris and his crowd. I never met him, sadly. He was a generation ahead of me, but…how do you know of him?"

"Nancy mentioned him. Briefly."

"So she told you about Minnie?"

"My great-great-grandmother—"

Bevan smiles warmly. "Indeed."

"She told me a little, but not enough. I guess it's why I'm here. I know snippets, but not the full story. I gather Minnie and Emery were close. Nancy referred to Emery as Minnie's soul mate."

"Yes, I believe they were happy together."

"In that case, do you know anything about a butterfly necklace that might have been made here?"

Bevan muses, puffs out his cheeks.

"With a drop moonstone? Glassy wings?"

"Yes—"

"Come with me."

Jess's heart quickens. She follows Bevan through a maze of corridors, some adorned with tapestry panels, some with wallpaper and flock, into an elegant sun-filled white room that looks out across the lawn. Bevan points to a collection of barns at the bottom of the hill.

"Down there, Emery's workshops. Some fine things were made in those buildings. But now...*this* is what I want to show you."

He plucks a framed photo from a nearby cabinet and hands it to her.

"This is the necklace you described, I think."

Jess gazes at the image. There is Minnie, in those same wide-legged trousers, the butterfly at her neck, standing next to a tanned and ruggedly handsome mustached man, whose white shirt is only half-buttoned, sleeves pushed up so that his sinewy forearms are on show, ready for work.

"Oh yes!" she says with a surge of excitement. "This is Minnie! And this is the necklace! This is it!"

"How remarkable," says Bevan. "How did you know about it?"

"Nancy asked me to find it for her, the real necklace I mean. She told me Minnie had made it here. It was then passed down through the generations. I guess you could call it an heirloom. I remember my mother kept it in her jewelry box. I used to love getting it out, but... that was years ago. At some point it went missing. To be honest, I'd forgotten it even existed until Nancy started asking for it. She called it the True Love Necklace."

Jess stares at its image, hanging graciously from its creator's neck, and riles at the thought of it being boasted about in "who's who" magazine features, courtesy of a fame vacuum like Stella Weston. Jess draws the photograph of Minnie closer, absorbing its details, her hotline to the past. The allure of Emery Floyd is not hard to see—his brawny physique and smiling eyes suggest an appetite for life. She can almost feel his vitality around her. The True Love Necklace chose well!

"So they were a couple, right?"

"Yes, although they never married. I gather Minnie had a difficult ex-husband who refused to grant a divorce. Such things being a rarity in those days."

Robert Belsing, thinks Jess. Whatever became of *him*?

"She never used her husband's name," Bevan explains. "She was always known to our family as Taylor. I should also show you these—"

He opens a drawer, and in it, there is a selection of metal tools: files, pliers, a small hammer, and a chisel.

"You'll see they've been engraved with an "M. T.," which we took to stand for Minnie Taylor."

Jess gasps. They are perfect, aged but perfect; the very tools her great-great-grandmother used to scrape and craft. Her personal set. Jess smiles to herself, glad that Minnie, having been denied the chance to follow her passion for so many years, was finally able to believe in herself as a jewelry designer and own her own tools.

"May I touch them?"

"Of course."

She lifts out the chisel, turns it in her hand, trying to imagine the way Minnie would have worked it in tiny movements, refining, smoothing, beautifying.

"Do you have much of her stuff here?"

"Just these, I'm afraid. We found them in the workshops when we were clearing out. Rats had got in, destroyed a lot of the fittings, but we saved what we could. Although there is, of course, the sketchbook—"

Jess's eyes light up.

"Minnie's?"

Bevan shrugs. "It's just a few drawings, some memoirs. Been left on the bookshelf for years, gathering dust. Useful to you?"

"Hugely."

"Then I'll fetch it."

He shuffles to the corner, to a library nook with rows of books and thick, green curtains. After a minute's search, he pulls a battered leather-bound tome from the top and presents it to Jess.

"The spine's a little sad, so watch you don't lose all the pages, but here, you might as well have it."

"Really?"

"Maybe it will tell you what you want to know," he says, smiling.

"Oh, thank you," says Jess, hugging the sketchbook to her chest, thrilled at the thought of this firsthand insight into Minnie's world, her eye's view, her personal thoughts made concrete.

"So did Minnie stay here a long time?" she asks, curiosity spiraling.

"Well, yes. Pel Tawr was considered her home. She and Emery had a daughter, the famously audacious Anna, but of course you probably know all about Anna—"

"I know the name," says Jess, regretful. "Nancy was always sparing with the Taylor family history. She never liked to dwell on the past."

"Yes, of course," says Bevan. "We talked about lots of things, her and me, but there were certainly a few topics that were off-limits. For instance, she'd never let me ask about her daughter, Carmen—"

"My late mum."

"Yes. I gather she died young?"

"She did. She had a stroke."

"You poor dear."

Jess shrugs. "It's okay," she says breezily. "All a long time ago."

She hugs the sketchbook tighter.

"Tell me more about Anna, will you? From the little I know, she lived quite a life."

"Well, yes, she was known for her vivacity. She moved to Hollywood in the thirties. Like many young women of the time, she was seduced by the glamour of the silver screen, but Anna actually made it her reality."

"So the story about Nancy being born in Hollywood is true!"

"Indeed."

"Was Anna an actress?"

"No. Like her mother, Minnie, she had a passion for jewelry. She became a film-set jewelry designer, worked in various studio costume departments, worked on some big movies."

Jess gasps, delighted. She'd largely assumed the Hollywood claim to be something of a fantasy, but the truth is more extraordinary.

"I guess it's in the blood," she says, "the jewelry thing. I love jewelry too. Always have. But what a change, the Welsh mountains to the Hollywood Hills?"

"I don't think it bothered our Anna. Her mother may have loved the countryside, but the mountains proved zestless for her.

In adolescence, all she did was peruse buy-at-home dress catalogs, listen to jazz records on the house gramophone, and daydream about transatlantic travel. Adventure was in her sights."

"How old was she when she left?"

"Nineteen, maybe twenty. It was a bittersweet occasion I believe, for it was just after her mother—after Minnie—died. Typhoid. It swept through the area. I suppose this loss left Anna with a certain sense that she should now go forth and follow her dreams. Cinema was booming, so there were fast-growing opportunities in all the big studios. A month later, using the money her mother had left her and a little extra from the Floyds, she took passage on Cunard-White Star's newest liner, the *Queen Mary*. Four days from Southampton to New York, then a train right across the states. Quite a journey for a young solitary woman."

He thinks for a moment. "Jossop's," he adds. "That's it. That's the name of the jewelry company she went to work for. Nancy once mentioned it. Jossop's of Hollywood. And there was a producer, a man Anna got engaged to, a Christopher somebody…Christopher Roderick."

"Wow!" says Jess, overwhelmed. "I need to sit down and draw my family tree. There's so much to figure out, so much to discover. All thanks to the butterfly necklace."

"Well, isn't that the wonder of family heirlooms? They keep us connected to our past, with the people who've gone, yet to whom we owe so much."

"Yes," says Jess. "They really do."

"One wonders why it left your family, given what a treasure it is."

"I wish I knew. It's odd. I mean, I guess maybe it got mislaid when we moved house. We did that a few times after my mum died. Lots of change. Although"—Jess puzzles, thinks back—"the jewelry box always came with us, every time. My sister and I, we had it in our bedroom. We used to fight over it. So it stands to reason that the contents, including the necklace, would have come too, but...who knows? In your chats with Nancy, did...did she ever mention it?"

"No, I'm afraid not."

"One of her off-limits topics?"

"I believe so."

Jess sighs, then her phone trills: a message from Guy. For a moment, she hopes he is contacting her to say that he has the necklace for her; then equally, she fears he is messaging to say it has been melted down for scrap.

"Excuse me," she says, clicking on the message, nerves sweeping her stomach.

Jess of the Doughnuts,

Is your grandmother hanging in there?

I'm keeping my ringed fingers crossed for you.

And in the meantime, stay away from airplanes. And skydive instructors.

G.

Neither. Just something nice. Pointless but nice. She shuts off her phone then looks to the window. On the terrace outside she spies a stone sculpture of a peacock.

"Ah, I've seen a photo of Minnie holding a peacock," she exclaims.

"That would have been Percy. He roamed the estate for decades. Ruled the place, some say. Emery made the sculpture of him just before…" He pauses, shrugs. "Well, why not come outside and see it up close."

He throws open the patio doors, leads Jess out. The sun has warmed the sandstone flagstones, and the smell of fresh-cut grass hangs in the air. *They would have taken tea here*, thinks Jess. They would have admired the view. Maybe played some croquet.

"Here he is," says Bevan, patting the large but elegantly formed stone peacock. "Sculpture was just one of the crafts Emery excelled at. He could turn his hand to anything."

Jess places a hand on the peacock's back.

"He's so lifelike," she says. "He could strut right off his plinth, take a turn on the lawn."

But as the sunbaked stone heats her palm, she realizes there is something achingly sad about the way Percy looks out across the valley. Like he's waiting, forever waiting. She turns to Bevan.

"They *were* happy together, weren't they?"

"Oh yes," he says, "they had some very halcyon years together, a decade in fact, before—"

He stalls, casts his eyes down. Jess senses what's coming.

"The war?" she says, second-guessing the specter of the First World War—its cataclysmic impact on the early twentieth century.

"Yes," says Bevan. "Emery was slow to sign up. They all were. The conscientious objectors of Pel Tawr—there was an article about them in our local paper. But in the end, having been inspired by the war artists, Emery decided to play his part. He joined the Welsh Fusiliers, sailed out in May 1917, taking his sketchbooks with him. He was killed five weeks later. Drowned, of all things. The rain that year, it was dreadful. No-man's-land was a lethal quagmire, never mind the sniper bullets. Emery slipped off a wooden gang-plank while carrying supplies across the field. His body was never recovered."

"Oh god," says Jess, a chill in her soul.

"And that, I'm afraid, was where Minnie and Emery's love story ended, like so many of that era, all too briefly."

A wedge of sorrow catches in her throat.

"But they were *soul mates*," she protests. "That's what Nancy told me. The necklace brought them together. They were meant for each other." She sighs. "Soul mates forever."

"Ah," says Bevan, "there is a philosophy that the way of soul mates is to come into our lives to challenge us, move us forward. It's not the job of a soul mate to accompany us through our entire life or share every detail of our being. Once it's purpose has been fulfilled, the soul mate is free to disappear."

Jess nods, wide-eyed.

"Like Emery," she whispers. "He restored Minnie's joy after a bad marriage. He made her happy, gave her a child, and then...he fluttered away."

"Like a butterfly."

"Yes," says Jess, the necklace's translucent wings suddenly more pertinent than ever.

She stares at the sky, then turns to Bevan. "Thank you so much for your time," she says, tucking Minnie's sketchbook into her bag, along with the envelope of Nancy's photographs. "And for sharing your home with me. It's wonderful. It really is."

Bevan smiles, a glint in his eye.

"Consider it your home too."

"Yes," says Jess. "Yes, I suppose it is in a way. Thank you."

"Visit again. Whenever you wish. And…give my love to Nancy, won't you?"

"I will. Goodbye. And thank you again."

Jess walks away feeling wiser and warmer, and a little sadder for Minnie and Emery, their love cut so short. To finally find someone who's right for you, who lets you be you—your soul mate—then have them snatched away… It's too cruel. But as she hobbles down the lane, past the lazing sheep and hedgerows, toward her guesthouse, she cannot shake the necklace from her thoughts, the tiny green-blue cells of its plique-à-jour wings—because suddenly she sees in it not just life and love, but death too; the end of things, the transience of butterflies, their presence so rich, so brief.

Does this explain the "*OUI*" engraving? An edict to say yes while you can? Yes to what? With a shiver, she hastens forward. Having already faced her mortality, she knows only too well that every of drop of time is precious. So what, today, should she be saying yes to? Settling down or taking risks? Listening to her head or trusting her heart?

At last she reaches the village of Beddgelert. Surrounded by heathery mountains and pine forests, not one but two rivers winding through the village's streets, creating meandering chaos for cars and pedestrians. At every turn there is a humpback bridge, and on every corner, a trinket shop or ice cream parlor or accommodation to serve the summer walkers. Jess finds her guesthouse on the main street, a traditional stone cottage with log fires and the promise of Glamorgan sausages and fresh eggs for breakfast. It's a welcome sight after so much walking. She checks in and just about manages the final push upstairs to her bedroom, where she flops onto the ruched satin bedspread and pops a double dose of pain relief. The tablets will make her drowsy, but no matter. From the bed, she can see through the window, right across the forested valley. It's a view she'll happily stick with for the evening.

As the sun sinks low behind the trees, Jess makes herself comfortable with a mound of cushions, places her haul of Taylor memorabilia beside her on the bed, then digs out her phone. Tim, she guesses, will still be at work, planning in his classroom, eating a protein bar, loyal to his job promotion. She dials his number and he answers immediately.

"Hey, you," he says. "I hoped you'd call. I'm sitting here, boring myself stupid going through the staff lists for next term. There's still a post up for grabs, if I could only entice you, oh greatest art-and-design teacher there ever was."

"I'm thinking about it," says Jess.

"And one thing we really should start thinking about is the kitchen for the flat. The contractors want our instructions. I'll get some brochures, then when you're back, we can go through them. Seriously, Jess, can you imagine us waking up every day together? Lie-ins in our own bedroom—"

Tim beside her every night. What would that be like? It wouldn't—as Steph has decreed—be fireworks, but it would certainly be a soothing night's rest. Tim always sleeps deeply, as though he's been programmed to. Jess has noticed she wakes up refreshed whenever they share a bed, as though somehow, lying next to him, she absorbs all his orderly, calming atoms.

"I'll bring you breakfast in bed every weekend," he promises.

And he will, she thinks. He's that much of a gem.

"How's Wales?"

"It's fascinating."

"I miss you," he says.

"Miss you too," says Jess. "So what are you up to this evening?"

"I promised Duff I'd meet him for a pint and a game of Risk."

Of course. Thursdays. The habitual routine: real ale and board games with Duff on Thursdays.

Tim talks on, about a scandal at work and a bike crash that has put half his cycle team's best riders out of action, but his chat is disturbed by the intermittent buzz of Jess's phone. When she gets off the line, she finds a slew of messages from Guy, who has sent links to a Facebook page from a woman appealing for help to recover her engagement ring, which slipped off her finger while snorkeling in Spain.

Business opportunity? G.

Jess smiles to herself. Two job proposals in one minute, at opposite ends of the spectrum, from men who are at opposite ends of the spectrum. She doubts Guy is serious—his type rarely is—but she knows Tim is utterly serious. The teaching post gets a mention at every opportunity. Yes, she's interested. Yes, she sees how getting back into teaching makes sense. Yes, she understands that Tim is proud of his school, but…the constant encouragement is starting to feel like pressure.

She pictures them both, Tim and Guy, tugging on her arms, fighting for her attention; Agnes pulling from one side, Nancy from the other. She sighs, shuts her eyes, and turns her attention instead to Minnie's sketchbook. The stiff, yellowed pages reveal sketch after sketch, much like Nancy's, some gentle and detailed, some crude, of flora and fauna. At the back there are a dozen pages of writing, presented like a memoir. Jess marvels at the sight of her ancestor's elegant, looped script. She softens into her pillow and reads:

I arrived full of anxiety, having made my way alone, by train, then boat, then another train. I was greeted on the lawn by the youngest of the Floyd children, who seemed merely amused by my sudden appearance, clambering out of the pine forest like a wood nymph; but I believe they were rather used to sudden arrivals and departures, such was the bohemian way of their home.

I was then brought to the kitchen and given some soup and asked about my background. I said little, other than that I wanted to join the artists and that I had walked for a very long time. They were kind to me. A bed was made, and I slept nonstop for thirty-two hours. When I awoke, the sky was blue, the birds were singing, and such a lightness came over me.

In the parlor, I met Emery Floyd, the young gentleman of the house. As he talked, I could not help but be inspired by his mind. He knew the work of the Pre-Raphaelite Brotherhood and the campaigns of William Morris. He confided he had once wished to replicate their intellectualism by studying Eastern philosophy and medieval literature, but that wordy ideas were not his forte. He said he believed his true gift was in his eyes and hands, their ability to communicate with each other, and this I wholly understood.

In the weeks that followed, I noticed him watching me as I wandered alone on the grounds. The house was not without its social routines. Meals were communal, at set times of the day, eaten around a long wooden table, which had been crafted by Emery himself. Everyone was expected to help with chores and maintenance of the grounds. There was open access to workshops and tools, to encourage the creative forces, but I stayed away. I stayed away from all the high jinks too—the plays, the card games, the drinking, the dressing-up.

Other characters at the house were large and loud, with many opinions and just as many insecurities. They stayed up all night drinking absinthe, then did daft, grandiose things, like marching through the streets, draped in velvet cloaks, shouting the verse of William Blake. Meanwhile I walked alone, ate in silence, spoke little. Looking back, it's almost as though the shock of my transition had all but wiped out my character.

I think Emery could sense this. He gave me the space I needed, but didn't quite let me slip away. Once a day, he would seek me out. He brought me things—an unusual flower or tile or piece of embroidery, hopeful that it might ignite an opinion or comment. He introduced me to Percy, the resident peacock, who ruled the place. When he suggested I paint or maybe try my hand at metalwork, it made me wince. After years of being denied, I found it terrifying to be actively encouraged. I found it terrifying, but Emery's calm attentiveness softened my nerves, and as the spring rains eased and the lawn baked in the summer sun, my confidence returned.

I took an interest in the flower gardens, where Madame Floyd grew dahlias, euphorbias, and lilies. Their intricate beauty gave me the impetus to start sketching again, first the flowers themselves, then the birds and insects that inhabited them. The butterflies in particular drew my attention.

"The Callophrys rubi," said Emery one day, observing my sketch of a vivid green-blue butterfly. "This part of Wales is known for them, where they mate and breed."

As I sat on my knees among the buddleia bushes, deep-pink flower fronds cloaking me, a pencil in my hand, he told me that far away in Japan, butterflies had great symbolic value. They were thought to be the souls of humans, representing joy, longevity, emerging womanhood, even marital happiness.

"Sometimes they place them on young women's kimonos," he told me, holding my gaze, "in the hope that they'll attract a soul mate."

As he spoke, one of the same green-blue butterflies landed on my thigh and a deep reasoning burrowed into my mind that this force of beauty should be the subject of my first jewelry creation. If I could only capture the translucent delicacy of its petal-shaped wings, its ephemeralness— there for a moment to land its love, only to flutter away moments later.

As though reading my thought, Emery took my hand and led me

to his workshop, where he furnished me with tools and materials and taught me the basics of silversmithing and stone setting. He had little knowledge of the elaborate Lalique enameling techniques that I loved so ardently, but did his best to re-create the effect. He never once saw outrage in my desire to make jewelry. He just saw magic.

We grew closer every day. When my butterfly pendant was finally finished, he told me I should be proud, then he handed me an engraving tool.

"You must mark your work."

"Mark it?"

"With your name, your insignia, so that the world knows that you, Minnie Taylor, created it."

For a moment I considered whether to attempt my signature or just my initials, but then it came to me—a word in my head, somehow more meaningful, more potent than any other. Oui!

Yes to art.

Yes to freedom.

Yes to love.

Overcome, I struggled to fit the clasp, so he fixed it for me and placed it gently around my neck. As his fingertips caressed the silk of my skin, I knew he wanted so much to kiss me. And I wanted him to, but my tender heart trembled at the thought and I cowered.

That evening we took a boat out on the lake. As we rested in the middle, I could not resist leaning over to admire myself in my necklace. Gazing at my reflection, I tipped too far forward and hit the water with a splash. Emery screamed to me.

"Minnie!"

I saw him drop the oars, jump in after me, but I couldn't stay above the surface. The more I tried, the more I sank. I felt the life leave my lungs, and I knew I was drowning. Then I saw him again, grasping into the sun-flecked depths, diving forward, seizing my arms, and pulling me to the air. He forced my face to the sky, and with a strength that I'm sure was born from pure adrenaline, he heaved me back onto the boat, where I spluttered and gasped and stared, awestruck, into his eyes.

And so, not wasting any more time, no longer holding back, he leaned down and kissed me, and it was a kiss of such intensity that all my demons were vanquished in that instant—a kiss of true love. I reached for my necklace, felt it there against my heart, and suddenly it seemed like the loves and lives of the whole world—not just mine and Emery's—were bound within its form.

Minnie Philomene Taylor. Pel Tawr, 1918.

Jess reads it again, herself in awe: the incarnation of the True Love Necklace explained by Minnie herself. There are a few more pages of notes about jewelry materials, plus a list of flowers and their Latin names, but it's this account that means the most. Through it, Jess finds a sense of closeness to Minnie that wasn't there before. The fact that they both had a brush with mortality intrigues her. A hundred years apart and the life lesson is the same: Never take happiness for granted.

And Minnie's happiness clearly lay with Emery. Her adoration of him exudes from every sentence. It was *their* necklace. Jess thinks of all the design masterpieces she's seen in galleries around the world, some about joy, some about suffering. To what extent does a creator's intent become imbued in the creation itself? Here is a necklace made with love, for the sake of love, but can the quest for a soul mate really be *bound within its form*? Such a lovely idea.

"If only it were true," she whispers, shutting the book, her thoughts twirling in circles.

Chapter Ten

IN AGGIE'S KITCHEN, OVER A PLATE OF HOMEMADE GLUTEN-FREE macaroons and kombucha tea, Jess shares the spoils of her trip to Wales.

"Is that really Nancy?" asks Steph, as she paws over the Denmark Street photos. "And is that the necklace?"

"It is."

"It's lush. *Why* didn't you buy it?"

"You know why," says Aggie. "It was too much money. Plus we were pipped to the post by a most *unfortunate* human."

Jess squirms, aware that Aggie is putting more emphasis on the word *unfortunate* than necessary. Does she know something? Can she smell the chemicals of attraction? It is possible, of course, that she has read Jess's text messages and seen her and Guy's ongoing interactions. It's a pet habit of Aggie's to "accidentally" see the pop-ups on other people's mobiles. But whatever she knows, she won't say directly. She'll just lace her chat with knowing looks and meaningful nods.

"Who do you think Paul Angel Photography is?" asks Steph.

"I'd love to know," says Jess. "I'd ask Nancy, but—"

"Oh, Jess, I meant to say, while you were away, the hospital called.

They said Nancy's picked up a bit. Your visit must have boosted her. Anyhow, the old bird's clinging on. For what I don't know."

For the necklace, thinks Jess, as a ray of sunshine illuminates the kitchen island.

"Perhaps I should speak to our dad?" she says, thinking out loud. "Maybe he'll be able to fill me in on a few details. I should call him."

"Ugh, really?" says Aggie. "Like he'd care. The last time I spoke to our dearest, darling father all he wanted to talk about was Eileen and her cruises. He didn't ask a single question about me. Or you, for that matter, Jess. No 'How's it going, girls?' or 'How are my grand-children doing?'"

Jess nods. On this, she and Aggie agree. Their relationship with their father, Richard Barrow, has rarely born fruit. There was no dramatic falling-out, just a slow disintegration of the bond. It didn't help that, a decade ago, he met Eileen, remarried, moved to Kettering, and had two more children, twins, Rosie and Ben. He'd come to Jess's bedside after her accident, but as soon as he'd real-ized she was going to survive, he'd sloped back to his Other Family shadow world, despite promises to visit every week. He'd gone awk-wardly, apologetically. And it was this that dismayed Jess most, his toadying loyalty to his high-maintenance second wife. More than that, the sense that he knew it was wrong, was *embarrassed* by it. Yet he still did it.

Jess sighs.

"Maybe you're right."

Between sips of tea, she talks on. Aggie is only vaguely impressed to learn that there is truth in Nancy's Hollywood claim, but Steph is chuffed at the prospect of being related to a movie mogul. Jess catches her checking her reflection in the oven door, looking over her shoulder, pouting like a movie star.

"I never heard the name," says Aggie dismissively. "Christopher Roderick? Doesn't ring any bells. Probably made B movies."

Jess is about to suggest they look him up, when Steph, two steps ahead, waves her phone and presents the Christopher Roderick Wikipedia entry.

"'Christopher Arnold Roderick, 1904–1972,'" she reads. "'Hollywood movie producer, best known for the box-office flop *Descent of the Sun*. Roderick went on to direct a series of low-budget horror films in the late 1930s, but postwar, his career went into decline.'"

"There we are," says Aggie with a self-satisfied smile. "A Hollywood has-been. I knew it."

"Does it say anything about his personal life?" asks Jess.

"Just that he died of lung disease and that he lived with his partner…Bernard."

"Bernard?"

"Bernard Almer. That's what it says."

"Okay," says Jess, her mind ticking.

"Oh, and there's this," Steph continues, "'Roderick's mansion on Hollywood Boulevard, having been untouched since his death, has recently been acquired by the Golden Age Restoration Trust and is now open to the public.'"

Jess's eyes pop wide.

"How cool is that! We have to go! We have to see it!"

"Can we?" Steph grins. "Mum? Can we go?"

Jess claps her hands with glee, while Steph hops up and down like an excitable kitten.

"Oh, *please*," says Aggie. "No one is going anywhere. This is sheer whimsy."

"But it's our bloodline," says Jess, "our heritage!"

"I wonder what Bernard has to say about that. Live in the present, Jessica. Never mind the lavender marriages of the Taylors of yore. For all we know, it's a bunch of nonsense that our great-grandmother was engaged to a movie producer. I never heard the name Christopher Roderick before. And if he and Anna *were* together at any point, one can only wonder what kind of relationship it actually was—"

"Maybe he identified as bi?" says Steph.

Aggie sighs, rolls her eyes. "I'm not sure they used that term back then. Anyway, why are we even discussing this? Think about the here and now. What about your new flat, Jess? Your kitchen plans?"

Of course. A house project, Aggie's favorite kind of project. No doubt she already has a Pinterest board set up and has been rabidly pinning images of tiles, backsplashes, and integrated dishwashers, testament to her impeccable taste and extensive wallet.

"Think of all the gadgets you'll be able to get," she pesters. "You'll need a NutriBullet and a decent coffee machine. Bean to cup, obviously. And a KitchenAid."

Jess shakes her head.

"You're the chef of the family, Aggie, not me. I'll be fine with a gas hob and a saucepan."

Aggie huffs. "You mean you're denying me the opportunity to purchase household appliances? How could you?"

Steph steps between them. "You two, honestly! Grow up!"

Then everyone is saved by the clatter of the letter box.

Aggie fetches the pile of letters, hands one to Jess. Casually Jess accepts, expecting another hospital bill, then sees a handwritten address and unfamiliar lettering. With a rush of self-consciousness, she lifts the seal, peeks inside, and spies the stiff, gilded edge of an invite.

"What is it, Aunty?"

"Oh, nothing."

"Looks like a card."

"It's just…a circular."

Aggie eyes her suspiciously.

"I better go," says Jess, "get on with some jewelry post."

She hastens to her room, the envelope pressed against her chest, mind bursting. An invite. Guy van der Meer has sent her an invite to the Capital Gala. Her heart starts to race involuntarily. Dangerous territory, she knows it's dangerous territory, but it feels so deliciously tantalizing. How did he get her address? That took some effort. Okay, so the address is blatantly on her website, but still…the Capital Gala! What is his game? What is he *playing* at? Does he expect her to come? Does he *want* her to come? Is this about the necklace…or about her? She checks the date of the event: *Saturday 6th August*. Nearly two weeks away. But Nancy may not survive that long. Then what? Then it will all be in vain.

Thank you for the invitation. Am I expected? Jess (of D-nuts)

Well, obviously. That's the point of an invitation :) Guy

I'll think about it.

How is she anyway, your Big G? Hanging in there?

She's okay, thanks. For now.

Wanna hunt?

Hunt?

Hunt for treasure. Then have coffee. And cake. The sun is shining. Come to Portobello, my territory. I'll take you to my favorite jewelry shops.

Presumptuous.

Just get on the Tube, will you? It'll be fun.

Jess shuts off her phone, feels her heart pounding in her rib cage. His cheeky confidence, his focus on her… She's certain it's all for show, yet it feeds her self-worth, makes her feel prized. What did she have planned anyway? Wrapping and posting a box of diamanté hair slides. Working her way through her tedious and painful list of physical exercises. A good walk is physical enough, surely? She chews her lip, stares at the clock. Tim won't finish work until six, then he'll have cycling and then he'll probably want to grab a pint at the Star. He won't even have to know.

Okay, she replies.

Message sent, she cups her mouth with her hand. That's it. She has crossed a line. She has agreed to a non-necklace-related meetup with Guy van der Meer, almost qualifying as a date. She knows she should be ashamed of herself, but while she's scared of the lie that this is starting to become, deep down, she realizes she is more scared of the thought that, perhaps, with Tim, she is *living* a lie.

Portobello Road—with its bohemian street-market a mix of food, antiques, curios, fashions, and trinkets—thrives in the sunshine. The area has seen its fortunes rise and fall, then rise again, neglected for much of the twentieth century and gentrified in the eighties by an influx of the fashionable, young, and affluent. Three centuries ago, it was a country lane leading to a farm, which then became a network of elegant crescents and terraces, which were crowned in 1864 by the arrival of Ladbroke Grove railway station. Which is where Jess meets Guy.

Notably he is on time, wearing a slim T-shirt and wide-legged trousers, like a throwback from the Rat Pack, befitting the vibrant surroundings. His greeting—a smile and a peck on the cheek—is a mix of warmth and wry conceit. Jess senses he's pleased to have tempted her here, the cat that got the cream with the diamond in it. But his eyes belie him; beneath those errant curls there is a candid all-in glow.

He buys two strong coffees, then paying no regard to her stiff gait and walking cane, he strides off through the stalls. At first indignant, struggling to keep pace, she then realizes her left leg can move a little faster than she'd thought. It's simply a matter of willing it. She has grown so used to the people in her sphere always slowing down, making exceptions, making sure she's okay, that it's become her default. But here, now—chasing Guy's heels—she wonders if she can in fact push out, do more.

"So you like art nouveau?" says Guy, as she catches up with him, a little out of breath, but smiling.

"I do."

"Me too. I like that it's ornamental, yet deeply earthy. Hard to define, but if it was a Shakespeare play it would definitely be—"

"*A Midsummer Night's Dream*?" says Jess. "Magic, love, and a hint of the macabre?"

"Exactly."

They approach a stall of dream catchers. Jess picks one up, runs her fingers through its feathered fronds.

"Do you think Stella Weston appreciates the enigmatic qualities of art nouveau jewelry?" she asks pointedly.

"What can I say," says Guy, shrugging. "She's got a thing about butterflies."

"Oh, how adorable."

"Jess, she's no fool. But yes, her main aim in life is to get good coverage in fashion magazines. And no, your necklace doesn't mean to her what it clearly means to you."

"Because I worry," says Jess, replacing the dream catcher on its stand, "about how she's taking care of it. Plique-à-jour is known for its fragility."

Guy stops, gives her a look.

"Don't you just trust me?" he says.

"That," says Jess, flicking the ground with her cane, "is an interesting question."

"You need to trust me, Jess. I'll get your necklace for you."

"I'd like to believe you, and in a way I do, but trust is earned. Otherwise it's just wishful thinking."

"You and that force field," he says with a grin, leading her to a stall of midcentury retro cuffs, embellished with colored stones.

"Which one's your favorite?"

"The aubergine one," says Jess, pointing to a deep-hued lump of amethyst.

"Aubergine?"

"You might say purple, but I believe it to be *aubergine*."

Guy laughs.

"I see why you're a jewelry nut. You like color. Let me show you this."

He leads her to another stall, displaying trays of brooches bearing the same distinct gem combination: green peridot, purple amethyst, and white diamond. She recognizes them immediately: the colors of the suffragette movement, worn by thousands of women in the early 1900s to enhance awareness and encourage solidarity for women's votes.

"Joy to the eye is one of jewelry's more minor tricks," says Guy.

"Agreed. The best stuff reflects more than mere aesthetics. Political allegiance, for instance. Religious devotion. Tokens between lovers. *Soul mates*." She catches his eye and bites her lip, tormented by his out-of-bounds attractiveness. "Sometimes I wonder if there isn't real power in the heirloom jewels we covet. They're not just static keepsakes. They've been through so much, *seen* so much. Surely they carry some trace of this within them?"

Guy shuts his eyes as though the intensity of the conversation is getting under his skin.

"I'm sorry," says Jess. "Have I said something wrong?"

"Oh, no," he says, adjusting his leopard ring.

Then he grins, blinks.

"What I'm thinking is why…*why* is it that when I talk with you, I get the feeling I've known you all my life?"

"That's such a line!"

She goofily pushes him away, deflecting the forces that keep drawing them together.

"It's not a line," he argues. "You are *so* suspicious, Jess. You've already made your mind up about me, haven't you? You're convinced I'm some feckless, womanizing playboy—"

"Yup."

"So why agree to meet me?"

"For the kicks." She shrugs, realizing she has no answer. No appropriate one, anyhow.

They walk on, bodies so close they're almost touching, oblivious to the crowds of shoppers and tourists in their periphery, past the rows of colorful Georgian terraces with neat front gardens and the shops selling vintage shoes, old vinyl, military memorabilia, Indian sari silk, belt buckles, and designer cupcakes.

"I love living in Portobello," says Guy. "There's always something random to look at."

"Can't be cheap. Do you rent?"

He smiles, a little shamefacedly.

"Sort of…not really. I, um, occupy Stella Weston's mews house."

"Rrrright."

"I know how it sounds, but she needed a tenant, someone she could rely on, and I needed a roof. Stella has several properties around the world. She flits between them."

"So she doesn't live in the mews house with you?" says Jess, keen to unveil the exact machinations of Guy's relationship with Stella.

"Sometimes. When she's in town."

"Just friends?"

"Just friends."

"With benefits?"

"Questions, questions," he says evasively. "If you must know— and keep it to yourself—Stella's main romantic interest is a Greek dot-com billionaire whom she sees twice a year. They sunbathe on his yacht in Mykonos and…she thinks it's love."

"Sounds a bit sad," says Jess.

"It is. I mean, Stella's world, it's extraordinary and remote. Beauty and fortune have given her everything, yet she's one of the neediest people I know."

"You care about her, don't you?" Jess ventures.

"I do. She's been good to me. But look, Stella and I are close, but we're not romantic close. We look out for each other, that's all. She's lonely. She wants a little loyalty in her life, so I do my best to be there for her."

"In exchange for social status and a crash pad in Ladbroke Grove?"

"Jess, that's so cynical. You say it like you think I'm using her, but Stella knows the score. She's all for helping me network and build my profile. It's a mutual thing." He huffs, folds his arms. "We all have to play the game at some point. That's just how it goes. So there."

"Okay, okay," says Jess, surprised by this sudden turn of defensiveness, his got-it-all-sewn-up confidence turning sour. "If you say so."

"I do," he says curtly, pulling his cards in.

They come to a churros stall. The smell of hot, sweet batter and melting chocolate is intoxicating, and it breaks the mood.

"Rude not to," says Guy jovially, before ordering a large portion with extra cinnamon sugar—successfully swerving away from any further scrutiny of his personal life in the process.

Through the sunny air, they walk on, but Jess remains unsettled by Guy's blurry meta-signals. *What was that*, she wonders—a glimpse of insecurity? A smoke screen? Or a straight-up dose of shady man-baby fuckwittery? Either way, she feels cautioned, reminded to keep her distance. A self-professed game player: dicey territory, no matter how gorgeous he is. At least with Tim, she always knows where she stands. He's decent to a fault and it's so refreshing. Tim, whom everyone loves. Whom *she* loves. The "good one" she's finally bagged. So what's she even *doing* here with Guy? She gives her pelvis a poke.

Perhaps she's ovulating, hormones rocking her judgment. Then he turns to look at her with those deep-set sparkly eyes. Most definitely the hormones.

"So what of the other Taylor women?" he asks as they walk on. "Explain what I'm getting into here—"

"Getting into?"

"Well, clearly I enjoy your company—"

"Steady," she whispers, a flush brightening the apples of her cheeks. "Save the schmooze for someone who'll buy it."

Guy shrugs, unperturbed.

"They all buy it," he quips. "It's just I don't always want to sell it."

"Oh no?"

Jess cackles. Truth or lie, she doubts she'll ever know for sure. She sips her coffee and smiles to herself, amid the aromas of spicy street food and the shouts of stall traders.

"Since you ask," she says, pausing to admire a cluster of china figurines, "I've embarked on a mission to find out what I can about my Taylor roots, about where the necklace came from. At first I just wanted to understand why Nancy was so desperate for it, but now it's given me a heap of questions about my entire family. I'd like to know more, because…sometimes I feel like a stranger to myself. Does that make sense?"

Guy nods wistfully.

"Yeah, it kind of does."

"My family is very fractured," she explains. "My mother died young. She had a stroke. I was only six so I don't remember much about it, but it meant that my sister and I were left with my dad, who hasn't been the greatest of parents, and with my grandmother, Nancy, who was… Well, let's just say it was a brusque kind of love—"

"Formative?" says Guy, as he picks up a figurine, examines the base, then places it back.

"That's one way of putting it."

"And what do you know about your mother?"

"She only got to thirty-three. Shit luck. She was an illustrator like Nancy, worked for a publishing company. Carmen Victoria Barrow née Taylor. I took the Taylor name back when I fell out with my dad. I believe she was talented. I used to like looking at her drawings. God knows where they are now. Probably in a dumpster somewhere. My dad, he had to…purge."

"Do you remember her well?"

Jess smiles.

"Only in my dreams. I think of her now as this beautiful dark-haired princess with green eyes and perfect teeth. I remember her showing me the necklace—"

"*The* necklace?"

"The very one," she says, holding his gaze. "I also just found out I'm possibly related to a Golden Age Hollywood producer—"

"*Hollywood?* So why are you here? Why aren't you drinking wheatgrass in Beverly Hills?"

"I don't like wheatgrass…but I'll visit one day. I'd love to find out more about my great-grandmother, Anna, about her life there. She made jewelry for the movies apparently."

"I like her already!"

"Yes, she sounds fascinating. I think maybe she's the ancestor responsible for my adventurous streak."

"Adventurous streak? If you have an adventurous streak, then what are you waiting for? Get on a plane and get yourself to Hollywood."

"What? Just like that? Just go?"

"Ah sorry, maybe you're not such a fan of planes—"

"No, it's just"—she sighs, shuts her eyes, runs her hand down her hip—"spontaneity… It's not really my thing anymore."

"Nonsense."

She hangs her head, deflated.

"Look at me. I can't do things like I used to. My body won't play ball. I can't simply jump on a plane and go here and go there. I'd love to, but…I *can't*. If I sit too long, I seize up, and if I walk too far, I get exhausted. Everything's an effort. Everything takes planning. And sometimes…sometimes everything just *hurts!*"

If Tim were at her side right now, he'd smother her with hugs, tell her she's safe, and promise to make her happy wherever she is, whatever her limits. Guy, meanwhile, gives a nonchalant shrug.

"Can't?" he says. "Or won't?"

Jess tenses, caught by his judgment.

"Seriously," he continues, cajoling. "Hollywood's not as far away as it sometimes seems. I go to LA all the time. Stella has a house there. She likes to throw parties—or rather, she likes people to throw parties for her. It's in the hills, got a great pool."

"Lucky you. Nice perk."

"What I'm trying to say is, if you ever want a traveling companion, someone who knows Hollywood like the back of their hand…I'd be happy to oblige. In fact, what I'd do," he says, eyes lighting up, "is take you to *Old Hollywood*."

"Old Hollywood?"

"Trust me, Old Hollywood's your vibe. You'll be in costume-jewelry heaven. So many stories. *So* much decadence. Musso's. I'd take you to Musso's. It's this restaurant on the Boulevard, near the old Egyptian Theatre—you'd love it—called the Musso & Frank Grill. I tell you, Jess, it hasn't changed in *seventy* years. It's like stepping back in time."

The way he talks, nonstop, with so much enthusiasm, is infectious. It reminds her of someone, but she can't think whom.

"Sounds amazing," she says. "And I will go. Eventually."

"Ah," he says with a clap of his hands. "Stop the excuses. Go now. There's no time like now."

"Yeah, yeah," she says drily, hobbling on, aware that while a stroll down Portobello Road with Guy van de Meer is an inappropriate flirtation, a rendezvous on another continent is at a whole other level.

Chapter Eleven

NANCY LOOKS THINNER THAN EVER. HER BREATHING IS SHALLOW, but her eyes still just about bear that twinkle. At the side of the bed, Jess has the envelope of Nancy's Denmark Street photographs in her hand, hopeful that the sight of them might stir Nancy's memory, ignite a reaction. She scatters them on the blanket, those vibrant images of teenage Nancy staring back.

"Look," Jess whispers. "This is you. This is *you*, Grandma, as a young woman wearing the necklace! It's not the actual necklace, I appreciate, but"—she squeezes Nancy's hand—"I've been working on that. I'll have it soon, I promise."

She flips one of the photos to reveal the sticker on the back.

"'Paul Angel Photography, 1954,'" she reads. "Who is Paul Angel, Grandma? Do you remember when these were taken?"

Nancy's gaze is fixed to the ceiling. Jess waves the photo in front of her, one of the best, in which she's standing with her arms folded—a hint of her future attitude within that demure fifties circle dress—but there is no discernable response.

"I've been squirrelling around," Jess persists, "seeing what I can find out about our Taylor women. I went to Wales and discovered these photographs in your desk at the cabin. I'd love to know the story behind them. Your cabin's fine, by the way. Still standing—just. And I met with Bevan Floyd, who sends his best wishes. What a nice human! He showed me around Pel Tawr and told me all about Minnie and Emery and the making of the necklace. He even gave me Minnie's sketchbook. And he talked about your mother, Anna, about her going off to America. So it's true? You *were* born in Hollywood."

She pats Nancy's hand, expecting more silence, then suddenly Nancy springs into verbosity.

"Oh yes, on good days, my mother was impeccable," she exclaims. "She'd set her hair, arrange her jewelry—earrings, brooches, hairpins, bangles…she brought them *all* with her. On bad days, though, she'd just lie on the sofa, drinking sweet sherry, endlessly lamenting her beloved Zedora—"

"Zedora?"

"Yes, Jessy, with the gilded toilet handle that Lucille Ball was rumored to have broken."

Jess laughs. "Now you're really confusing me! What on earth is a Zedora?"

Nancy looks pensive.

"It's all gone now."

"What?" say Jess, tensing. "What's gone, Grandma?"

Nancy sighs.

"Her life. My mother's glamorous life. All her stories… They became nothing more than stories, from a world we'd never get back. *Wake up*, I used to think. *Face it, move on*. I knew better than to join her in the shadows of nostalgia, Jessy, because while those stories always began with jubilance...they finished with tears."

Jess rests her chin on her hand, puzzled that these remarks don't match the audacious and vivacious image of Anna she'd had in mind.

"What happened, Grandma, to make her so regretful?"

Nancy scowls.

"That's Anna's business."

"But—"

"We came back to London and lived in a terrible place."

"Are you talking about the tenement block?" says Jess, remembering how Nancy had sometimes talked of a grimy flat in Poplar, where she'd spent her early teens.

"That place," she scowls. "The surrounding streets were still pitted with bomb damage. No running water, damp in the walls, TB in the corridors, never a clean sheet, and the only working kitchen facilities were located on the second-floor stairwell, shared with three other families, who had shouty boys who got on my nerves."

"So what on earth happened to Hollywood?"

Jess leans in, hopeful for an answer, but the way Nancy looks vacantly around her, it's clear her focus is starting to drift—the scenes of her life ebbing and flowing in no coherent order.

"'You should marry the grocer's son,'" she says with a twisted Welsh American accent, which Jess assumes to be an impression of Anna's. "'The grocer's son has something about him. Choose your suitor well, my girl. Don't make the mistakes I made.'"

Nancy leans toward her photo, taps the necklace with her fingertip.

"My mother thought our butterfly would attract the grocer's son," she recounts. "With all her dramatics, she pressed it into my palm and said it would be in my interest to try it out on him."

"And did you?" says Jess, gripped.

"Absolutely not. I hated that dolt."

"Oh."

After a moment, Jess picks up a few more of the Paul Angel photographs.

"So what about these images, Grandma? You're wearing the necklace in them. What are you here...fifteen...sixteen maybe?"

Nancy grins impishly.

"Yes, I skipped school," she whispers. "That was my best dress. I wore my best dress so that no one would know I was an O Level student with a Woolworth's uniform. I skipped school and took a Routemaster to the center of London."

"To Denmark Street?" says Jess, reading the words on the sign. "The beating heart of the rock-and-roll scene. So did you want to be a musician?"

"Goodness no. I was looking for a pawnbroker."

"A *pawnbroker*?"

"My mother was reckless with our finances, wasted everything on nail polish, sherry, and cigarillos. I wanted money she wouldn't know about so that I could buy food and stockings. I'd heard about the pawnbrokers from neighbors, places you could get quick cash. So when she gave me the necklace, I took it—"

"*You* pawned the necklace?"

"Not quite."

Jess puzzles. "Then—?"

"I jumped off the bus at the first shop I saw, on the corner of Denmark Street, only to discover I was too early. Schoolgirl eagerness. The shop wouldn't open for another hour, so I took the necklace out of my bag, clipped it around my neck, and"—she smiles suddenly—"for just a while, I walked up and down the street, feeling sophisticated. I remember I saw a man with horn-rimmed glasses, guitar strung over his shoulder. He gave me a nod, then disappeared into a tatty building advertising itself as a recording studio. Then I admired a pair of women dressed in matching polka-dot fit-and-flare dresses. They were giggling and singing as they walked along, their voices sweetly harmonious. Glamorous, but in that ragged, haven't-slept-all-night kind of way... I knew the touch. Then as I crossed the street, I noticed I too was being admired."

Now there is a fulsome twinkle in her eyes.

"He was there in a trilby hat," she whispers, "hunched over his camera. He looked up and signaled for me to wait. At first I thought better of it and walked on, but he called after me. His accent was cockney, like my neighbors, and that was reassuring. 'Don't rush off!' he said. He told me his name was Paul, then he threw out his hand and I didn't know what to do, because I'd never shaken a stranger's hand before. He said he liked my necklace, asked if he could take a photo of me wearing it. He said he knew the style: turn of the century, art nouveau. 'If you ask me,' he said, 'it's due a revival. I bet you, in ten years' time it'll be all the rage.' So I removed it and pushed it into his hands and I told him: 'My mother wouldn't want you to take my picture, sir, but if you like my necklace, I'll sell it to you.'"

"And did that work?"

"He pushed it back to me. But then…he noticed my malnour-ished limbs and offered to take me to Gideon's Café to buy me a breakfast. He promised he wasn't a sleaze, said I could ask anyone on the street. They all knew him. He said he photographed musicians—Petula Clark, Lonnie Donegan, Frankie Vaughan. He told me it was his business to capture them looking sharp, respectable. He said some of them come from the United States, stars like Little Richard and Nat King Cole. So I told him"—she puffs out her chest—"that *I* was born in Hollywood. He said I'd have to tell him all about it over a fried-egg sandwich.

"As he spoke, he lifted his camera. And I started posing, not sure whether I was doing it right, but doing it nonetheless. And"—she closes her eyes as though reliving the moment in her mind—"I shut my eyes and began thinking about how outraged my mother would be, only to realize I didn't care. When I opened my eyes again, Paul had lowered his camera and was gazing straight at me. It made me feel quite peculiar, like everything in my soul was leaping. Then as he gazed at me, Jessy, his eyes, huge and blue with long, dusky lashes, I sensed them scanning the necklace at my neck…and that…that, I think, was where the magic happened."

Jess sighs, entranced.

"So it was Paul Angel," she whispers. "*He* was your soul mate. The necklace brought you together. Oh, Nancy—"

Nancy smiles, such a smile, one that Jess has never seen before, an inner radiance shining through.

"What happened to him, Grandma? Did it work out?"

At this, Nancy snaps her eyes shut. She turns away and refuses to speak more, leaving Jess with the feeling she has just acquired more questions than answers.

Chapter Twelve

THE TRAVEL AGENT RAISES HIS BROW.

"Tomorrow?" he asks.

"If possible," says Jess, crossing her fingers.

The agent taps his computer keyboard. Meanwhile Jess smiles and floats through the moment. The impulse that has carried her here—to Abbotts Travel on the corner of the high road, with its window adverts promising the cheapest flight deals available—hums in her chest. She yearns to find out more about Anna, who now seems rather more complicated than she'd taken her for; to uncover more Taylor secrets while Nancy is still able—just about—to fill in the missing details. Jess knows it's a risk, that Nancy could decline at any time, but she also knows, given the opportunity, what Nancy would do if she could. She can almost hear her voice in her head: *You're a Taylor! Get on that plane!*

"Okay." The agent strokes his beard and turns the screen to face her. "Leaving what time?"

"Hmm," says Jess, her thoughts drawn to the Capital Gala at the end of next week; her chances of recovering from jet lag, combined with Nancy's chances of hanging in there. "I'm kind of on a time limit. Maybe…first thing?"

"Spur of the moment, eh? Good for you."

They both grin and the hunt for a deal begins.

An hour later, Tim matches the travel agent's surprise.

"Tomorrow?" he says. "Los Angeles? *Tomorrow?*"

"Real cheap flights," says Jess, beaming. "I reserved two. The agent can hold them for an hour. I just thought—"

Tim scratches his head, gives a confounded sigh.

"I'm not sure you did think, Jessy. Otherwise, you'd have considered the fact that I simply can't drop everything and go off for a random week of jollity."

"But the school holidays have started. Why not have a surprise break? Besides, it's not a week, just a few days."

"All that way for a few days?"

"Loads of people do it," she says, realizing that by "loads of people" she means Stella Weston. "I–I want to do it for Nancy and, well, we hadn't made any other plans, so—"

"That's because we're buying a home, Jess. Normal people don't splurge on new flats and luxury holidays in the same month. We have to be sensible about this."

"It's not luxury," Jess protests. "The flights were a bargain, and we can stay in a hostel."

Tim balks.

"I'm forty. I don't want to stay in a hostel."

"Oh, come on, it'll be an adventure."

Jess sighs. This hasn't gone the way she'd hoped. Meanwhile Tim paces the floor until, ever considerate, he manages to find something nice to say.

"Thank you for the thought. I do love your spirit, Jess, but ultimately it's an adventure I wasn't counting on. You know what I'm like. I need a plan. I need routines. Besides, I've entered a cycle series, three races over three weeks—"

Jess twitches, fearful of turning into Aggie, who bitterly complains about being a bike widow, while Ed backs up his calendar with cycling meets, because cycling, he claims, with close-to-the-knuckle humor, is the only time he can be himself and not some dried-up house slave.

"More cycling?"

"I thought you liked me cycling," says Tim, pulling her close. "What it does to my thighs—"

She casts her eyes to his tight bulked quads, the physical attribute that first got her attention.

"I do like your thighs," she says, "but I also like having a life."

"Well, if you really want a holiday, maybe we could go away at the end of the summer, late August? Do something that'll be easier on your hip? After all, you're supposed to be resting and healing, not taking last-minute long-haul mini-breaks. In fact, if you fancy it, we could join Collette and her boyfriend. They've hired a villa in Portugal, and they said anyone's welcome to—"

Jess glowers.

"I don't want to go Portugal with Collette and her boyfriend. I've never met her boyfriend. And I have this theory that Collette thinks I'm strange. And, ultimately, I don't want to rest and heal.

I want to live. I want to do it all and go *crazy*. Think about it… Hollywood!"

"Jess, I *can't*." Now he is churlish. "It's too last-minute. I can't get my head around it. And, to be honest, all of this sudden adventure-seeking spirit of yours is frankly rather maverick."

"As you wish," says Jess, sniffing the air into her lungs, "but I'm taking that flight."

"On your own?"

"On my own."

And so they part, neither side winning, neither side losing, but with a distinct sense of disconnect wedged between them.

At the airport, among the holiday crowds and families, Jess finds a seat and eats sushi alone. She's traveled plenty, so airports don't faze her, but it occurs to her that this is the first time she has flown since her unhappy return from Mexico. Her cane stacked against her chair, a cocktail of courage and unease seeps into her blood. It's a big, wild step. But somehow, she understands, it's a step she needs to take, a little bit of her old self returning, reminding her that she is still Jess Taylor, whatever that means.

"Well, cheers to that," she says, as she glugs from her water bottle, before feeling her phone buzz, a message from Guy.

So that dinner? How about tomorrow? G.

He's certainly persistent. She thinks for a moment, then replies.

Can't. I've taken your advice. J.

She attaches a photo of her boarding pass, and knows—*hopes*—it will incite a different response from Tim's. Indeed, straightaway Guy sends a page of emojis, expressing various states of shock and delight.

These tacky little fellas are trying to say GOOD FOR YOU. G.

Jess smiles and is about to shut off her phone when he messages again.

So yes to dinner then? Musso's. Saturday, seven o'clock? G.

Ha-ha. J.

Then as she scoops up her backpack and starts the long hike to the boarding gate, he messages one more time.

May you find what you're looking for. G. x

And out of nowhere, the sentiment of this, or maybe the laden addition of the kiss, makes her burst into tears.

The heat gets her first, then the big sky, which stretches overhead, a brilliant blue forever, brightening the hills and streets. How much it must have changed since Anna first arrived in the 1930s. And yet, everywhere Jess looks, there are remnants of that history in the streamlined curves of the deco buildings and the elegant villas. As she walks the length of the Strip, she feels them all around her, the ghost whispers of Anna Taylor's life. Anna from the mountains, with passion in her bones and designs in her head, among the colonial-style boutiques with their weather vanes and flower boxes, the black-tie supper clubs with their neon signs and palm-fringed entrances, the hills in the distance, the drifting heat, the women so tall and stylish, the men so suave—what did she think? What did she feel?

With three days to herself, Jess feels dizzy at the thought of how to fill them, but she has made a list: her Hollywood DNA. Firstly, she will seek out Christopher Roderick's mansion, see if she can join one of the Golden Age Restoration Foundation tours. Then she will hunt for evidence of Jossop's Jewelry, the company she was told Anna worked for. Lastly, once her personal Hollywood connections have been plundered, with whatever time is left, she will embrace the standard touristy things: the Egyptian Theatre, the Walk of Fame, Rodeo Drove. Maybe a little of the Old Hollywood that Guy talked about. Plus the obligatory walk up to the white-lettered sign, although she doubts her hip will accommodate it. The flight, as Tim foresaw, has taken it out of her somewhat.

After a hearty brunch of Americanos and blueberry pancakes, Jess grabs armfuls of brochures from the coffee-shop window. There are tours for everything, promising all that Tinsel Town has to offer, with names like the "Ultimate," the "Big One," and "Dream Homes of Beverly Hills." Her attention is eventually drawn to an unassuming, cheaply made leaflet for a house tour, bearing the logo of the Golden Age Restoration Foundation. She tugs the dog-eared leaflet free and gives it a closer inspection. The main image features an old-style Spanish mansion with castellated turrets and dusty-pink walls. And in the top corner, in italics, is a word that strikes her heart: *Zedora.*

Her beloved Zedora.

She'd had no idea what Nancy was referring to, but now it's obvious. Zedora must have been the Hollywood house where Anna lived. The cogs of her mind start to whir. With her heart in her mouth, she reads every word of the leaflet. "Support Hollywood heritage," says the tagline. "See Zedora, a historic mansion in danger of being pulled down for development. Former home of Golden Age movie mogul, Christopher Roderick. Tours every day."

She stares, mesmerized, the pieces of the puzzle slotting into place.

This is it, she thinks. Hollywood history, sure, but it's a little piece of *her* history too. She checks the time of the tour. Midday. Perfect.

Away from the tourist-mobbed landmarks, Jess finds herself among rows of gritty streets where art galleries and strip malls hide bistros and tattoo parlors, then on steep, sleepy lanes where elegant homes in traditional styles promise the "old." Following the map on the leaflet, she takes another right turn, then at the top of the hill she sees a turret. Those deep-pink sunbaked walls, she thinks, what memories do they hold? Pool parties, dinners, sunset cocktails, and *surely* a scandal or two?

At the gates—rusted filigree ironwork, bearing the name Zedora—Jess is greeted by the Restoration Foundation tour guide.

"Welcome," he says with an unexpected monotone, pointing to the name on his pin badge: Jackson.

Jess and Jackson are soon joined by a young man from Hungary, a group of Korean students, and an elderly couple from Alabama. Jackson ushers them into Zedora's scrubby, overgrown grounds and clears his throat.

"With so many prestige mansions within a few square miles," he says as though reading from a script he's extremely bored with, "you might wonder why you've arrived here. Hollywood has its share of ultra-modern palaces with every amenity going. You name it: hidden champagne vaults, helicopter pads, personal spa suites, and cinema rooms. But rewind for a minute and follow me. The true prestige is in the past. This is where the long-gone stars of the silver screen had their feuds, their affairs, and their fun."

Fun? thinks Jess wryly. Jackson makes the entire prospect sound devoid of fun, but whatever his commentary lacks, at least her imagination can fill in the gaps. They proceed to the front porch, and the tattered oak door is heaved open. Jess fidgets with anticipation, as the spoils of Zedora's faded decadence are offered to her. The first treat is a swirling marble staircase gracing an enormous hall, flanked with sculptures of gilded cherubs. The gilding is a little lackluster and the marble is chipped, but the feel is there. Beyond the hall she sees a living room with mirrored walls, arched windows, and an ornate rococo fireplace. To the side, there is a row of shelving, which would once, she imagines, have been stacked with film scripts, magazines, and bookends shaped like lions. There has been some attempt to furnish the rooms: Italianate velvet sofas, a console crowned with a vase of ostrich feathers, a glass coffee table with imitation bamboo edges, and a sunburst wall clock, so reminiscent of the art deco era.

The living room leads to a kitchen/dining room—and the lingering suggestion of finger buffets and gimlets. Jess finds herself drawn to the far window, to a glimpse of the terrace and swimming pool. The water in the pool is a shade of green that does not incite bathing. In fact, the whole house has seen better days—to call it a museum is perhaps stretching a point—yet to Jess, it has *much* to say.

The fun Anna would have had! How exactly did she manage the maneuver: the Welsh mountains to all this! Evidently the house was Christopher Roderick's, but how did the pair of them get together? Jess wonders, with a flutter in her belly, if the True Love Necklace had something to do with it.

She tries to imagine Anna—rouge, lipstick, and neat pin curls—pirouetting into the heart of 1930s Hollywood society. The era of the blond bombshell, of Marlene Dietrich, Jean Harlow, Bette Davis, Joan Crawford, and Katharine Hepburn. Did Anna meet them? Did she dress them? Did she fit sweet-bright glass brooches to their lapels? Suddenly the air seems alive. Jess strokes the glossy walnut veneer of a nearby table, tickles the fringes of the lampshade that dangles over it. Anna is with her, she is certain.

"Excuse me," she says, pestering Jackson, "can you tell me anything about Zedora's occupants? I'm especially interested to know about a couple called Anna Taylor and Christopher Roderick. They would have lived here in the 1930s."

"You've been doing your homework," says Jackson sagely. "Records tell us that the house was built by the Roderick family in 1926. Christopher Roderick remained here until his death in the early seventies."

"And he was a movie producer, a successful one by the looks of this place?"

"Debatable. He is best known for the 1936 swashbuckling blockbuster *Descent of the Sun*, which, in some circles, is considered to be one of Hollywood's most overblown follies. But fortunately for Christopher, the Roderick dynasty was wealthy enough to absorb a flop. They weren't trying to be big in Hollywood. They *were* Hollywood. Nonetheless, in Christopher's final decade he was a reclusive figure, his directing career virtually forgotten. He lived here alone with his long-term life partner, the celebrated choreographer, Bernard Almer."

"Ah yes…on that matter, do you know how things finished up with his wife, Anna Taylor? She was a costumer, made jewelry for the movies."

Jackson hesitates. "Christopher never married."

"Oh." She shrinks back. "But…he was engaged once…perhaps?"

Jackson shrugs.

"It wasn't unheard of for gay men in Hollywood to conduct relations with women in order to conceal their sexuality, so in answer to your question, maybe, but there is no official record of this." He pauses, thinks for a moment. "There is, however, an unconfirmed rumor that he fathered a child. You'd have to look at birth records to be certain—"

Jess brightens, stands to attention. Nancy? Could this child be Nancy? As the tour group files to the next room, she lingers at the window, absorbing every color, every detail. What next? A Roderick/ Taylor DNA test? A hunt through the local birth records? No. Deep down, she knows it isn't proof she's looking for. It isn't legal certificates and inheritance rights. It's a sense of kinship, an affinity with her backstory.

So how did it play out? Christopher Roderick from his "dynasty," with his mansion and his pool; an engagement that never resulted in a marriage; an illegitimate daughter who rarely talked about her upbringing; and Roderick's subsequent commitment to another man. All said and done, Jess can only wonder whether Anna's life at Zedora was as rose-tinted as its walls.

Eager to uncover the next piece of her puzzle, Jess escapes the house tour and searches "Jossop's" online. She is amazed to find that the company is still trading as a jewelry business, proudly boasting its historic credentials: *Jossop's. Since 1925.* Its headquarters are now a store on Rodeo Drive. Tired of the walking, Jess hails a cab, but the roads are busy. Frustrated to be frittering away precious moments in traffic, she stares from the window and daydreams. She spots the famous landmark Egyptian Theatre, with its pyramid frontage and lofty palms, then a nearby restaurant sign snags her attention: Musso & Frank Grill.

She puzzles for a moment, then remembers that it's the name of the restaurant Guy described. Nothing flashy. Its bland exterior makes it almost ignorable, and yet...she remembers the way Guy described it, the passion in his voice, his warm charm and ever-expanding enthusiasm. She winds down her window, and as the warmth of the Hollywood afternoon floods into the cab, she leans out with her phone and takes a photograph of Musso's. Then before she can question herself, she sends it to Guy with a message.

Tempted? J x

Immediately, she regrets her action, realizing such a gesture cannot be construed as anything other than flirtatious. She shoves her phone back in her bag, scrunches her face, berates herself. Why blur the lines? It's not fair to Tim. Even if he doesn't understand her desire to fly to LA, that doesn't mean he deserves betrayal. So thank goodness Guy doesn't respond to her message, bringing the flirtation to a sound and sensible dead end.

Jossop's of Rodeo Drive. The window displays say it all. The kind of jewelry that makes her shudder—big, blinding bling, solely aimed at demonstrating wealth and status, favored by ladies who lunch and host charity balls. Jess pushes open the door, expecting to be wafted with a you're-not-our-typical-client vibe, but is greeted pleasantly by an elderly woman with sharp eyes, wearing an equally sharp suit dress and an edgy plastic choker that betrays her tolerance for the gaudy merchandise in the window.

"Hello, dear. How can I help?"

Jess smiles, wondering where to start. "I–I'm afraid I'm not here to buy jewelry. I'm on something of a mission."

"A mission? Well, that does sound exciting."

"I believe my great-grandmother may have once worked for this company, back when it made costume jewelry for movies."

"Ah, we certainly made jewelry for the movies. All the studios used us. MGM. Warner. Universal. From 1925 right through to the early fifties."

"You don't anymore?"

"Sadly no. Other companies got in the way, doing things on the cheap, cutting corners. Jossop's always prided themselves on making costume look convincing. Bette Davis loved one of our emerald-effect brooches so much that she took it home with her. But when producers would no longer pay for our high standards, we started to focus on retail. I'm Ellen. Marti Jossop, our founder, was my grandfather."

Jess smiles, feels an instant kinship with this woman.

"How lovely to meet you."

"You too, Miss—"

"Taylor. I'm Jess Taylor."

"Please to meet you, Miss Jess Taylor. So tell me about this great-grandmother of yours—"

"Her name was Anna Taylor. I believe she worked at Jossop's in the 1930s. She came from Wales originally. I don't suppose you'd remember? Or have any employment records? Or anything that relates to her? She got engaged to a movie producer. You might know of him…Christopher Roderick—"

Ellen nods.

"I do indeed. Christopher produced *Descent of the Sun*, which was Jossop's biggest-ever project. We made nearly four thousand separate items for that movie. 'We don't make the fine stuff here,' Marti used to say. 'We just gotta make it *look* like the fine stuff.' It's no secret that picture turned out to be a dud, but production chucked every shiny thing they had at it, so we chucked our shiny little selves in there too, made our name from bangles and cutlass clips. For years, the ruby skull-and-crossbones brooch was Jossop's signature piece. It even got popular in Paris. Several fashion houses tried to copy it.

"Back then, of course, we weren't the high-class jewelry shop you're standing in now. We had a huge warehouse on the Boulevard, near Colombia. Mostly storage with workstations and dusty floors—it was a hot mess. Marti liked it that way, but when I took over in the seventies, with the way the business was changing, I knew it was time for an upgrade. So we came to Rodeo Drive. Do you like jewelry, dear?"

"I love all kinds of jewelry."

"So you take after Anna—"

"Then you know about her?"

"I know *of* her. I know she played a part in Jossop's success. Wait a second. I have something that might interest you."

She disappears to the back of the shop, then returns with a box.

"This is a bunch of keepsakes that we took from the old premises when we moved. Take a look."

She pries off the lid of the box, revealing piles of invoices, pamphlets, and a few black-and-white photos of lighting rigs, costume rails, jewelry samples, and props—mostly swords and barrels. She sifts through them with her manicured red talons.

"Here," she says, removing one of the photographs and presenting it to Jess. "This might tell you something."

Anna! It's clearly Anna—those unmistakable Taylor cheeks! Jess grins; her great-grandmother, suddenly vivid in front of her, all the way from the 1930s! As she draws the photograph closer, observing every detail of Anna's rayon day dress and pin curls, her hands start to quiver. Right here, this is her ancestry, her kin, the origins of her existence.

Anna is not the only person in the photograph. She appears to be midwork, fitting a faux bronze cuff to a sweaty-looking actress in a gold lamé playsuit. The look of concentration, the slight but natural smile on her lips, suggests she is only semi-aware of the lurking camera lens.

"That's on set, preparation for the 'pirate slave' scene," Ellen explains. "Marti used to say Anna was the darling of the costume department. Had a real soft spot for her, with her instinct for color and an eye for what worked, always making sure everything was symmetrical. She was liked by the cast, too, because she didn't just care about the appearance of the costumes, but about comfort. Look at those gem-encrusted shoulder straps that poor girl's wearing, hideously scratchy, but Anna would have made sure they had enough padding."

Jess's attention is drawn to a young, suited man standing behind them, slightly in shadow.

"Who's that?"

"That, dear girl, is Christopher Roderick. No doubt wading in, about to insist those bangles are fitted tight." Ellen rolls her eyes. "That man," she says, with an irritated tone, "was the bane of Marti's life. Apparently he constantly demanded more chains and bangles, then the minute he came on set, he complained the jangling drove him nuts. Told us we needed to make *silent* jewelry."

"Was he a good producer?"

"He was a fastidious daddy's boy. Uptight and snappy tempered, leaned too heavily on his prestigious family name. Marti thought he lacked the gifts a talented producer needs, used his bullishness to hide it."

"Oh."

Jess cannot hide her disappointment, having hoped for a soul mate with flair for Anna.

"Didn't stop his popularity with the young women of the chorus and crew however," says Ellen. "Since he was young and handsome, they'd collapse into giggles whenever he came near, taking bets on who'd catch his eye. But not Anna. She was a shrewd one. She listened to their gossip, silently fixing their jewels, not letting on she was curious. My guess is she knew an opportunity when she saw it. She listened and watched and got to understand everything she could about Christopher Roderick, then slowly, surely, she positioned herself in his sight line. Bumping into him in the parking lot, being in the right place when he was calling for assistance. Not enough to look overeager but enough to get her noticed."

"You think she engineered it?" says Jess.

"Put it this way," says Ellen, "Anna joined the set of *Descent* as a costume junior, but by the time the movie wrapped, she had a ring on her finger. A nice one too, Marti told me. A fine, fat cushion-cut diamond with sapphire insets. Got coverage in all the gossip columns. They celebrated at the Trocadero. Here—"

Ellen passes Jess another photo, this one of the exterior of the famous Café Trocadero with its Italianate roof tiles, topiary bushes, and red carpet welcome.

"Definitely an upgrade from the Casa Casanova, which was the Jossop crowd's usual hangout. The Trocadero was special. The building doesn't exist anymore, demolished in the name of progress, but in its day, it was *the* place. Fred Astaire went there. Cary Grant. Lucille Ball. Christopher was friends with all of them."

Jess beams, recalling Nancy's seemingly arbitrary flourish: *the gilded toilet handle that Lucille Ball was rumored to have broken.* Then she remembers the melancholy that followed, Nancy's downcast description of sad Anna, lamenting the glamorous life she'd had to leave.

"So…although Anna and Christopher got engaged, they never actually married," she says, hopeful that Ellen Jossop can shed more light on the mystery. "Perhaps it was something of a lavender relationship? I heard Christopher ended up with a man called Bernard Almer."

Ellen shrugs. "Ah, Bernard, yes, lovely man, the yin to Christopher's yang. You're right. I expect the engagement, unfortunately for Anna, had little substance behind it. In the end, the Roderick/Almer pairing was no surprise to anyone, but in the thirties and forties, it wouldn't have 'belonged.' Christopher clearly felt obligated to maintain a straight image, while waiting for Hollywood morality to catch up with itself. As for Anna, whether she understood what she was getting into or not, the engagement certainly gave her the opportunity to quit working twelve-hour days and languish in all the nicest boutiques and restaurants."

Jess sighs, frustrated, unsatisfied. She doesn't deny Ellen's take on the situation, but surely Anna would have wanted more than a mere illusion of love. In what way was Christopher Roderick her soul mate? Her eye then catches on a crumpled film script, or more specifically, on a doodle scribbled across its back cover: written in pencil, outlined in a childish heart, the initials A. T. and A. J.

"A. T.?" says Jess, delighted. "Could that be Anna?"

Ellen picks the script out of the box, smoothing its corners before flicking through the pages.

"Hmm. It's from *Descent*. Could well be Anna."

"So who's the A. J.? Did Christopher Roderick have a nickname?"

Ellen ponders this, looks thoughtful.

"A. J.? My guess is that stands for Archie Jossop, Marti's nephew. He hung around here in the thirties, helped Marti out. Had a five-second dream of becoming an actor. Perhaps he had a crush on your Anna? It's possible their paths crossed. Nice fellow, full of heart, could talk the hind legs off a very tall donkey. Not in Christopher Roderick's league though. Archie's parents were corn farmers."

"I see," says Jess, curious.

"Who knows?" says Ellen. "Such a long time ago. Dear Archie. We lost track of him when he left the States. He went to Europe to fight during the Second World War, and we never heard what became of him. But take the script if you like. Take it all, the whole box. Doesn't serve anyone while it's cluttering up my back office. There are a few bits of Archie's in there if you're interested, letters and such. Marti kept them aside, in case the boy ever returned, but… sadly it wasn't to be."

"Thanks," says Jess, accepting the box eagerly, thinking only of rushing back to her hostel room and pawing through its contents.

The hostel is quiet. The afternoon sun streams through the slatted blinds, highlighting the dust in the air, while aromas from the communal kitchen—stir-fry and paprika soup—seep into every space. Jess has paid extra for a private room and is now glad about it because she can rest her back in peace. She creates a nest of cushions on the floor and places Ellen's box in front of her. With vim in her fingers, she pries off the lid.

Most of the items are paraphernalia from Jossop's: impersonal receipts and invoices, a couple of catalogs. At the bottom of the box, however, Jess finds a photo that cheers her: another image of Anna. This time she's standing next to a fake anchor, and at her side, looking her way, is a tall, scruffy, wide-grinned lad—not Christopher—arm clamped around her shoulders, almost lifting her off her feet. Could this be Archie Jossop? Jess holds the photograph to the light, eager to penetrate its secrets. Through the poor-quality grain, she can see, just about, that Anna is wearing the butterfly necklace, and the sight of this thrills her.

She digs into the box again and, as Ellen mentioned, finds a bundle of unopened letters held together by a rubber band, addressed to Archie at Jossop's. She pulls the band off and sifts through them, plucking out flyers for lawn mowers and DIY stores and a few uninspired postcards from someone called Bob Symmons. She is left with a pair of handwritten airmail envelopes, yellowed with age, postmarked from London. The handwriting on both envelopes is the same, although the postal dates are more than a decade apart: June 1949 and February 1961. Her heart thuds. What to do? The envelopes are still sealed, their contents unseen by anyone, let alone their intended recipient. If Jess opens them, she will be the first.

"Come on, Archie," she whispers, digging her nail beneath the gummy seal of the earliest of the two. "What have you got for me?"

As she unfolds the thin sheets of paper inside, she scans straight to the top corner and sees what she'd hoped she see:

Anna E. Taylor
Flat 64B Chadwick House
Dock Road
Poplar
London E14

Her mouth drops open as a deluge of emotion washes through her. Love letters. *Please* let them be love letters! She steels herself, smiles, and reads on:

24th June 1949

My dearest Archie,

I hope you remember me. Our time together was brief, but it has stayed alive in my thoughts, so I'm writing to jog your memory and see if you might perhaps reply. My name is Anna Taylor. We met in Hollywood before the war, August 1936. You might remember a terrible pirate movie we both worked on called Descent of the Sun? *I'd just joined Jossop's costume department and your uncle Marti, the company's owner, introduced us. He called me "Miss Anna."*

Do you remember? You were sitting beneath a studio lamp, eating a baloney sandwich, when he called you over. He joked, saying you were his protégé. He said he'd done you a favor, getting you away from the family farm, that there was no money in crops anymore, "not since those jellybeans on Wall Street bled our economy dry." He said he'd pulled some strings with the director, got you a gig as Deck Hand Number Twenty-Seven.

"It's a start, right, Archie?" he'd said, then he told you to take me across to the Descent set and show me how it all worked. You stood up straightaway and gave me the warmest smile I'd ever seen.

"So, Miss Anna," you said, "we're doing a pirate movie. It's a goddam mess, but the studio brass has it in their heads that if the costumes look good and the leading lady sparkles, no one will notice their crummy script. Soon enough everyone

from downtown to upstate will want fake ruby-studded skull brooches. You see, we aren't just making movies here, Anna. We're making trends. We're setting the pace for the rest of world. That's how it is. You interested?"

Oh, Archie, I loved your accent, your constant patter.

You walked me around, and the set was everything I hoped it would be, full of people with purpose. I did my best to keep pace with you, but your legs were almost up to my shoulders and, truly, I could feel my heart beating madly with the excitement of it all. I remember you brushing your hand through a row of frilled shirts, asking:

"You wanna be an actress?"

"No," I said. "Why does everyone assume I want to be in front of the camera?"

"Because they all wanna be in front of the camera," you said.

"But I'm not them. I'm me."

Then you turned to me with that wide, easy grin of yours.

"So you are," you said, before stumbling into a four-foot fake anchor.

"Who left that there?" you said, laughing.

Then your eyes dropped to the necklace at my neck, took in every curve and line. Do you remember that necklace? A sea-green enamel butterfly with a moonstone?

"Well, that's the prettiest thing I ever saw," you said. "You don't see that no more. Now it's all about jazz and angles and the plastics. Personally, I like the old style. It's got class."

And I told you that although the necklace was old-fashioned, I loved to wear it because whenever I wore it, I felt its good energy warming my soul. You asked me where I got it, so I explained my mother had given it to me moments before succumbing to typhoid fever, that she called it the True Love Necklace. And you looked at me and you said: "Is that so?" And it was a full minute before we managed to shake off the buzz.

Jess pauses, looks up. So *this* was the moment, Anna's soul-mate moment—the necklace, like a charm, binding and tightening, pulling them into each other's spheres. She shuts her eyes and imagines the scene, amid the hectic studio clatter: Anna and Archie, just them, only them.

She returns again to the photo, to the man standing beside Anna. *Definitely Archie*, she thinks, surveying his height and genial smile. And yes, the butterfly looks outdated, its decorative, nature-inspired art nouveau form too fanciful for a world that was shouting about modernity, with geometric jewelry made from newly invented materials such as Bakelite. Working in the jewelry business, no doubt Anna had her eye on it all—the possibilities and ideas of the art deco era, but still she wore her outdated butterfly necklace.

Do you remember our first date, Archie? Well, yes, it was our ONLY date, but what a night! I'll never forget the bumbling way you asked, tripping over your words, sweetly goofy.

"I don't want to be forward or nothing," you said to me, "but there's this new diner, right on the junction with Gower

Street, called the Casa Casanova. It only opened a fortnight ago and it does this brisket and everyone's raving about it. And you know, on my wage I can just about afford the fries at Hamburger Jack's, but for a really special girl, I always thought I'd take her to the Casa Casanova. I'd do that for her. Except...I never met this girl. So here I was, thinking I'd never get to taste the goddamn brisket everyone's so hot about, and then"—you looked at me then, wholeheartedly—"I did! I met her! And now I'm gonna take her to the Casa Casanova! And the wine's gonna be real nice and the brisket's gonna be a knockout and the whole world's gonna be butterflies from now on."

And I just stared at you, mouth open.

"So," you said, "how about it?"

"You talk too much," I said. "Truly. You say everything that's in your head, and it's...messy."

"I know," you said, swiping your hand, as though you never considered it a problem. "At least that way, we won't have those awkward silences. So how about it, Miss Anna? Can we eat brisket together? Tonight?"

"Yes," I said.

You picked me up at seven—every detail is in my head— and in the back of the taxi, you talked. You talked. And you talked. About the streets, the hills, the sky, the stars, the movies, the buildings, the jobless, the president, the banks, the banknotes, the state of Europe, the musicians fleeing Germany, the drawings you did as a child, and the farm in Maryland where you were raised. And then, at the dinner table, where the *brisket was indeed succulent and tasty, you talked even more, like a never-stopping train of thought. And something about your chatter, and the candlelight and the cocooning red-velvet walls, made me feel very heady and very happy.*

When you finally tired of talking, you downed your martini and told me it was my turn. So I told you all about my upbringing in North Wales and my home, Pel Tawr. About my father, Emery Floyd, who'd drowned in the Great War after tripping on a gangplank and falling into a muddy sinkhole, and how I liked to think that the reason he'd tripped was because he'd been distracted by something beautiful. You were so kind, Archie, assuring me that this was most certainly the case. And I told you about my mother, Minnie, who'd taught me to grow hollyhocks from seeds and had never been able to marry Emery because she was still married to a mean man from Paris who'd locked her in a bedroom for weeks. And about how the Floyd family had never judged her for this, because they were liberals. And you told me you were a liberal, too, but I had to wonder if you actually knew what that word meant.

We shared the most enormous ice cream for dessert, and as the band struck up, you grabbed my hand and pulled me onto the dance floor. Thanks to a few martinis, you had me learning the steps of the St. Louis shag before I even had time to untuck my napkin. Already I was second-guessing what a future with you would be like. More zest than even I could handle. And as we jigged and spun, I felt joy like I'd never known.

At the end of the evening, you walked me back to my

boardinghouse and wasted no time taking hold of my hand, making it clear how you, too, felt. At the front door, we kissed. It was my first kiss, and it was soft and sweet and everything I'd wanted. I went to bed with the memory of it and the smell of your shirt and the swell of happiness in my stomach. The thought of seeing you the next day at the studio made me quiver. How quickly one falls in love in Hollywood!

The next morning, with a near skip, I took the streetcar to work. I kept a look out all day, but you were nowhere on set. Eventually I found the courage to ask Marti, who just shrugged and nudged a camera cable with his shoe.

"He had to leave, Anna, first train this morning. His pa's taken sick, dying sick. He's gone back to Maryland."

So I asked when you'd be back.

"Ah, kid," Marti said, "there's things to be seen to, a farm to be run. I'd say that's the end for Archie's acting career, not that he really had a prospect, with those ears, but hey——"

Archie, I just stood there, staring into nothing. At midday I took to the powder room, sick. I looked in the mirror, held my hand to my butterfly necklace, and felt it inside, that the best thing ever had just become the best thing that never happened.

It broke my heart, Archie, the way you left, cutting short our chance. Sure I've met other men. I've even been engaged. Who is Archie Jossop anyway, I used to say to myself, with his surplus chat and goofy smile? But, you know what, I stopped wearing my necklace after you left. It didn't seem right and I didn't want it damaged, so I wrapped it in a silk handkerchief and kept it in my dressing table, every evening making sure it was still there, what with my roommates and their wandering hands.

Oh, Archie, I hope this letter finds you well. You may think I'm silly to be pining for you like this, a decade later, still clinging to the memory of the few days we spent together. You're probably thinking I should get over it, move on, but it would mean so much if you'd just reply. So that, one way or another, I can stop pestering myself with the thought of what could have been.

With fondest feeling,
Anna Elizabeth Taylor

Jess folds the letter, heartbroken for Anna. So what happened to Archie? Clearly he never returned to Jossop's or received his mail. Because he didn't want to or because he couldn't? She reaches for the second letter, postmarked 1961. She presses it between her fingertips, prays that it holds clues to a True Love happy ending.

14th February 1961

Dearest Archie,

I write you again, my Valentine, in the thin hope that this letter will reach you. Since you never replied to my previous letter, I'm at a loss. Of course, there's always the possibility that you read my last one and dismissed it, but my hunch tells me otherwise.

If I know you at all, Archie, I know you have a good heart. And a good heart would reply to my plea, if only to let me down gently. The fact is I still think of you. So much has happened since I knew you, and sometimes I feel quite despairing of it all. I torment myself that if I'd done something more to keep you, followed you to your farm maybe, or made Marti track you down, then I'd be good. Ah, hindsight.

You know at Jossop's I made the scrappiest bit of nickel shine like platinum. These days I don't get the chance to make things. I had to move to London. Here, all I do is try to soothe my boredom with television soaps, but then I just end up shouting at the screen, outraged by all the cheap wigs and ridiculous earrings. At least my creations looked authentic. Jossop's knew what they were doing.

So much sparkle and ambition left in the dust. It hurt me, Archie. It physically hurt to walk away from my life in Hollywood. I guess that's why I still think and talk of it, to keep it alive. Memories are my comfort. The other women on the block where I live mock me. They think I brag. But honestly, if they'd seen that peacock wallpaper, all that good china, those box-fresh crystal champagne coupes, the pool, the cocktail parties. If they themselves had witnessed the sight of Clark Gable eating shrimp in my dining room, they'd put their sneers away.

You see, after you left—don't be mad—I caught the eye of Christopher Roderick, the producer from Descent of the Sun. *He liked me. He thought I was smart. The moment he asked me to marry him was one of the most elevating experiences of my life. Little Welsh Anna engaged to a Hollywood producer!*

Our engagement party, open bar at his mansion Zedora, was the talk of the town for months. An orchestra played in the lobby. We had a full dance floor in the courtyard. Two naked baseball players canoed in the swimming pool—that's true— and the fountain overflowed with pink champagne. Christopher agreed to everything on my wish list. He even okayed my full-length Schiaparelli feather gown. Oh, it was beautiful. What I'd give to wear it again!

All of it, Archie. I had all of it. Then I walked away. Because there's one thing I now know: you can't fake true love. That feeling I had—that giddy, gorgeous, swooping feeling I had the night I ate brisket at the Casa Casanova with you—not a single second with Christopher ever felt like that. As much as I love a marble staircase, Archie, no mansion is worth my soul. The truth is, my engagement to Christopher, and all the spoils that came with it, were nothing more than a sham. Despite his quick and showy proposal, he wasn't in love with me, or even particularly interested in marrying me. He delayed and delayed our wedding plans, avoided all talk of it. In the end, I stopped asking. Our one romantic clinch, in the early days following our engagement, had been awkward and clinical. The fact that it produced our daughter, Nancy, has been nothing short of remarkable. After that, he hardly touched me. Sometimes I got the feeling I disgusted him.

Do you remember us, Archie? Do you remember our kiss?

All the time, you had this running monologue, and I just wanted to shut you up and dive my hands through your hair, because your eyes sparkled and your lopsided smile was so natural and free and you weren't like anyone I'd ever met.

Well, it wouldn't surprise you to know that Christopher showed as little interest in our daughter as he did in me. At the end of the fall, 1948, after weeks of arguing, I made the decision to seek something better. I'd done it before, when I left Wales, so I knew I could do it again. With Nancy still only eight years old, young enough to benefit from a fresh start, old enough to feel the pain of a disinterested father, I began to pack our things.

At first I thought I'd go back to the mountains, to Pel Tawr, where my father Emery's family still lived, but as I sat out the five-day transatlantic boat ride, Nancy at my side, a sense of shame got to me. I'd left the mountains for a reason. I couldn't return to rural life. Besides, I'd read in a letter from one of my cousins that the house had been overrun by the army, of all things.

The capital appealed, where the fashionable lived. London, surely, needed costume jewelry designers of distinction! But, goodness me, Britain after the war was a shock to the senses, and I soon learned there was limited appetite for well-crafted pot-paste bangles, not when a loaf of stale bread was being hailed as a miracle. In my cocoon across the ocean, I'd had no idea how tough it had been, how the poverty and rationing and bombing raids had bitten great chunks out of my homeland. With no more money and no obvious way of making money, the true calamity of my decision to leave Zedora rained down on me. But it was a calamity I had to live with. For my dignity. For my daughter.

I've now come to understand that with Christopher, I was merely a foil. He prefers the company of men. This, in itself, doesn't bother me. I guess it's the fact that for years, he didn't confront it, was content to use me as cover, stringing me along like I was nothing but a tool for him. When actually I could have been—Oh, Archie!—I could have been so happy with you!

So here I am. Sometimes, during these long days alone, trying to block out the drabness that surrounds me, the only thing that settles my nerves are thoughts of us. I write this for you, and maybe for myself, because if nothing else, it gives me a bit of hope. No one else listens or cares. They think I'm some drunken has-been with an overactive imagination. Even my own daughter tells me I'm ruinous.

So perhaps you've forgotten me completely and are wondering whom this mad, ranting, airmail-writing female could be. Perhaps I've not meant anything to you. But perhaps—just perhaps—you still think of me sometimes?

I do hope so.

Forever yours,
Anna Elizabeth Taylor

Jess sits back, blinking, absorbing every detail of what she's just read. Clearly by the sixties, poor Anna's bitterness had set in. Yet this second letter isn't entirely without hope. Where, she wonders, has Archie been all this time? But then she thinks back to what Ellen said about him disappearing after going to Europe to fight in the Second World War, and the dread thought rises inside her that Archie met a similar fate to poor Emery Floyd, another casualty of another war, in some unmarked grave in Belgium.

She sighs.

"Oh, Anna."

All that pining in vain.

On the second day of her LA exodus, Jess's physical challenges get the better of her and she is forced to spend most of the afternoon lying down. It's a frustration, but one she tolerates, because after her encounter with Anna's love letters—which she rereads again and again—the rest of Hollywood seems brash and soulless. On her third and last day, a little recovered, she joins a bus tour for the full hit of Hollywood hot spots, then takes a final amble down the Boulevard, absorbing the sights and sounds of the sun-filled evening: the buskers, the street artists, the party crowds. She is reminded of her early twenties, when she traveled extensively, welded to the buzz of new destinations, the tantalizing idea that life in parallel places is always happening, whether you're there to witness it or not. Could Tim ever understand this? He certainly didn't buy into the Hollywood adventure. With a tickle of regret in her belly, she takes a photo of the sunset and sends it to him, adding a message:

Miss You x

The second it's sent, however, she questions herself. Yes, her choice to take the trip was rash, but only because he *made* it feel that way. It could have been fun, but *he* made it feel irresponsible and silly. She bristles, walks on, head pounding with doubt. Is she actually missing Tim? Or is her text simply fulfilling an obligation? What would LA with Tim have been like anyway? A riot of spontaneity and adventure, or a teacher's timetable?

In her rumination, she loses track of her steps and ends up at the Egyptian Theatre, where the sun casts long shadows across the Boulevard. In front of her is Musso's, and she thinks fondly of Guy's praise for it, his suggestion that they should eat dinner there. The thought of food appeals. The walking has given her an appetite. Not that there would be a table. The whole place looks like it's heaving. But out of curiosity, she decides to get a closer view.

The interior drips with old-school glamour: high ceilings, dark wood paneling, and upholstered leather booths. Each booth has its own hat rack. How many famous movie people, she wonders, have hung their fedoras here? A waiter in a bolero jacket shimmies past, holding aloft a tray of prime rib, balanced on the very tips of his fingers. She hastens to leave before having to face the embarrassment of being asked for a reservation she doesn't have, glad that she has at least seen the restaurant for herself. But just as she's pulling open the door, a familiar voice bears down on her.

"Jess Taylor! What are you walking out for?"

She blinks and spins around, only to see Guy Arlo van der Meer, in the flesh, standing beside one of the oxblood-red booths, wearing a vintage Hawaiian shirt and slacks.

"I told you," he says, with a tone that suggests it's perfectly normal she should find him here, halfway around the world, "this is *the* greatest place to eat in the whole of Hollywood. Come, sit down. I got us the best table."

She is speechless. Her feet don't move. Meanwhile Guy gives the waiter a nod.

"Two of the house martinis please, Sergio," he says, beckoning her forward. "And, Jess, don't look so freaked out. We made a date."

"We did?"

"Come *on*," he says, ushering her into a seat. "Sit down. Check out the menu. You have to try the mac and cheese."

"But—?"

"Seven o'clock, Saturday night. Old Hollywood. I told you… we'd do dinner."

"But I thought you were joking—"

"I sort of was, but then you sent me that photo and…it was *very* tempting. One thing you'll learn about me, Jess, I always follow temptation."

Jess just blinks, her thoughts cascading.

"It was bit of a gamble to hop on a flight," he continues, "but as it turns out, you've honored the date, only twenty minutes late."

"Except I didn't," says Jess, staring ahead of her. "I just happened to be passing."

She bursts into giddy laughter. How is it that they are both here together? A feat of flirtatious engineering? Or a touch of True Love fate? With her mouth still agape, she claws her way to reason.

"I cannot believe you came all the way here, just to take a chance on meeting me for dinner. You made all this effort...for *me*?"

Guy smiles.

"Doesn't seem like an effort. It seems...I don't know...*fun*. You wanted me to, right?"

He holds her gaze, those eyes sparkling, making her feel like she is his number one, the only woman in the world, the only one that matters. It's intoxicating. Without her having yet sipped the coming martini, her head is already spinning.

"You are good," she says, wagging her finger at him. "*So* good. I mean, *this* is a gesture. There aren't many of my species who wouldn't be flattered, but—"

"Too much?"

Jess shrugs, keeps her answer to herself, cautious to admit that while, yes, it is way too much, it is also mind-blowingly brilliant. And now all she wants to do is snuggle in and get lost in the moment. Nevertheless she flashes her Tim badge.

"It's too much for someone who already has a boyfriend, which I do," she asserts, determined to keep her loyalties intact.

Guy nods.

"I hear you, Jess. I haven't forgotten about Education Tim, but I really like your company, so...can we at least settle on friends?"

Jess smiles, teases the corners of a napkin. "Okay," she says. "Okay. Friends it is."

Guy looks at her and beams.

"Great," he says. "Let's order, shall we?"

～❦～

The rest of the evening passes in a glorious, if slightly surreal, bubble of elation. They eat the Musso favorites, chops and fettuccine, washed down with martinis. They talk boundlessly about Hollywood costume departments, the trickery of the camera, fake beards, and cleavage brooches.

"So how is my necklace?" says Jess as dessert is finally served.

"*Your* necklace?"

"Mine by proxy."

"I believe it's doing fine. More to the point, how's your grandma?"

"She's okay. She's hanging in there. Tough old girl."

"I bet. Tell me about her."

"Well, she certainly liked a cause. She used to wear a jacket covered in Amnesty International badges, and apparently back in the eighties, she was regularly arrested for getting mouthy with policemen during public demonstrations."

Guy laughs. "A spirited soul?"

"She had a certain passion in her, yes. I'm not sure she was the world's most loving mother. Or grandmother for that matter, but she made an impression on me and I'm grateful for that. She traveled a lot, eventually settling in North Wales, where she built her own log cabin and lived liked a hermit. I went to check on it, and you know what? It turns out that's where it all began—"

"What did?"

"The necklace."

Jess opens up about Pel Tawr and Bevan Floyd and Minnie's diary and the story of the necklace's creation. She then explains everything she's discovered about Anna in Hollywood. When she's finished, Guy interlaces his fingers across his chest and gives a long sigh.

"Oh, Jess, talk about the wonder of lost-and-found jewelry. That's incredible. No wonder you're on such a mission to get your necklace back." He lowers his eyelids, looks into his lap. "Just so you know," he adds, "I deeply regret selling it to Stella."

"Well, I'm glad you understand," says Jess. "It's not just a piece of jewelry to me."

"No," says Guy. "It's your history."

Her eyes drop to his leopard-head ring. She would like to ask him about it, his own family heirloom, but when he senses her looking, he cups it, presses his hands into his lap, a warning not to probe. So instead she dives into her slice of dessert.

"I have to ask," she says, between mouthfuls of vanilla-scented cheesecake. "Is this normal behavior for you, to jet across the world for an evening?"

"Normal-ish. Can't say I do it weekly, but spontaneity is definitely in my nature. I like to get on a boat or a plane or a kayak... and just *go*. Arms wide open to whatever I find."

"Arms wide open," she repeats thoughtfully. "I like that."

She bites down on her spoon as a memory flashes into her thoughts, of herself—her *old* self, before the accident—up in the foothills of Mexico, standing on the ridge at dawn, the jungle canopy beneath her, shrouded in mist; how the beauty of the moment made her throw her arms wide open. Where's that self now? She smiles ruefully, points her spoon at Guy.

"No responsibilities to consider?" she asks.

"I built my business so that I could live on my terms," he replies. "I get to travel and focus on the things that interest me. No paper clips on a desktop. No boss to answer to."

"Apart from Stella Weston?"

"That's different. We're friends."

"No kids?"

"Not to my knowledge. I'm not sure kids are for me. There are plenty of excellent parents out there doing a sterling job, so I'll let them take the glory. I'll just be the cool, globe-trotting uncle who flies in for dinner every now and then, tells good stories, and slays everyone on the PlayStation." He catches her eye, a twist in his lips. "Is…is that an issue for you?"

Jess blinks, flusters.

"Why would you think it's an issue for me?"

"In case you wanted them."

"But…we're not… This isn't…" She sighs, shuts her eyes. "Just friends, remember. I'm in a relationship, as you well know. I'm committed."

"Committed? That sounds very…dutiful."

"I mean *happy*. I'm happy."

He glares at her from the rim of his martini glass, with a *Yeah, sure you are* glint in his eye. Suddenly—and luckily, thinks Jess—they are distracted by the arrival of a large dining party. The waiters scurry around, making space.

"Looks like the bigwigs have arrived," whispers Guy. "There are at least three well-known directors in that crowd."

Jess cranes her neck.

"Don't make it obvious," he chides, laughing. "This is where they come to be 'normal.'"

When it is time to leave, they are both joyous and drunk.

"What a way to spend my last night in Hollywood," says Jess. "I mean, talk about filmic—"

"You know what we should do?" Guy slurs, his curls flopping. "Go to the sign. Since it's your first visit and all."

"The Hollywood sign?"

Jess stares down at her legs, just about sober enough to appreciate that alcohol, night hikes, and walking canes are never a good mix.

"You know it was originally a real estate advert," says Guy, "been there since 1926. Nothing says old Hollywood like a bunch of white plastic letters, huh? Let's do it. Let's go."

"I can't," she says.

"Can," he argues, then swoops her up in his arms. "I'll carry you there if I have to."

"Stop!" she shrieks, giggling, half-aghast, half-delighted. "I'm heavier than I look!"

He spins her around and flings her over his shoulder, the strength in his arms thrilling her.

"Don't make me go!" she cries, beating his back. "I heard there's snakes up there!"

They get a few yards up the path and then, exhausted, he drops her to her feet.

"You win," he says, heaving a breath. "It's a tacky trip anyway."

"This entire place is tacky."

"Not Musso's"

"Definitely not Musso's. Musso's is great. I'll always remember Musso's."

Her words trail off as, suddenly, she realizes where this is heading. He grasps her hand. The gesture shocks her into stillness. His warm fingers wrap around hers. The intent is unmistakable. Every cell in her body wakens, arrows of desire shooting up her arms, through her heart, to her soul. In the valley beneath them, the lights of LA twinkle, a fairy blanket at their feet. Silent now, he stares at her. This is it. He's about to kiss her. And she would *really* like him to.

But…

She pulls away, snaps to reason, inwardly berating herself for her recklessness, for the sneaky, disloyal clinch she has gotten herself into.

"I'm sorry," she says, shielding her mouth with her hand. "I can't… I just *can't*."

Guy pouts. "Right. Okay."

"We said 'just friends.' I love your company, Guy, but I have to think of Tim."

His eyes roll. "Of course. Education Tim."

"Don't say it like that. Tim's great."

"Sure he is."

"I won't betray him," she asserts. "Oh god!"

She throws her head back, feels wrought with frustration, her conscience torn in two.

"Thank you for surprising me and making me feel brilliant, but you have to understand it can't go anywhere. I'm not a cheat. I've been on the other side of cheating, and it's hideous. Besides, my flight is super early. Really, I–I should get back to my hostel—"

Guy sighs.

"Come on," he says, resigned. "Let's get you a taxi."

Chapter Thirteen

"WHAT THE HELL? WHERE HAVE *YOU* BEEN?" THE INQUISITION, courtesy of Aggie, begins the moment Jess walks through the door. "You look *rough*."

Jess groans and shivers—the dehydrated aftermath of the worst hangover, coupled with a ten-hour sleepless flight.

"I feel rough, thanks," she says, staggering through the hallway to the kitchen where she immediately pours and downs a pint of water. "I'm a husk."

"So?" says Aggie, fixing her sister a Berocca with water and offering her a handful of mystery vitamins.

"Don't ask," says Jess. "It was some kind of lost-weekend thing."

"Lost weekend? Really? Tim told me you suddenly demanded a trip to Hollywood."

"I didn't demand. I invited him. He said it wasn't convenient, so I went alone. My god, it was just a mini-break, a few days abroad. No crime has been committed."

As she says this, her insides churn. Aggie gives a haughty sniff.

"Tim says—and I agree—that there is something amiss."

"What? Because I decided to have a last-minute holiday?"

"Because you're being all mysterious and you keep covering your phone up and—"

"Oh, Aggie, you're overthinking," says Jess, pummeling the ache in her forehead. "I'm fine. I'm just reminding myself to live again."

But not too much, she thinks, still reeling from the sting of what her phone had shown her postflight. As soon as she'd landed, before even collecting her baggage, like a clingy, insecure teenager, she'd switched it on and looked up Guy's profile. Having tortured herself about him for the entire flight, she'd been hoping for a sweet text or at least an expression of regret that their extraordinary evening—their surprise dinner of dinners, one of the surrealist, loveliest nights of her life—had ended so abruptly. Instead she'd found a dozen images of him partying, shirtless, around a neon-lit pool, with several young women and, in particular, Stella Weston. None of the images were incriminating, but the aftertaste was nonetheless sour. So much for flying out just for her! For all she knew, he'd had the trip planned all along, one of his Stella Weston jet-set perks.

Well, she thinks, at least now she can feel glad she didn't give in to lustful want and, most importantly, she didn't jeopardize her future with Tim, who would never sneak off to an LA after-party or spin bullshit stories about flying across the world just to "be in her company." She swallows Aggie's vitamins, her nerves crackling, as she thinks of all those others who, in the beginning, made her feel so special and wanted. She knows the pattern. As soon as they hook their catch, they throw it back.

"Don't worry. I'll call Tim," she says, yearning to be back in the nook, safe and secure, her head cozy against his warm, comforting chest.

"Yes," says Aggie, clapping her hands together. "That's a start."

Later that evening, after sleeping all day, Jess makes her way down to the kitchen in a haze of queasy-stomached jet lag for something to eat. At the TV room door, which is slightly ajar, she overhears Aggie and Ed talking quietly between themselves.

"What is it, you think?" says Ed. "I mean, she jokes about having a quarter-life crisis, but this is getting out of hand."

Immediately Jess knows they're talking about her. Steph, their other favorite subject of analysis, is still firmly in the teenage rebellion zone, the quarter-life yet to come. As for the midlife, well, that's anyone's game. With a wince, Jess lingers, listens in.

"Oh, I don't know," says Aggie. "Some long, bloody quarter-life if it is. She's finished her thirties. Really, she needs to be getting her act together now, not running off to random corners of the world on a whim. I thought the shock of the accident would be the catalyst, make her grow up. And things were going so well with Tim, but—"

"Maybe it's her pain medication? I've watched her, Aggie. She pops some pretty strong stuff—"

Because I have to, thinks Jess. *Because if I didn't, I'd be on my knees, gibbering in a corner, begging for relief from the agony of my mangled pelvis that's been pinned together with seven metal plates.*

"Talk to her," Ed continues. "If she'll listen to anyone, Aggie, it'll be you."

"I wish that were true," says Aggie, "but honestly, she's a law unto herself. Always has been."

"You'll sort it out, love. Just keep steering her in the right direction."

The right direction? Jess bristles. *According to whom?*

Will they never see that she has chosen her lifestyle rather than failed her way into it? Or that Marcus genuinely prefers the valleys of Minecraft to the local park? Or that Steph adores Jared the Vegan regardless of his inability to provide a John Lewis marble countertop? Aggie and Ed mean well, she has no doubt, but she is not their puppet, not their pet project. She is and always will be her own person, who can make decisions for herself. Fury brewing inside, she retreats, resolving that the quicker she can move out, the better, and then her relationship with Tim can be *her* business—no one else's.

Overwhelmed by the need to hear his voice, she calls him, no longer bothered by what kind of mood he'll be in. All she wants is comfort, the reassurance of his soft, kind tones.

"Tim?"

"Jess!"

"Oh, Tim, it's so nice to hear your voice. Listen, I'm really sorry I left like that, with an atmosphere between us. Did you get my pictures? I should have sent more, but I thought… Anyway…now I'm back…and…are we okay?"

"Jess, we're *fine*. I was a bit sore at first, I'll admit, but then I thought, yeah, I'm being a boring middle-aged person. I should have gone with you. It was a lovely idea. I'm sorry too. I missed you."

Relief washes over her. That's Tim, his response more mature and dignified than she could have hoped.

"Can we hang out?"

"Of course."

"And can we move in together quick?"

"Definitely."

She smiles into the handset, enjoys the sense of him, an anchor in a storm. And while she hates to admit it, Aggie is right. It *is* time to get her act together, to embrace the things she's supposed to want. Her feelings toward Guy… Surely they are nothing more than self-sabotage, her mind's topsy-turvy way of testing her commitment to grown-up life, proving to herself that she's ready. The fine four: marriage, home, career, babies. Definitely ready. Guy Arlo van der Meer can party in Los Angeles all he likes. He can also sweep her off her feet, try to carry her off into the Hollywood Hills. He can even dare to fire her passions by nearly kissing her. He can do all of those things and more. But he can't, and she's pretty certain of this, ever make her feel secure.

Aggie lies awake in bed, Ed snoring beside her, eyes fixed to the spotless white ceiling, questions stampeding through her head. What is Jess up to? All this sneaking around, disappearing to the other side of the world, being secretive on her phone. It's like having another Steph. Oh god, they're peas in a pod! It doesn't suit a thirty-year-old to be behaving like a teenager though. This needs to be brought into check.

She tosses and turns, stretching the bedsheets, giving Ed repeated prods to stop him spluttering. No, Ed isn't perfect. He's hardly a thrill—never was. But together, somehow, they mesh. He lets her do what she does best: organize the show. Is she bored with him? Sometimes. Is he bored with her? Well, he's not allowed to be, but if he is, he tolerates it. He accepts the fact that *this* is family life. It doesn't have to be fireworks and show-ponies and spontaneous trips to America. It just has to…function.

Oh, who is she kidding? Ed has tuned out. And that's the truth of it. She and Ed function because they're both in a state of permanent distraction. She keeps herself busy ruminating on everybody else's problems. While he just dials down the volume. But at least they're not swinging from one disaster to another, like Jess has done all these years. No roots, no security, and endless heartbreak. The money she's wasted, dossing about in a no-responsibilities paradise, ripe to be exploited by the next self-obsessed flake that walks into the backpacker dorm!

There's no future in *that*. And those eggs aren't getting any fresher. She'll want children soon. And Tim is a sure bet for that. He talks about it all the time. They'll be late starters—there'll be almost a generation between their children and Aggie's—but all to the good. She was only nineteen when she gave birth to Steph, spent her twenties rocking prams and wiping bibs. And her thirties resenting it. But hey.

She must make sure Jess works things out with Tim. Maybe she should talk to him, alert him to all this shifting sand? It's not interfering. It's just…guidance. Jess doesn't know what's best for her. But she deserves happiness, after everything she's been through.

Next worry on the list: tomorrow's "chat" with Steph's head teacher. Address the "phase." Fair enough, teenagers need phases. Goodness knows, she had a few! The year she went grunge, the bad jeans, that ill-fitting woolen dress, and the jacket with the daisies on it...but these were just clothes, paired with a few CDs. They didn't lead to extreme beliefs about meat eating or banking, and they certainly didn't entice her to put her future prospects on the line. Skipping class? She *never* did that.

Aggie shudders. *Oh, Steph.* If she could only make her daughter see the amazing future that lies ahead of her. She'll give her all the support she needs. She'll pull her out of that school if she has to, get her into the private place on the hill. The money for the Mercedes, she can sacrifice it. Whatever it takes to turn Steph away from the dead-end disaster that is Jared Fisher.

Pushy maybe, but at least Steph has a mother to push her, which is more than she and Jess ever had. With a pang of anguish, Aggie throws off the duvet. Jess doesn't understand. She was too young to remember the details, but Aggie has them etched in her memory. That necklace—the arguments it caused. The door slamming, voices erupting, the vehemence between the only two people those girls had. Her father, usually mild-mannered, screaming at Nancy, telling her she had "no idea of the insult...no respect...no care!"

Nancy yelling back, "You had no right!"

Jess thinks the necklace is something joyous, some wonderful tribute to her beloved Taylor ancestry. But as far as Aggie can tell, none of those women ended up with secure, happy marriages. No wonder Jess is like she is. Perhaps it's in the genes.

Chapter Fourteen

ON THE MORNING OF THE CAPITAL GALA, JESS VISITS NANCY'S CARE home, her bag brimming with Jossop photographs, the doodled film script, and Anna's letters. The thought of sharing these treasures with Nancy gives her goose bumps, but when she enters the room, a team of nurses is around the bed.

"It's okay," says her favorite nurse, the one with the Victorian locket. "We've finished our checks now. Go ahead, spend some quality time together. I'm sure she'll be glad you've come."

As she says this, she lightly touches Jess's arm. Jess understands what the gesture means: the time is coming. She catches the nurse outside the door.

"How long?" she says, realizing there's no other way to ask.

"We estimate around forty-eight hours," says the nurse. "Maybe a little less. Maybe more. We'll keep you updated, so if you want to be with her at the end you can."

Jess swallows, stops herself from tearing up. Suddenly she wishes she could bottle up that fierce, eccentric, independent spirit and preserve it forever. With a sigh, she goes to Nancy's bedside, takes her hand, and starts a monologue, hopeful that if Nancy can't respond, she can at least hear and be comforted.

"I took a leaf out of your book, Grandma," she says, her voice high and tremulous. "I went on another trip. You'd be proud of me. Last minute, I booked myself three nights in Hollywood. And you wouldn't believe the time I had. I went to Zedora, Grandma. Oh, if I could take you, I would."

She pauses, wipes her eyes.

"I also went to Jossop's," she says, rummaging in her bag, pulling out the *Descent of the Sun* script. "The owner gave me this. Look, it's your mother, it's Anna, her initials on the back of Christopher Roderick's movie script. Did…did she ever talk about someone called Archie with you? I think he meant a lot to her. I think…I think he was the man she was *really* in love with."

At this, Nancy stirs. "And so I told them," she cries out, "all that glitters is not gold!"

"Nancy?" says Jess, leaning in.

Tell me, she thinks. *Tell me everything.*

But Nancy sinks back, lowers her eyelids.

After twenty minutes of silence, Jess concedes defeat and kisses her grandmother goodbye. Just as she's leaving, however, she hears another murmur from Nancy's lips.

"My necklace," she whispers. "Did you get it? Paul is waiting."

"Not yet," says Jess, heavy-hearted. "But I will. Hold on, Nancy, and I *will* get for you."

In a daze, Jess takes a cab to Denmark Street. Her tears for Nancy still at the surface, she knows the street will have changed since Paul Angel's photographs were taken and, sure enough, as the cab pulls in, the ciphers of urban development surround her. New buildings, new cladding, new windows. But she is pleased to find hints of the street's rock-and-roll past still humming from its walls, its blue plaques, and the few remaining rare and vintage guitar shops. How much longer the hum will last is anyone's guess. The city is changing all the time.

She walks up the street, then halfway along, beneath a scaffolding-covered eighteenth-century terrace, she sees the remnants of a shop sign, the words *Angel* and *Photography* just about visible. She rushes to the window, but the cement floor and "Under Development" posters give nothing away. The sign, with its dated lettering, is clearly not the most recent incarnation. The ragged edges suggest it has been previously covered over, maybe multiple times: different shops, different eras, different prospects. She backs away, then stumbles into a man walking the other direction.

"Oh sorry!"

"No worries, love."

Jess's attention catches on the man's Celtic cross earring and steampunk skull pendant. She takes in the rest of him: late sixties, leather jeans, band T-shirt, concentrating on his hand-rolled cigarette.

"You okay, love?" he says, noting her red eyes and teary, blotched cheeks.

"Uh, yes, thanks."

She moves on, but from the corner of her gaze, she sees the man enter Gary's Guitars opposite. She pauses, turns to him.

"Excuse me," she calls. "Do you work here?"

He nods.

"Do you know much about *this* place?"

She points to the empty shop.

"You looking for somewhere to rent?"

"No, I–I'm just curious about the sign. Paul Angel Photography."

"Ah, that's well old. It's been a drum shop since, then a T-shirt printer, then a deli-café…along with all the other deli-cafés. As for what it'll be next, who knows? Hopefully nothing corporate is all I can say. But yeah, Paul went out of business decades ago."

"You knew him?"

"Sure, he and my old man went way back. They were good mates."

Jess brightens.

"Really? It's just I'm doing some research, family stuff."

The man shrugs. "Well, come in the shop," he says affably. "Have a brew. I'll tell you what I can."

She obliges with a smile, wondering perhaps if someone, some-where is deliberately putting these Taylor messengers in her way. Bevan Floyd. Ellen Jossop. And now the aging rocker from Gary's Guitars.

Inside, the shop is a tatty but dedicated space for musicians and amp enthusiasts.

"I buy and sell rare models," he—Gary?—explains. "The older, the better. I like the way they sound. Obviously the technology was a bit more basic back then, but the *care* that went into them… I mean, you go to shops now and see rows and rows of anything and everything. Some of it so cheap, it looks like it knows its imminent future is landfill. Too much stuff everywhere and no heart in any of it. Do you play?"

Jess laughs. "I can thrash out a few three-chord clangers. I formed a girl band in high school. We were called the Lucky Bitches. We mostly covered Brit pop hits."

"Blimey!"

"Don't worry. The drummer and I fell out after our first gig."

"Musical differences?"

"Yes. And the fact that we were both snogging the same boy. So, are you Gary?"

"I'm Nick. Gary was my dad. He started the shop back in 1958, on the crest of the music boom. I took it all on when he died, the guitars, the lifestyle, the stories…everything. I see it as my duty, you see, to keep the history going. Denmark Street, there's no other place like it."

He passes her a tea in a chipped mug.

"Please," she says, "tell me about Paul Angel."

"He was already in business when my dad set up on the street. Music photographer, one of the best. Proper gentleman. Old school. Never took the piss. Not like nowadays."

Jess takes out a few of Nancy's photos and shows them to Nick.

"Could you tell me anything about this woman? Her name is Nancy Taylor. She's my grandmother. Paul Angel's label is on the back."

Nick studies the images. "Well, I never! That's his girl. That's Nancy!"

"So you know her?" she says, wide-eyed. "They were together?"

"For sure. They were inseparable."

Jess blinks. For as long as she can remember, Nancy had lived alone. That she'd ever had a romantic life seems extraordinary, but there he is: Paul Angel.

"Looking young there," says Nick. "I only knew her when she was older. Mind you, she always seemed young compared to Paul. Is she—?"

"She's really poorly. She's dying."

"Oh, I'm sorry."

"Eighty-two."

"Good innings, at least. Did she find someone else?"

"No. No, she didn't."

"Such a shame," says Nick solemnly. "Five decades. That's a long time to be a widow."

"Oh no," says Jess, heart sinking. "What happened?"

"Heart attack. One hot May morning in 1969. But I tell you what, his funeral was something. I was just a boy, but I was made to put on a suit and pay my respects. I remember it vividly, heck of a turnout, testament to how much Paul was loved by his industry. But for Nancy, it was too soon."

"I bet it was. So what were they like? Do you remember?"

"Always together. Bit of an odd pair, mind. The age gap was close to fifteen years, which caused a few wagging tongues and raised brows."

Jess laughs. No doubt Anna was one of the tongue waggers, her chances with the grocer's son and the convent school spiraling down the drain.

"Seemed to work perfectly for them though," says Nick. "They ran Paul Angel Photography together. 'Gentleman Paul,' as he was known, became one of the most well-respected music photographers of his day, always flattered his subjects, looked to bring out the best in them, no matter what whiff of scandal or degradation was in their midst. They had a daughter, Carmen, named after the opera."

"Yes," says Jess, beaming. "She was my mother."

"Of course," says Nick, as though the pieces of the puzzle are slotting into place. "Paul was a doting father."

"Aw, that's nice to hear."

"Fancy a strum?" he says, gesturing toward a rack of acoustic guitars.

"Thank you," says Jess, distracted by the sound of Nancy's voice, the last thing she said to her: *Paul is waiting.* "But I need to get going."

She thanks him again and makes for the door. Halfway down Denmark Street she stops, takes out her phone, and calls Guy's number. They haven't spoken since Hollywood, since he sneaked off to party at Stella's LA pad, making her feel like a gullible fool. Should this be discussed? Is it even important when all she needs is to get Nancy's necklace, then never see him again?

"Hello," she says, voice clipped.

"Jess," he says, with cheer, "of the Doughnuts. Funnily enough, I was about to call you. Recovered from LA?"

"Yes, thank you."

"We had a lovely time, right?"

"I suppose."

"What does 'I suppose' mean?"

"It means I'm not in the mood for small talk—"

"Oh. So how about big talk?"

"How about *no* talk? I'm calling because, once and for all, I need to get the necklace."

"Er, yes, but you do realize it's the Capital Gala *today*? Stella is primed for the red carpet, very much loving that art nouveau butterfly—"

"Good for her," says Jess, "but I need my necklace."

Her emotions bubble. She doesn't want to cry again, not to him.

"It's happening," she says. "The nurse told me she reckons forty-eight hours. This is the one thing I can do for her to send her off in peace. You *have* to get that necklace for me."

She can hear Guy sighing, under pressure.

"Look," he says, "maybe there's a way we can speed things up. Just come to the gala. Be my plus-one. I sent you a ticket, which wasn't easy by the way. The security at these things is insane. Anyway, here's the plan: we'll let Stella have her showcase moment, then we'll get the necklace off her immediately after. I'll say it needs repairing or something, then you can steal it into the night, Cinderella-style, get it to your grandmother ASAP—"

Jess brightens. "Will you honestly do that?"

"Jess, I'll do whatever I can."

Jess sniffs, restores herself.

"Somerset House, the Strand," says Guy. "Stella will be on the red carpet about five thirty. Let her get a few snaps, then it'll be yours. And until then, just keep giving Grandma the elixir."

"Okay."

"And…since I'll be rocking a tuxedo, don't forget your best dress. It'll help the mission if you blend in."

Jess blinks, caught by the idea of Guy in a tuxedo, realizing that, despite the desperation of it all, some deep, inscrutable, shameful part of her cannot wait to see him again.

Chapter Fifteen

TIM STANDS AT JESS'S BEDROOM DOOR, WAITS FOR HER TO NOTICE him. She appears to be reorganizing her wardrobe, all her best things strewn across the floor—shoes, scarves, and of course, the obligatory jewelry chaos. There is redness in her eyes, a hint that she's been crying. This grandmother stuff is crushing her. Aggie is right; what Jess needs is cheering up. Her advice, as always, is on point. He grips the gift-wrapped box behind his back, gives a little cough.

Jess looks up.

"Tim? Oh, hi. I–I didn't think I was seeing you until later."

"You weren't, but, well, I thought I'd call by anyway to see my love."

"Aw," she says, cuddling into his embrace.

"So what's all this?" he quizzes. "Decluttering? We won't be short of wardrobe space in the new place, while it's just us two anyhow—"

"No, I–I was just…"

She pauses, shrugs, stares down at the ensemble of pale-blue organza beneath her feet. There it is again, that faraway look in her eyes. Life would be so much easier if he had a mind-reading talent, one that could give him the assurance he needs, whenever that mystery distance creeps between them.

"I have something for you," he whispers, keen to reclaim her focus.

He presents her with the box. She gazes at it and smiles.

"What's this?"

"Just a gift, knowing that you've been missing a certain butterfly necklace."

Now her eyes brighten. She's delighted. Or is it puzzlement? He can't quite tell.

"Open it," he encourages.

Hopefully, the box lid says it all. She'll know from the brand name of the jewelers what's coming next. He grins, holds his breath.

"*Ah,*" she says.

The way her eyes sail across the bright silver butterfly charm pendant within, she is…astounded.

"Do you like it?" he urges. "It's to make up for the one you didn't get."

"It's…it's…"

Jess really *is* astounded. She doesn't know what to say. He mustn't put words in her mouth though—a bad habit of his, to fill silence, to coach people through their reactions. He breathes deeply, grins some more. All he wants is affirmation: *Yes, I love it and I love you!*

"It's…so *sweet.*"

"Do you want to try it on? You could wear it tonight."

"Yes. I…could."

He takes it from the box and places it around her neck, turns her to the mirror, and they both admire her reflection.

"The shop assistant told me it's sterling silver, with something called cubic zirconia. That's the sparkly bit. But…you know more about this stuff than I do. I just thought a nice piece of jewelry, to make you smile. Something you can pass on one day, maybe, if we have a daughter?"

He tickles her ribs, and she squirms and turns and buries her face in his arms. That's more like it. Somewhere in the back of his head, he hears his mother reminding him to treat women well, which is something he can certainly trump his brothers on. He was always good to Cassidy, which would have been fine had she not decided she wanted the kind of excitement that came in the form of a gym instructor with a motorbike.

He was good to Cassidy and she screwed him over.

But he won't pass it on. He'll be good to Jess.

Because Jess is deserving. Jess is everything.

It's sweet, thinks Jess. *It is sweet.*

So very sweet. But *awful*.

And it doesn't matter that it's sterling silver. It could be solid platinum encrusted with emeralds, and it would still make her heart wilt. It's just not *her*. It's so new. So crudely designed. And so very, very, very shiny. It could never compare to Minnie's True Love Necklace, the ions and atoms of four women's lives absorbed into its links and curves. This, on the other hand—she knows the brand, has always avoided it—is nothing more than department-store shelf filler, along with a million others like it.

To make up for the one you didn't get.

How could it? How could it possibly? He doesn't get it. He doesn't see that if it weren't for Minnie's necklace, and the part it played in uniting her with Emery Floyd, then Minnie would never have gotten pregnant and given birth to Anna, who would never have famously "gone to Hollywood," never met the doubtful Christopher Roderick, presumably never had Nancy, who would never have had Carmen. And without Carmen, of course, there would be no Jess, no Aggie, no Steph, no Marcus. None of them. So to say it's a necklace doesn't do it justice when, really, it's a birth rite.

But still, she appreciates Tim's gesture. Like the Stratford City new-build apartment, every item needs a beginning. It's only a necklace. She shouldn't be ungrateful. Some people go all their lives hoping their loved one will be thoughtful enough to buy them jewelry, or even just a bunch of daffodils, or a coconut Toblerone. Yes, he bought her bad jewelry, but doesn't every partner make that mistake once in a while? She stares at the pendant, the way it wanly rests against her breastbone. Maybe some people just need educating, guiding into touch…except, how *can* he be so out of touch with her taste in jewelry? When it is pretty much the foundation of her core, the reason she jumps out of bed in the morning!

"Aunty Jess!" Steph bowls in. "You said you wanted a second opinion about what to wear to the…uh…gala—"

She stops in her tracks, stares hard at Tim.

"Hello, Stephanie," he says.

Jess can tell by his voice that he'd like Steph to disappear fast— and that the word *gala* and all of its Cinderella connotations has caught in his throat like glue. Meanwhile Steph stares down at the pale-blue organza effort.

"Is that what you're thinking of? It's gorge!"

Jess winces, glances back and forth between the two of them.

"But it's only games night at the Star?" says Tim, eyebrow raised. "No need for the prom gown."

"Yes, but…as Steph mentioned—I was about to tell you—I *am* coming to the Star…but before that, I'm attending a gala. In town."

His eyes narrow and immediately she feels villainous. Steph, either oblivious or superbly astute, nods at Jess, then backs away.

"I'll be back in a bit," she says. "I've got just the bag to go with that. I'll dig it out of my room."

Thanks, mouths Jess.

"What *gala*?" says Tim, hands now clamped on his hips.

"It's the Capital Gala," says Jess, lowering herself to the bed to rest her hip. "Not my thing, although always fun to dress up, but… it's…a jewelry event."

"Oh. And who are you going with?"

"Just…a mate." She hates lying. She can't lie. "The truth is, I'm going to get the necklace back. *The* necklace—"

"You mean you're going to meet that Guy person?"

She exhales, drops her chin. "Yes."

"Right." The coldness in his voice says it all.

"I just want the necklace. For Nancy."

He clenches his jaw, stares at the ceiling, as Aggie breezes in.

"Well," she says, grinning at the ill-fated charm pendant dangling from Jess's neck. "Oh, how—"

Jess assumes she's about to say *lovely*, or *pretty*, or some such gleeful adjective, but at the sight of the tense jaws and frown lines, Aggie falters.

"I was just about to see if you guys wanted a G&T, but"—she backs away—"when you're ready."

Alone again, Jess softens, reaches for Tim's hands.

"I'm sorry," she says, trying to smile, to steer them back to comfort.

But it's too little, too late.

"Whatever," he growls, grabbing his jacket and marching out.

Jess removes the charm pendant, places it back in its box. The act feels barbarous, but time is running out. Her emotions all over the place, she hastens to don the blue dress. Steph skips back in with a glint in her eye.

"Here's the bag. Oh, you look ace. What was wrong with Tim?"

"Nothing. Everything. Men."

"I get you," says Steph with a consenting nod.

Dressed and ready, Jess sneaks down the stairs, hopeful she can exit the house without any more scenes, but Aggie is there, waiting in the kitchen, consumed by one of her low-voiced chats with Ed. They both look up as Jess enters the hall, staring at her through the shadows.

"What?" says Jess, snapping at their darkened faces. "Don't look at me like that!"

"Jess… Ed and I, we're concerned. We don't understand what you're playing at—"

"Playing?"

Aggie shrugs, a gesture that implies she deserves a full and frank explanation.

"That's the problem." Jess scowls. "You think I'm still at the *playing* stage. You treat me like a naughty schoolgirl, sneaking out without your permission."

Aggie rolls her eyes.

"If you don't want to be treated like a schoolgirl, Jessica, then don't behave like one!"

"Aaaarrrrggghh!" Jess rages, shaking her hands at the sides of her head.

Everyone with their opinions! Everyone with their concern! She storms out, slamming the door, fire burning in her belly, fury for the sister she adores but can never appease, never match, never truly be.

~⟢~

Somerset House, the Thames-side venue for the Capital Gala, its neoclassical magnificence buzzing with paparazzi, is red-carpet ready. Clutching the invite, Jess approaches the entrance, her walking cane clattering on the cobbles. She looks around for Guy, but can't see him anywhere. Guests keep arriving—a few celebrity faces she recognizes: a TV chef, a singer, and a news correspondent who happens to be wearing an excellent set of baroque pearls. Jess shows her invite to security and is welcomed through the gates, but alone she feels self-conscious. Everyone else seems to know each other.

The early evening sun cascades into the forecourt, flooding the pale stone floor where horses and carriages would have once alighted.

Jess can't help imagining the arrival of Regency women—their empire-line dresses adorned with aquamarine ribbon chokers, coral cameos, and diamond hair bandeaus—and on their arms, the Darcys and Rochesters of the day, somehow finding their way to heroism, despite a few dubious personality "quirks." Was it easier then, she wonders, when a woman's choice of suitor was governed by strict codes of social etiquette?

She glances around, but there is still no sign of Guy. Suddenly, she sees how tenuous this all is, a fanciful plan to meet at a ball—like some jumped-up fairy tale. Now she really *does* feel like a schoolgirl again, waiting for her crush Danny Dobson to meet her at the cinema. The sink and sting, when she realized Danny wasn't late, wasn't held up. Just wasn't coming.

With a despondent sigh, she checks her watch, then her phone. Maybe, like Danny Dobson, Guy has other plans? Should she even be surprised, given his antics in LA and his self-proclaimed on-my-own-terms attitude to life? She clenches her fists, releases them, her frustration for the necklace escalating, and then...

He emerges from the shadows of the colonnade, gorgeous in his formfitting tuxedo, a fluster in his sunlit eyes as he looks into the crowds. He is searching for her. She knows it, senses it. Against her better judgment, her chest fills with lightness. He looks *so* lovely. And now she has a choice, to either wave her hand and get his attention or walk away without him ever seeing her; how that would uncomplicate things, freeing her to live the rest of her life as planned with Tim, ensuring that the brief time she and Guy have spent together remains nothing more than a commitment test.

But Nancy's necklace. Regardless of Guy in his sexy tuxedo and Tim with his sweet but ill-judged jewelry gestures, regardless of *all of it*, she is here to get Nancy's necklace. And that is that.

So she waves, calls out.

"Guy! Over here!"

"Jess!" He waves at her. "Wait! I'll come over!"

Her mind fills with thoughts of their night at Musso's, the moment she first saw him there, the magical shock of it, their laughter, their near kiss...then the sting of those pool-party photographs. *Don't!* she warns, shutting her eyes, chasing out her desire. *Don't be fooled!*

When she looks again, she sees he is flanked by two glamorous women in red dresses and Cartier. And there behind him, looking the other way, is Stella Weston. The supermodel turned influencer, with her party pad in LA and her mews house in Portobello Road, tall and willowy, olive-skinned, straight chestnut hair parted in the center, framing her high-defined cheekbones, her flowing white gown making her look like a Grecian goddess. Immediately self-conscious of her shortness, her roundness, her walking cane, and her general lack of Grecian goddess dress, Jess hugs herself.

"Jess!" says Guy, swooping her into a two-peck greeting. "Sorry, I should have warned you it would be a nightmare to find each other, but here we are"—he holds her gaze—"so let the fun begin. You look lovely, by the way."

"Thank you," she replies, urging herself to remain annoyed about the LA party/false pretenses fiasco. Annoyance, she remembers Aggie telling her, after Matteus sent his heartless "can't do this anymore" text, is a fruitful thing. Stay annoyed. It stops you getting hurt.

"Let me introduce you," says Guy, leading her toward Stella.

Jess steadies herself, determined not to appear overawed, but as Stella approaches, the first thing Jess's eyes land on is the necklace. Any semblance of calm is eclipsed by envy. Why should that beautiful butterfly adorn the neck of someone who clearly doesn't need extra adorning? All that Taylor energy bound in its sea-green wings, giving it vitality, giving it grace, now on the skin of a stranger! It looks wrong, unbearably wrong! Jess shudders, tucks her hands behind her back to stop herself from reaching for it.

"My necklace," she mumbles, flush-cheeked.

"Yes," whispers Guy. "She loves it. She's already had a bunch of compliments."

"Has she now?"

"Easy," says Guy, catching her snippiness. "What is it with girls and their cattiness?"

"I'm not being catty. It's just… I just…"

She sighs, takes a breath.

"Okay," she says, pulling herself together, lifting her shoulders. "Let's do this."

Guy taps Stella on the shoulder.

"Hey," he says. "I have someone I'd like you to meet. This is Jess Taylor. She's a jewelry dealer. Like me. She has business selling vintage and retro pieces. I tell you, she's got a great eye."

Stella graces her with an air kiss. Close up, she smells like citrus fruits. But for all her exquisite poise, she barely manages to make eye contact. Her focus is all over the place, constantly monitoring who else is out there, who else is more popular, more powerful.

"Lovely to meet you," says Jess as politely as she can. "What a perfect evening."

"Yes," says Stella, distracted.

"And"—she cannot *not* comment—"what an extraordinary necklace!"

"Thanks."

Stella raises her fingers to the tips of the butterfly wings. *Don't you dare break it*, thinks Jess.

"Out of curiosity, do you know when it was made?"

"Uh…it's vintage."

"Of course. It looks vintage. I wonder what era."

She can feel Guy's eyes boring into her, yet there is a hint of a smile on his lips, suggesting he's also enjoying the sport of it.

"Uh…an olden-day era."

"She means it's from the early twentieth century," says Guy, maneuvering himself between the two women.

"Yes," says Stella dismissively. "Twentieth century."

She looks past the two of them, waves at the TV chef, then turns to the paps with perfect aplomb, her camera-smile radiating seduction.

Stick to this, thinks Jess. *This is where you excel.*

"*Jess*," says Guy, taking her by the hand. "Why don't we get you a drink?"

"Great idea."

They walk toward the hall, and as Guy sweeps her past the doorman, Jess can't help but feel important to him again, welcomed and wanted. The sound of a harp drifts up to the painted ceiling, a fairy echo above the fizzy chat. In every cell, she feels it, the buzz of being in the center of things. Not on the side, but the very center. From whom, she wonders, does she get her love of a fancy party? Not Nancy. Definitely not her mother or father. But maybe there's a gene that skipped a few generations, a partying gene? Anna. It's got to be Anna!

From the nearest waiter, Guy takes two Bellinis, hands one to her. They chink glasses and sip the sweet, peachy nectar.

"So…are galas your day-to-day thing?" Jess asks, leaning back against a fluted pillar.

"Nah," he says, the angles of his body mirroring hers, subconsciously creating a private Jess-Guy zone. "They're my weekend thing. Day-to-day, I'm on my super yacht in Monaco."

They both laugh and the feeling crackles between them again, that zesty connection that refuses to dissipate.

"You look very, very, very, *very* lovely by the way," he says.

"You've used that line already."

"Why do you always assume it's a line?"

"Because I know your type."

Touché.

But Jess can feel the annoyance eroding. The way they throw these comments back and forth like confetti, it's impossible to resist. Every inflection feels tantalizing, teasing, playful. They huddle so close that their bodies almost touch, blended energies. A tray of canapés—little pastries sprinkled with edible flowers—is momentarily offered to them, but the waiter, sensing their intimacy, retracts and sashays onward. Through the dark, Jess catches sight of Stella. She is working a line of photographers.

"She *is* beautiful," she comments.

"Don't say it like that."

"Like what?"

"Like you've just bitten into the most luscious-looking apricot, only to discover the inside is watery. She's actually a blast when she gets going. It's just"—he raises a brow—"she rarely gets going."

"You know, you have very active eyebrows," says Jess, the Bellini going straight to her head, aware she is now feeding the flirtatious air between them.

"So I've been told," says Guy. "I try to control them, but they always get the better of me. I should probably get them their own Instagram account."

"Ah," says Jess, daring to raise the thorny subject, "as for Instagram accounts—"

Guy scrunches his face, a classic *What have I done now?* look.

"You and Stella had fun at your LA after-party, did you?"

"You've been cyberstalking me?"

"I woke up wondering about you, that's all, after we'd had such an amazing night…that hadn't quite ended in the way that I think you hoped… Anyway…it's all irrelevant now…"

"Why bring it up then?" Guy smiles at her from the rim of his glass.

"No reason," she says.

"I'm glad you thought it was an amazing night, anyhow."

He moves closer. She can smell his aftershave, the scent of musk and vanilla. The urge to run her hands through his hair, pull him close, draw him in… She feels it overwhelming her, grows dizzy with it—the tingle, the yearning, the thought of his hips pressed against hers. Surely the only way she can quell this crazy want is to...

Suddenly a woman with a black bob and glittering diamond choker is in their sphere.

"My favorite jewelry dealer," the woman drools, showering Guy with intruder kisses, completely ignoring Jess. "Guy, darling, there's someone I'd like you to meet—"

She pronounces it *Gee*, like the French. Jess inwardly cringes. *Gee, darling* sounds so affected. It just doesn't feel very...Guy. How does he stand it?

"Have you heard of General Phillips?" the woman continues. "Absolute smasher. He and my husband were at Sandhurst together. He's been looking into the whereabouts of his great-grandmother's brooch. Very distinct, has his family crest on it. And a big ruby. Anyway, he thinks he's traced it to Cape Verde, but he could use your help. First though, darling, you owe me a dance—"

Within seconds, Guy is in this woman's arms, twirling onto the dance floor. He doesn't seem unhappy about it. In fact, he seems to revel in the attention of this posh, bobbed vulture. A triple cocktail of disappointment, envy, and anxiety prickles through Jess's body. She retreats to the other side of the pillar, where she downs the rest of her drink. When she eventually finds the stomach to peer around the corner, she sees Guy so immersed in the dance, it's as if he's completely forgotten her existence.

As he turns, however, through the swirling lights, he catches her eye and smiles. And it feels like a truthful smile. So she allows herself this little concession: that his devotion to this woman is perhaps purely business, a schmooze with a client. That his truth is not in this room. Not with Stella and her prestigious friends and her press frenzy, but somewhere else, somewhere…with her.

When the song ends, he breaks away and, much to the bobbed vulture's vexation, he returns to *their* pillar.

"Another drink?" he asks.

"Shouldn't you be schmoozing?"

"I *am* schmoozing."

"Not with me. With…your people."

"They," he says, staring at her squarely, "are not my people."

Jess grins, privately pleased.

"So now that Stella's had her fashionista moment, can we get *my* heirloom please?"

"Sure. What's your plan?"

"I thought *you* had a plan—"

"I did. And it's worked."

She stares at him.

"I'm here for the necklace," she asserts. "Nothing else."

"Well, I was thinking I could tell Stella that the catch at the back appears broken, and that rather than risk losing it, I'll 'look after' it for her. I'll smother her with compliments, reassure her that she doesn't need bling to shine, that sort of thing." He shifts, looks a little uneasy.

"Thank you," says Jess. "You're not nervous, are you?"

"Of course. It's Stella…and I'm lying to her."

"A small lie, for a good cause."

"Which could get me into a whole heap of trouble. Seriously, if Stella gets wind of this, she'll be livid. I'll be struck off the Christmas list."

Jess scoffs.

"Nonsense. Prince Charming, you'll always come out on top—"

"So I *am* Prince Charming? Thanks for the compliment."

"I'm not sure it's a compliment," Jess quips. "Charming doesn't always mean *charming*."

"There it is again," says Guy, gliding his hands to indicate an invisible shield between them, "the Jess Taylor force field."

Meanwhile, from the corner of her eye, Jess sees Stella moving away.

"Quick," she urges, "go to it."

"Okay, okay. Mission engaged. But I can't promise Stella will fall for it. If she senses I'm messing her about, I'll have to pull the plug."

"Oh, stop pandering to her," Jess scolds. "Just do it!"

"*Okay*," he shouts, waggling his fingers, grinning at her, walking backwards.

As Guy weaves into the crowd, Jess aches with the pull and push of her feelings. She twiddles her hair, presses her heels into the ground, rocks back and forth. She watches Guy approach Stella, whisper something in her ear. They both giggle, then disappear together, and from where Jess is standing, it doesn't look like he's said anything about the necklace, let alone that it's damaged and needs emergency repairs. Tense and nervy, she goes to the bar and orders another Bellini. Ten minutes later, the Bellini downed, Guy is nowhere to be seen. The barman offers her another.

"I better not," Jess says, drumming the bar top with frustration.

Her unease escalates. What are they up to? Where is the necklace? Should she message, or would that look like pestering? She steels herself and, instead, messages Tim to say she's sorry they parted on bad terms and that she'll be at the Star soon. He immediately FaceTimes her back, but this ignites panic. He can't see where she is. It will only inflame matters. He won't…understand. She backs outside to a quiet balcony, takes the call.

"Hey," she says overbrightly.

"Hey to you," he replies. "Look, Jess, I'm sorry I stormed off. It's just I feel like you're… Oh, I don't know, Jess… I just want it to be about us, okay? I get jealous, the way you do your own thing. It makes me nervous."

"Don't be," says Jess, the guilt plummeting like an anvil in her belly.

"Are you coming to join us?"

"I am," she says. "In a short while."

"And…have you managed to get your beloved necklace back?"

"Nearly," she says. Change the subject. "Are *you* having fun?"

"Yeah, good times. The guys have got us playing drinking games."

He pans his phone around, creating a 360-degree panoramic of the scene: the check-shirted geography department and the silver-chain math gang sipping pints of lager while Duff holds court. Jess hears the words *radiation* and *simulator* and realizes he is delivering one of his Duff-style physics monologues. She then catches a glimpse of the scene in the grand hall behind her, where two crystal-studded stilt walkers are breathing fire across the delighted crowds and a feathered burlesque dancer has just thrown her nipple tassels at the Lord Mayor.

"Love you, Jess," says Tim optimistically.

"Love you too," she says, the words exiting her mouth as though they've been shoved out.

Dazed, Jess circuits the hall, past the throngs of hedonists, the glitter cannons and the towers of crystal champagne coupes. The sense that anything could happen enthralls her. Games night with the Baxter Academy lot, the same people, same place, same conversations, every week, it just can't compare. But at least Tim doesn't keep her waiting or say one thing, then do another. And while he may not have the most gripping of lifestyles, his steadiness is his strength. It pervades everything he does. Whereas all of this—the grand gala of Guy's world—is fun for a moment, but ultimately it's fluff. Once the loudspeakers have been dismantled and the glitter swept up, surely it's just another empty space. No substance. No security. In her anguish, her thoughts do another one-eighty flip.

She checks the lobby, the cloakrooms, and the powder rooms, where a huddle of women are spraying their crotches with perfume. She then returns to the balcony where the lights of the Thames sparkle and the breeze from the river ripples her dress. She checks her watch again. If she doesn't get the necklace tonight, what will the consequence be? The thought of Nancy dying in agitation, denied her final wish, squeezes her heart. But it isn't just that... Somehow it feels as though *she* will suffer too; that without the necklace, without its energy, her own happiness will be set askew.

She looks into the shadows of the hall, looks for Guy one more time, then with a gale of regret, she makes her choice to go. She cannot keep Tim on hold any longer. It isn't fair. With a final glance across the moonlit Thames, she tucks her bag under her arm, leans into her walking cane, takes a step, then suddenly a warm breath tickles the back of her neck. She stills and gasps, as a pair of hands emerge beside her.

"*Shh!*" he whispers, softly slipping the butterfly necklace over her shoulders, his fingertips scintillating the cool of her skin.

He turns her toward him and their eyes meet.

"Happy now?" he whispers.

"Oh, yes," she says, breathlessly, reaching for her butterfly.

The necklace she has longed for, the Taylor legacy, *finally* around her neck—and through it, right here and now, she can feel the past in her blood, four generations of her family coursing into her veins, bolstering her: Minnie, Anna, Nancy, and Carmen. They are all here. She shuts her eyes. They are here within her, whispering their wisdoms.

"Thank you," she says.

And then, on impulse, engulfed by gratitude, she leans up on tiptoes and plants a thank-you kiss. Just a thank-you kiss, but it unintentionally misses the cheek it's intended for and lands straight on Guy's lips. The moment shocks. They both fall away.

"Sorry," she gasps, her walking cane clattering to the floor.

Before she has a chance to pick it up, Guy lowers his gaze to the necklace, to that fat moonstone, where it rests against her milky skin, a hypnotist's charm. He stares, mesmerized, then looks up at Jess. They were flirty before, but this, *this* is another level. This is it.

No matter how risky, how wrong, or how out of place, *this* is how soul mates feel.

Her reasoning mind rendered powerless, no longer in opposition to her lust, Jess shuts her eyes and gives in to the fervor. Her fingers entwine with Guy's. She shouldn't. She knows this. She has never been a cheat, hates cheating, but her heart is on fire, her breath so fast it's dizzying. And as she leans toward him, in the space where their lips hover, desperate to touch, everything feels suspended: every star, every cell, every hope...*everything* hangs in this moment.

So she dissolves into the pleasure of kissing Guy Arlo van der Meer. And it's wonderful. His kiss is both deep and tender and it makes her shiver, makes her feel like a queen of the silver screen. And all at once everything comes to life, the truth of her heart colliding into his, the bond between the wearer and the watcher, a tightening knot, declaring itself: undeniable, indelible.

Then the magic is broken by a vibration between their bodies.

"My phone," says Jess, hurtling back to reality.

She doesn't need to look at the screen to know that it's Tim. She shudders from her bliss, shocked, appalled at herself.

"Oh god...I don't know what came over me... I shouldn't have... I'm sorry, really sorry."

Guy grips her hands.

"Sorry?" he says. "Why be sorry? You went with your instincts. We both did. We could do it again. And again. And again."

He pulls her toward him, cups her cheeks with his hands, and she wants *so much* to let him, but the thought that she's building a life with Tim, one that is good for her, one that she needs is bigger than this. *Get real, Jess.*

"I'm sorry," she says again, then before he can argue or seduce her anymore, she hastens away.

Reeling, Jess hails a taxi cab. Her first thought is to direct the driver to Nancy's care home in Sydenham, but then she remembers it's past nine o'clock. The care home will now be closed to visitors. In desperation, she telephones the home's reception and is relieved when the favorite nurse answers.

"She's still with us," the nurse reassures her. "And she's perfectly comfortable. We're checking on her all the time."

"So she'll make it through the night?" says Jess, grasping for assurance.

"I'd say so."

"And tomorrow?"

"Well, it's impossible to say for certain, but for now she's hanging in there. We'll call you if anything changes."

"I'll come first thing tomorrow."

"Great. That'll comfort her, I'm sure."

Jess sits back, puts her hand to the necklace, and breathes. She feels relieved, but not relaxed. Her limbs are fired up with adrenaline and Guy is still in her head—the kiss that should never have happened. She cups her mouth, as though to bury the guilt. She was weak. She gave in to him, gave in to the moment. She could—*should*—go to the Star, catch last call, focus on Tim.

"Head to Wanstead," she says to the driver, resisting her reticence.

The lights of the Thames blur past the window, and as she sinks in her seat, Jess prays that the familiar sight of the Star will somehow cleanse her sins.

❧

Over at the window, there is Tim, being "The Man."

"You made it!" he says cheerily, a few pints into drunk.

Jess covers her startled edge with a smile. She hugs him tight, desperate to right her wrong.

"So did you get it?" he asks.

"Yes," she says cautiously.

"Show me."

His gaze drops to the sea-green butterfly at her neck. She waits for his reaction. But his face hardly changes, then he shrugs.

"That's it?" he says casually. "*That's* what all this fuss has been about?"

"You don't like it?"

She eyes him, wills him to be at least a little impassioned.

"It's…elaborate," he says. "I mean, it's certainly fussier than the one I got you. Here, have a drink."

He scoops her into a hug, hands her his pint. And despite the silent confusion snaking through her mind, she smiles and accepts and does her level best to join in. *Familiar*, she reassures herself. Not boring. Just familiar. And familiar is good. Familiar is secure.

An hour later, they return to Jess's room in the Hoppit household. Tim is drunker than Jess and in a buoyant mood.

"I need to ravish you," he says, pulling her toward him.

She wants to feel closeness. Closeness might help. So she flicks off her shoes, loosens the straps of her dress, determined to conjure the spark. Tim kisses her foot, but then retreats to the en suite bathroom. She hears him rooting around at the sink. He then pokes his head around the door.

"Forgotten my dental floss," he says. "Do you have any?"

It crosses her mind that, barely a year into their relationship, they should be obsessed with each other, rolling across the bed, stripping naked, making love with throw-it-in-the-air passion.

"I don't care about dental floss," she says.

"You should. Better than brushing—"

"I mean, I don't care about dental floss right now," she says, layering her words with seductive suggestion.

"Patience, Jess. Let me get a glass of water and put my phone on charge. I'll be with you in a second—"

She flops back, wilting into the ordinary.

Five minutes later, Tim reappears. He undresses and folds his clothes in a pile—so much for stripping naked! To be fair, with his triangular torso and big shoulders, he is rather lovely naked. And his thighs are undeniably shapely from hours on a racing bike. But the way he stands, pre-prepared, step-by-step, it's simply x plus y, which was fine last week and the week before. But...

He slips into the bed beside her, snuggles under the duvet and does nothing. Beer and tiredness have got the better of him and he is soon asleep, mouth sagging, nostrils flaring as though readying to snore. With a sigh, Jess loosens her zip. She will, she realizes, have to undress herself, but at least she'll have the warm security of his body beside hers. She pushes her dress aside and curls up against him. After a moment, however, she feels something digging into her neck—she is still wearing the necklace. She unclips it, but before placing it on the bedside table for safety, she holds it her chest, runs a finger across its chain links, feels the inscription on its back. Her thoughts surge: the way he slipped behind her, the way he gazed at the necklace, then spun her into his arms, the way they kissed.

It was a moment. Just a moment, an emotionally illegal moment, but it was one of those. It was a *OUI* moment!

And a *OUI* moment can't be minimized or dismissed. Nor can it be defined by a yearning for security or the avoidance of a "type." If it's there, it's there. She bites down on her lip, resolves to find a way out of this mess, a way to end things with Tim. There's no point settling for the familiar when your heart, in truth, wants something else.

Chapter Sixteen

THE NEXT MORNING, HAVING SLEPT LITTLE, JESS IS AWAKE EARLY.
Ignoring the fierce pain that is shooting down her lower back and
hips, she dresses, tucks the butterfly necklace in her bag, and takes
the first train to Sydenham. The walk to Nancy's care home is an
unbearable hobble, but she makes herself do it, one foot in front of
the other. As she approaches the reception, the staff are extra wel-
coming. *Ominous*, she thinks.

"Come along," says a nurse, ushering Jess along the corridor. "It's
good that you're here. We think it won't be long now. We were just
about to call you."

"You mean…it's time?"

The nurse nods, holding the door open for her.

"Right, okay," says Jess, gulping, collecting herself as she enters
the room.

Instinctively she feels for the butterfly necklace. All the effort
it has taken to get hold of it, all worth it for this, the last chance to
make a wish come true. Nancy is peaceful, her eyes slightly open.
Her breathing is shallow but rhythmic. The room, its beige walls

and plastic-coated furnishings, feels still and silent. Jess goes to the bedside, takes out the necklace, holds it to the light.

"I got it," she whispers. "Finally, Grandma, I got it for you."

Nancy stirs.

"Oh, Jessy, my lovely Jessy," she whispers, dry-mouthed, barely audible.

Jess takes her hand, places the necklace in her grandmother's palm, and closes her cold, frail fingers around it. Nancy tries to speak again, but it comes out as a gasp. Jess leans closer.

"What is it, Grandma?"

"Paul," she whispers, sighing with the effort, the words so delicate on her lips. "My Paul. He's waiting for me."

"He is," says Jess, eyes slick with tears.

"He was my true love, Jessy."

"I know."

Jess looks on, feels a rawness in her heart. She cannot mistake the similarities of her and Nancy's faces—that achingly familiar Taylor bone structure, the DNA that unites them.

Shakily, Nancy draws the necklace to her chest.

"Minnie," she explains, shutting her eyes, straining to get her words out, "Minnie poured everything she had into making our necklace. All her hopes, her dreams…and her soul…her *soul* went into it. And now it lingers inside."

Then with a sudden surge in her bone-thin arms, she thrusts it toward Jess.

"You…you want *me* to have it?"

"*Oui*," gasps Nancy, before collapsing back to her pillow.

Awed, Jess cups the necklace's delicate enamel and metalwork. The wings feel so *alive* in her hands. And through their energy, a thought starts to pester, that Nancy's desperation for the necklace was not for her sake but for Jess's.

"Nancy—" she begs, so many questions to ask.

But Nancy is silent.

"Oh, Nancy," Jess cries, her voice a siren in the quiet. "Not yet, Nancy. We've got some fun to have yet, you and me—"

At this, Nancy turns, very slightly, and she smiles with half her mouth. It is momentary, all she can manage, but it is enough to show Jess that she isn't sad.

She is at peace.

One hand holding Nancy's, the other holding the necklace, Jess waits and listens as Nancy's breathing starts to slow. She no longer feels anxious, simply aware of what it is to be with someone in their final moments. Silently, softly, the air changes. A hush fills the room. After a moment Jess looks to the window and is struck by the sight of a butterfly landing on the ledge. A small tortoiseshell, it sits perfectly still, then opens its wings and flutters off through the bright-blue sky, entirely unaware that the soul of Nancy Maria Taylor has just left the earth.

Jess calls Aggie, then with a sense of banal finality, she fills in the required paperwork, gathers up Nancy's belongings, and packs them in a box. She exits the care home in a daze, suddenly unsure, after such a monumental event, of what to do. Should she go home, carry on, mark it in some way? With a thud, she sits down on a nearby bench and stares at the sunflowers swaying in the breeze. Plants are growing. Birds are singing.

She takes out the necklace, and in the bright sun, she can see how tarnished the silver is, yet all the more beautiful for it. A mark of its life. And what a life! Jess thinks back to all she has learned, thanks to this necklace. About Minnie, so single-minded in her creative ambition, giving up on gossip in Parisian drawing rooms, abandoning convention, escaping to an Arts and Crafts commune in North Wales, falling in love, *really* falling in love, pouring everything she had into making this heirloom—all her hopes, her dreams, all the "yes" in her soul, which now lingers within the necklace's timeworn links and curves.

Is that what the inscription meant to Nancy, she wonders; that for the short time in the 1950s and '60s that Nancy and Paul Angel were together, they were a "yes" couple? And what of Anna, fiery with ambition, chasing her Hollywood jewelry dreams, ingratiating herself with movie producers, living the high life: marble staircases, gilded toilets, and A-list cocktails. Definitely a "yes" girl when it came to parties, but did she ever get a True Love "yes" moment with her soul mate? Poor Anna.

And finally, of course, Jess thinks of her mother, Carmen. She takes comfort in the thought that, perhaps, somewhere, in some unfathomable part of the universe, Carmen and Nancy are now together again, mother and daughter. She strokes her fingers along the tips of the butterfly wings, remembers the way her mother would cradle it in her hands; how she'd admire it, talk about it, treasure it, but never, to Jess's knowledge, wear it. Who, she wonders, did her mother have her "yes" moment with? Surely not with her father, the intractable and uninspiring Richard Barrow? It would be good to know, she thinks. She should ask—

She stops, shudders. Because there is no one now to ask.

In the days that follow, any lingering resentments and recriminations are pushed aside, placed on pause, as the new family landscape emerges. Aggie cuddles her children in a way she doesn't usually, which is strange and intense for them, and they wish things would go back to normal. Tim comes to the Hoppit house with flowers for both sisters and a huge tin of shortbread, should it be required. He sees Jess's teary face and, without a word, pulls her into an embrace. She feels comforted, enormously cocooned. And in his arms, it feels safe to release, to let it all out.

She wears the necklace all the time, even in bed at night, because, although she understands that Nancy is gone, something of her energy seems to remain within it. Aggie occupies herself with arrangements for the funeral, channeling any excess emotion into being purposeful. On Thursday afternoon she summons Jess to the kitchen island on the proviso of choosing buffet options for the wake. Once that business is out of the way, she slaps her hands on her knees, clearly poised to say something deep and meaningful.

"Anyway—"

Jess watches with caution, sensing an incoming lecture.

"Tim's been a star throughout all of this, hasn't he?"

Jess murmurs.

"All good between you two?"

"Yes."

"Because—"

Here we go.

"I've been doing some research." She gives Jess a hard, meaning-ful stare.

"Have you now?"

"On your new 'friend.' Guy van der...*whatever*..."

Jess bristles. She's been at the mercy of her big sister's "research" in the past, and it's never been pleasant. Aggie's discovery that Andrew the band promoter had a serious gambling habit, or that Mac the Irish musician had many, many, many baby mamas. All intentions good, no doubt to help, to show Jess what she seems so ignorant of herself: that the men she's attracted to are riddled with issues. Still, she sighs, puzzled as to why it should be such a point of interest.

"Aggie, I really don't think it's necessary for you to go giving him the third degree. You're wasting your time."

"Except...you met him in LA, didn't you? I saw it on your phone. And then this gala you went to? And goodness knows where else. And all those secretive text messages and the way you've been acting weird. My hunch is you've been avidly interacting with him—"

"It was to get the *necklace*."

"Oh, Jess, you can't tell me it was simply about the necklace, because...I'm your sister. I *know* there's something between you two." She sighs. "But what *you* need to know is—"

She pauses.

Jess bows her head.

"He's not who you think he is."

Aggie pushes her tablet in front of Jess and scrolls through her Pinterest board of "evidence."

"For a start, his name is not Guy van der Meer, as he claims all over his website and social media. He's not from a Dutch diamond dynasty, as various gossip columns imply. His name is Guy Davis. He went to school in *Ramsgate*, had a Saturday job in a chip shop, and got zero qualifications. So whatever elaborate backstory he's been telling you about, it's a load of old crock."

Jess's mouth drops open.

"So…he changed his name," she reasons. "Big deal. People do that all the time."

"The point is, Jess, if he's lying about his name and his family background, what else is he lying about? I've looked through his profile. I see it for what it is. He thinks he's some kind of international treasure-hunting playboy, living the jet-set dream. Look at this—"

She scrolls through photo after photo, Guy posing and partying, always surrounded by exotic locations, glamorous houses, sophisticated people.

"As exciting as he might seem, Jess, you can see he's just a showboater. Definitely not a keeper. I won't let you risk your future happiness."

Taut with frustration, her thoughts in free fall, Jess throws up her hands.

"Well, it really doesn't matter," she scolds, "because, as I've told you time and time again, there is *nothing* romantic going on between me and Guy van der…Davis…or whatever! We're friends. In fact, we're not even friends. So just…drop it, will you!"

She storms away, forcing one of the bifolds open, out to the garden, where the sky is metal gray. Aggie's revelation spins in her head. The warning is immovable: he really is a bullshitter. Another one. How did he manage to burrow so deeply under her skin? She clutches the necklace, panged by uncertainty, all that teasing, toxic desire bound up in its shimmering wings.

Of course it shouldn't matter. The passion she'd felt with Guy was an anomaly. A mistake. How could she ever doubt Tim? Tim who has been magnanimous since Nancy's death. Tim who at every turn has shown himself to be loyal and honest and emotionally mature. Tim who has all the traits that any salient person should want from their partner, who doesn't play games or kiss other people's girlfriends or turn up an hour late or sneak off to LA after-parties and act like it's no big deal.

But still…that kiss at the gala, it burns in her heart; that kiss was a "yes" moment.

Chapter Seventeen

As Guy lazes in the young grass of Green Park, hands clasped behind his head, Jess is in his thoughts. Her bright eyes and quick mind, the way they kissed when he slipped her the necklace. Normally at this stage in a flirtation, he'd be on the case, enveloping the object of his affections in a charm-offensive of calls, texts, and perfect dates. But with Jess, he doesn't dare. He doesn't want to scare or overwhelm her or get it wrong. She's already made it clear she has a certain opinion of him, and perhaps he's brought that on himself, but now he has to undo it. He has to prove to her that he's not really the player she thinks he is.

He has thought about little else for days, but has so far kept the reverie to himself, Stella being ultra-insecure this week. Here she comes with two ice-cold water bottles, having aborted her whimsical desire to Rollerblade (after the painful discovery that she wasn't good at it—and that there were paparazzi lurking). It has been a week of "doing things" with Stella, feeding her ego, keeping her buoyant and well-distracted from the news about her dot-com billionaire, Yannis, who has reportedly proposed to a Colombian swimwear model.

"Why the constant smiling?" Stella demands, thrusting a water into Guy's hand.

"I'm thinking about someone."

"Who? Tell me. Come on. It's time you spilled the beans."

"If you must know, it's Jess," he says. "Jess Taylor. I introduced you to her at the Capital Gala."

"Jess? I don't remember any Jess. Is she worth remembering?"

He sighs.

"She is to me."

"And where did you meet her?" Stella asks, flicking her immaculate chestnut hair. "I don't think she's on *my* radar."

Guy hesitates, unsure whether to mention the necklace. It has been a sore point between them since he smuggled it to Jess at the gala. He had rather hoped Stella would forget about it, end of story, Jess and her necklace reunited forever, but…Stella has been unusually picky. The night she had to give up the necklace for "repairs" was the night she also learned of Yannis's Colombian indiscretion. And now she keeps pestering for the necklace, almost as though she's convinced herself that the two events are interlinked; that getting the butterfly back, all "fixed," might also fix her and Yannis.

"Well?" she presses.

He fears she suspects something. Mind you, she always suspects something. She pulls herself up on her haunches, her flimsy skirt revealing two long, tanned legs.

"Let's just say we met in a haze of time," he explains.

"You like her?"

"We have a connection. And it's a connection I've never had with anyone else."

"Oh please, spare me, Guy. Connection? You're the Connection Casanova."

Guy laughs, then shakes his head.

"I'm telling you, Stella... This is different. This isn't about flirting or getting likes. This is real. It's real and it's messy and...suddenly I don't know what to do with myself. Because I like her. I *really* like her."

Stella just laughs.

"Oh, Guy, you're too cute."

Then she eyes him from the rims of her Prada sunglasses.

"But I have to ask, is she—?"

He knows what she's going to say.

"One of us?"

"No," he says. "She's a normal, cool girl. She doesn't care about postcodes and fine wines and the who's who of Chelsea. Doesn't need to. She's amazing as she is. And I want to talk with her all the time and make her laugh and be in her space and, honestly, she's like a lovely drug."

"Sounds suspiciously like infatuation to me. Not healthy, Guy. Lust/love. They're not the same thing, you know. Something tells me you'll obsess about her until the shine wears off, then you'll dump her and move on to the next. And then she'll assume you've dumped her after sex, which will really piss her off and probably fuck up the rest of her dating career. So just don't. Go. There."

Guy cogitates on this rather grim appraisal of his prospects, then climbs to his feet.

"No!" he says, suddenly animated, surprised by his own ferocity. "*No*. I like her. I really, truly like her. In fact, sorry, Stella, but I think I'm in love with her."

Stella glares at him, openmouthed.

She'll never tolerate him being in love with someone else. He can see in her eyes that she fears losing him, her most loyal, doting best friend forever, who tells her the truth, does as he's told, and always gives her first dibs on any good jewelry he comes across. He knows, deep down, that theirs is not a balanced friendship, but where would he be without her?

"She has something to do with my necklace, doesn't she?" Stella demands, eyes narrowed. "I *want* that necklace back, Guy. You said it was with the repairman, but it must be fixed by now."

Guy sighs.

"I paid for it," she asserts, her pout turning sour. "So it's mine. Get it for me."

"All right, all right," he says, stressed.

He hates this, the way he feels like her puppet. His role has been to keep Stella amused for the forty-five weeks of the year that she hasn't been with Yannis (now, seemingly, to become fifty-two). In return, he gets a rent-free home in a Portobello mews house, free trips to LA, and above all, an open door to London's rich list. He's built his business on reputation. And they like him. They value him. They *believe* him. But…at what cost?

He paces, under pressure, the tendrils of his past threatening to creep to the surface, reminding him of the life he's escaped from. All those sad kids in that care home in Kent where he grew up. What did they ever amount to? Selling crack to underage schoolkids going nowhere? Scrabbling for pennies to pay the electricity meter in sorry-sorry bedsit-ville?

No. He's risen up. He's used his guile and his charisma to make a better life for himself. He's gotten away from all that. He's become a success, despite no one caring whether he would or not.

So just keep rolling the dice, keep in the game.

"I'll call my man," he says. "You'll have it back by the end of the day."

Stella plants a sleek, glossy kiss on his cheek. "Thank you, baby," she coos. "Now, I'm thinking, what about Cannes this autumn? Should we go to Cannes?"

He grins. *Yeah. Why not?*

Wary of the reason behind Guy's request to meet, Jess hobbles toward his suggested venue: Hatton Garden, London's diamond center, *the* destination for affluent engaged couples looking for something twinkly to seal the deal. But despite the delight of these environs, her hackles are up. She can only assume he chose the venue to fit in with his "van der Meer" diamond-family charade. Whether she'll get the truth from him, she has no idea, which only serves as testament to how little she knows him. She steels herself, grimaces, resolves to be more annoyed than ever before.

There he is, leaning against a lamppost beside a glittering window display, in a moss-green shirt and gray jeans, oozing louche confidence.

"Ta-da! Another jewelry-themed destination," he says as she approaches.

His attention immediately falls to the butterfly necklace, the plique-à-jour wings poking out from the collar of her blouse. The sense of his gaze both thrills and enrages her. He then goes for a hug, but she pulls away. Clearly he presumed there would be the usual verve between them. Not today though. The rules of the game have changed.

"So I suppose you picked this location because it's familiar territory?" she snarls.

He shrugs.

"Diamonds?" she nudges. "The van der Meer family legacy and all that?"

"Oh, yes, sure"—he catches her eye, maintains the conceit—"although my family specialized in raw diamonds. A lot of the ice around here is synthetic. Not so good."

So he really does live this lie. Not only is he maintaining it, but he's embellishing it. Raw diamonds? *Really*, Mr. Davis? She glares back at him, scrutinizing the sparkle in his eyes.

"Everything okay?" he queries.

"All good," she snaps. "So…what was so urgent we needed to meet?"

"Well. I thought we could window-shop the diamond porn, then get a coffee or maybe lunch, and then—"

"Can't," says Jess. "I've got things to do."

"Oh."

His disappointment is palpable. That face, eyelids half-lowered, an unexpected hint of *But I like you* vulnerability, it feels—or at least it *seems*—genuine. She hadn't expected disappointment. All those early rebuffs she'd given him had been met with cocky, self-assured smugness. This one is different. This one bothers him, which can only mean that beneath the veneer, perhaps he actually does feel something true. She blinks, holds her breath, emotions surging.

Stay firm, Jess, she tells herself. *Don't fall for it.*

A smiley couple in matching gray business suits come to the shop window to ogle at the engagement bling. Their loved-up presence only amplifies the awkwardness between Jess and Guy.

"Please," she says, determined to sever the occasion before her judgment clouds completely, before she says or does something she'll regret, "if there's nothing else you want from me, I have to get on."

"Why do I get the feeling you're being funny with me, Jess?"

Jess shrugs, the weight of the butterfly necklace pressing against the base of her throat. Guy stares at her.

"Is it Tim?" he asks.

Jess sighs, lowers her head.

"I have a question for you," he says, fighting for closeness. "You say you're committed, but what if it's the wrong relationship? What if the person you're really meant to be with is standing in front of you right now? It could be, couldn't it? I mean, this *fizz* between us—"

Jess looks to the sky, the nitpicking opinions of Aggie, Ed, and Steph tearing circles through her mind.

"Fizz is not enough," she says. "That's it. I have to go."

"Oh, Jess, come *on*—"

He eyes the necklace, then smiles at her. He is thinking about kissing her, she can tell. The wanting, the resisting…it's a crazy, crazy torture.

"You're just a diversion," she says.

"Brilliant. Great. What's not to love about diversions? Although I could be the main journey, if you like. Really, try me. Watch me become an excellent main journey—"

"*No!*" Jess asserts. "How many ways do I have to say it? We're not a thing. We can't be."

"Well, if that's the case," he says, pride wounded, recoiling like a scolded animal, "I might as well put it out there… I need the necklace back. Stella wants it. You've had your favor, so now, please"—he holds out his hand—"let me return it to its legal owner."

Jess glowers. She hasn't yet told him of Nancy's death. Fair enough, but still, it's as if it's not just the necklace he's asking for, but the very memory of Nancy, so raw and unprocessed.

"I'll give you the money for it," she implores, barely able to look at him. "I'll go straight to a cash machine now."

"It's not about the money, Jess. Stella wants her necklace. She's nagging. My neck's on the line. I helped you out—I was happy to, more than happy—but you should have known it wasn't a permanent fix."

"But you said…*you said* she wouldn't miss it—"

"Well, she has and that's that. My loyalty's to Stella. I mean, she's someone I'm actually *enough* for."

"Nancy's gone," Jess admits. "She died on Sunday morning. The funeral's next week."

Immediately Guy softens, comes toward her.

"Oh, Jess, I'm so sorry. I didn't know. I—"

He pulls her into a hug, whether she wants him to or not. She can't deny that there is comfort in his arms, that her heart races, that his smell makes her tingle, that his hair against her cheek is sensuous. But then—perhaps she's being paranoid, just imagining it—then she becomes aware of his fingers at the back of her neck. And it feels as though they're working their way toward the necklace clasp. Her blood cools. She backs away.

"You were about to undo it!" she accuses.

"*No.* I was just comforting you. Oh, for god's sake. I can't win, no matter what I do. But you know what? Out of all of this, Jess, technically, legally, the necklace is Stella's. She paid for it."

"This isn't about legality," Jess rages. "It's not even about you or me. This necklace"—she hastens it from her neck, nearly ripping the chain in her fury—"is about my life! And now you're demanding it back like you really don't get it! Just take it," she hisses, pushing against him in anger. "Take it and fuck off back to Ramsgate!"

Guy flinches.

"Yes, that's right," she says. "I've seen through the 'diamond family' bullshit." She glances down at the leopard-head ring. "You're nothing but a lying fake, Guy *Davis*."

He stares at her, mouth open. But before he can argue or say anything constructive, she is away, wielding her cane as though it's more a weapon than an aid.

Chapter Eighteen

THE BREAD IS DRY AROUND THE EDGES. IN HER SCRUTINY OF THE buffet, Aggie is underwhelmed. They should have known to cut the loaves last. No one likes a stale egg sandwich. She looks to Ed, who is busying himself with the bar staff, hopefully setting a limit on the tab; then to Marcus who is buried in a copy of *Gaming World*; and to Steph, who has her cheeks sucked in as she takes selfies. Mourning chic. Dear god.

It was a somber service, and now this wake, in the oldest of Shoreditch's pubs, promises to be quietly excruciating. Aggie is at least pleased with the bouquets of white lilies on the tables (not that Nancy would ever have complimented her for her efforts), which make up for the curly bread crusts. The guests are few. Jess will cite Nancy's old age and singular lifestyle as the cause of such a small crowd. No doubt she'll claim Nancy would have wanted it like this, far too forgiving to acknowledge that a certain disagreeableness of character drove everyone away.

Aggie looks cautiously over at her sister. Jess is no longer wearing *that* necklace, but it's hard to tell whether this is a good or bad thing. She hasn't spoken much this week. Today she looks wan, like a sad doll. Lost a bit of weight, perhaps? It shows in the hollowness of her eyes and the way she leans on her cane. Really, it's as if she's in a permanent state of semicollapse.

Hooray for Tim, who patiently fusses over her, brings her tea, finds her chairs, and rubs her shoulders. And thank goodness that the discussion regarding that "other" male distraction seems to have sunk in. Once the grief is out of the way, hopefully things will fall into place: Jess and Tim, the happy pair in their new home. The Hoppit House will get its spare room back. Steph will stop playing aunt-versus-mother. And Aggie herself will be reassured that the responsibility of her little sister is in good hands. Who knows, maybe this time next year, she'll be helping choose a wedding dress. She has the details of a great little bridal shop, specializing in vintage, right up Jess's street. A year after that, maybe she'll be selecting baby clothes. She'll have to impress the matter on Jess. That window of fertility doesn't stay open forever…

The family pile their plates with chicken wings and vol-au-vents, then gather at one of the beer-sticky wooden tables. The chat flits between school matters, favorite television, and cycling races. And then, just as Aggie is finishing her first glass of warm, white pub wine, a specter appears in the doorway: their dad, Richard Barrow. They have spoken little in the last two years and seen each other even less. Richard has gained weight and failed to buy new clothes to accommodate it. He has also, Aggie notices, lost a few more hairs. Overall, it is not a cheering sight.

Has Jess noticed? She glances at her sister, who is busy trading ketchup for butter. She knows Jess has found their father's disinterest difficult. Perhaps, thinks Aggie, this explains her poor choice in men. But here he is, Richard Barrow, come to pay his shabby respects. She'll have to get Steph to put her phone down and offer him a sausage roll. They must be polite. At least be polite. A funeral is definitely not the time to dredge up old hurts.

"Hello, girls," says Richard, with a sort of shuffling warmth.

"Hello, Dad," says Aggie, smoothing the way.

"This looks cozy…nice spread… Am I too late?"

"You missed the service, but you're in time for what's left of the buffet—"

Looks are passed around the table, no one quite sure what to say. It's Jess who relaxes the weirdness as she breaks into a startled smile, then shuffles along the bench, making space for her dad to sit. Aggie can see it in her eyes, that distinct blend of fondness and aversion, the one that makes her want to hug and punch him in one go—she knows it too well.

"Richard," says Ed. "Good that you've turned up. Something to drink? We're running a tab."

"Er…a lager would be nice, thanks."

Ed rises, clearly grateful for an excuse to exit the scene. *Typical*, thinks Aggie. No doubt he'll be hoping it will all be done and dusted in time for the rugby.

"Eileen and the twins send their condolences," says Richard. "They couldn't make it, what with school and everything—"

"Sure," says Aggie crisply.

"I've got to ask, did she…did she go quietly?"

"She did as it goes," says Jess. "I was there."

"Oh, Jessy," says Richard, eyeing her with some vague attempt at fatherly concern. "I hope you aren't—"

"What?"

"Too sad. After all, you were always her favorite."

Classic, thinks Aggie, lay it out square and blunt, rub it in. Jess: the favorite. They sit in silence, while Marcus wriggles and makes the table rattle.

"We weren't expecting you to come," says Jess eventually.

"Well, for all our differences," says Richard, "somewhere inside I had a soft spot for the old girl. She picked up the pieces when your mother passed. Did her bit."

He folds and unfolds his arms as though not quite sure where to place himself. His eyes dart from daughter to daughter. Aggie struggles to give him anything other than a hard-glazed glare, so he lingers on Jess.

"How are you doing, girl?"

"I'm okay, thank you. I'm lined up to see a specialist. It's not been a great week, but overall the hip's much better."

"And your jewelry? Last time you said you were setting up some kind of online jewel business. Is that—?"

He gestures to the butterfly charm pendant, which Jess has layered over a plain black shift dress. Aggie is so glad she's finally taken to it, such a sweet gesture from Tim. Okay, it's a little naff and indistinct, not Jess's usual style, but it's the thought that counts. And to be fair, it's surely a standard that husbands buy their wives a ropy bit of jewelry every now and again. Ed certainly has. The solution is simple: take it back to the shop, get vouchers instead.

❧

Tim holds Jess's knee, urged to protect her. Be polite, it's a funeral after all, but he knows the last time Jess spoke with her father, it wasn't pretty. There was some argument about how he'd stopped visiting her when she was broken in the hospital. His own daughter! What a selfish human. Suddenly, Tim feels glad for all the normality and stability his own upbringing has furnished him with. His dad, always there for him at birthdays, holidays, graduation, every cricket match, every cycling race. He'll pay it forward. He'll do that for Jess. He'll be there for her and their children. Always.

She's got his necklace on. It's a good sign. She'll never admit it, but it suits her. A more sedate look—perhaps it will help the world take her a bit more seriously. Whatever. He's just glad she's wearing it and that she's back on board. For a moment it seemed like he was losing her; like sand, the more he grasped, the more she slipped through his fingers. Perhaps it was the stress of losing her grandmother? He must be patient. And he *must* get her to apply for that teaching post. A proper focus might help curb her restlessness.

The cycle of life, he thinks. With every ending, there's a beginning. Nancy is gone, but the future is theirs. Momentarily he shuts his eyes, sees tiny hands, a little face staring back at him, a baby full of love and neediness. It was denied him last go-round, but this time…maybe in a year or two…he'll have his wish. He should get a ring maybe? Now that the charm necklace has been approved, maybe she trusts his jewelry choices. There's that place in London with all the posh diamonds. Hatton something? Hatton Garden. He digs out his phone and makes a note, when all this is settled, to speak to Aggie about ring ideas.

Obviously he should start by introducing himself to Jess's father, man to man.

"Mr. Barrow," he says, aiming for sleek geniality. "I'm Tim."

"Call me Richard."

"It's excellent to meet you at last, in spite of these sad circumstances. You're probably already aware, but I'm dating Jess. We're moving in together. Perhaps we should sit down, have a chat some time? Share a pint?"

He's not quite the in-law Tim imagined—golfing days, family lunches, walks in the forest. But there you go. Jess is the important one. Keep things upbeat, pull these tenuous family ties together.

"So." Tim stands up. "Another round, everyone?"

"No, no," says Richard. "Allow me."

"No, please, my turn," Tim insists.

"Honestly, it's my turn," says Richard.

"Yes," say Jess and Aggie together. "It's definitely your turn, Dad."

Guy paces, runs his hands through his curls. Timing. Perhaps the timing is wrong. Or completely right. How can he know? He just has to go for it. He stares at the pub door. Jess is in there. She's captive—although that's a terrible word—but the point is, he has to get her on the spot, grab her attention, and open her eyes. He can't let her make excuses and run away again. They could be great together. He knows it. And he's pretty certain, beneath the bluster, that she knows it too. He sighs, takes a breath. What is this? *Butterflies?* For the first time since childhood, he actually has butterflies. She—Jess of the bloody Doughnuts—is giving him butterflies. He can only hope she likes big, embarrassing displays of heartfelt honesty.

He twiddles his leopard ring, draws strength from its presence. He sighs again, then with a now-or-never push, he makes his way into the pub, spies her through the crowd.

Jess is weary. Her father, her sister, Tim…*all* of them seem hell-bent on crowding her today. She knows they mean well, but if they could see inside her head, they'd understand how scrambled it is. She just needs space, time to breathe. She gets up, clatters from the table, heads for the toilets, then halfway across the pub floor, she is stopped in her tracks…

Guy stands square in front of her, takes hold of her arms.

"Jess," he says, eyes more sparkly than ever; that impish, impulsive smile bursting from his face.

"Wha—what are you *doing* here?"

"Don't talk," he says, still smiling. "Just listen."

She glances around her, aware that everyone in the room is now looking in their direction.

"I'm really sorry about Nancy," he says. "I realize what she meant to you. Is that your family?" He nods to the table, the opened mouths. "They look like a good bunch." Then he lowers his voice. "Except for your sister, with the judgy eyes, which are boring into my back right now. Not convinced she's a fan, but...the thing is, Jess, what I've come to say is this—"

He fumbles in his pocket, pulls out a purple box. He stares at it, then offers it to her.

"Of course, if you'd rather stick with high-street replacements..." he says, scrutinizing the silver charm necklace dangling from her neck. "I mean, really, Jess. After all we talked about, please tell me you're only wearing that because your niece and nephew gave it to you."

"It was Tim, actually," she says, hoping he'll take the hint and keep his voice down. "Tim gave it to me."

Guy gives her a look, such a look, then blows a rush of air through his mouth.

"The thing is," he says, fingers trembling as he opens the box, "I made a mistake. I got all petulant and demanded the necklace back when I shouldn't have, because what I truly understand now is that this butterfly is meant for you."

He removes the True Love necklace from its insert and offers it out. Jess's mouth falls open, part shock, part wonder. The necklace, back where it belongs. She knows that everyone, including Tim and Aggie, and her father at the bar, are all watching; that a tide of outrage is about to descend on her. And yet she feels caught in the rare, alluring magic that the necklace imbues—the interplay, the spark it ignites between observer and observed. Not just a body ornament, but an enchantment.

"I've sorted things out with Stella," Guy explains. "I've told her I'm done, quitting the trap I've been in. I gave her back the money for the necklace. She thinks I've gone insane, and judging by her last few messages, she's pretty pissed off, but if that's what it takes to prove that I want to start something—"

"Start something?" Jess blinks, glances at Tim. "What do you mean?"

"I want to start an adventure. With *you*, Jess."

Before she can articulate a sound response, he cups her cheeks in his hands, takes his lips to hers, and kisses her with such passion and power that her eyes are forced shut and her body feels weightless. The rest of the room blurs. The smell of him, the feel of him; she tingles all over, melts into his touch, unable and unwilling to resist. His lips are so soft, his body warmth so soothing, but...

"Stop!" she cries, shaking her head. "You can't just turn up here with all this...fanfare. You can't come at a person, out of the blue, kiss them in the middle of their grandmother's wake, with all their family watching, and their boyfriend and—"

"Is that the bit that bothers you?" says Guy. "That your family are watching, because—"

"Oh, there is so much about this that bothers me, Guy. Don't you get it? We can't *do* this. It's not meant to be. I don't trust you. You're not the trustworthy type. And that's no good for me. We can have all the sparkly, doughnut-based moments we like, but if the foundation isn't there—"

Guy throws his head back, exasperated, but *still* smiling.

"Why are you so determined to shove me into a 'type,' Jess? I'm just...*me*. Sure, I'm kind of flawed. And, yes, I've got some questions to answer, but give me a chance. Get to know the me I am, versus the me you think I am. I can't promise we'll live happily ever after. I can't make assurances that we'll spend the next twenty years setting ourselves up with a mortgage, marriage, mini-mes, and life insurance. I won't guarantee that it'll be roses every minute of every day, but what I can tell you is this… From the moment we met, something clicked in my head. And I think it clicked in yours too. Am I right?"

"I–I—"

Her instincts curl and coil—that fear in her soul, so deep and primal, telling her she cannot, must not be fooled again.

"I am indeed Guy Davis." His eyes are wide and purposeful. "Which is a really bland, crappy name that I decided I didn't want, but that doesn't mean I'm not capable of being truthful. I mean, if you want the truth, Jess, the fact is, I started calling myself Guy van der Meer because it gave me confidence. With a name like that, I became important. I *felt* important. Suddenly, I was a diamond heir with a rich history, rather than Guy Davis from Ramsgate."

He holds up his leopard ring.

"It's not an heirloom, Jess. I bought it in a junk shop six years ago. My parents were nasty, penniless fuckups, so I grew up in foster homes. By the time I was sixteen, I'd had fourteen different addresses, six different schools, and no qualifications. But I wanted better for myself, so I moved to London and I made it work. I bought this ring with my first decent paycheck, then I made up a whole story in my head about how it had been left to me by my wonderful father."

He stares at it and laughs.

"Silly, really, but you know what? Sometimes when I look at it, I almost *believe* in that father."

He looks at Jess, eyes pained.

"I promise I'll tell you the truth about my life, about the games I've played, the mistakes I've made, and the ways in which I've risen above them, if you'll just give me the time. Because you're the one, Jess. You're the one I can be myself with."

She senses he's about to kiss her again. But there is Tim, lurching toward them with the most furious deputy head glower on his face.

"Mate," he says, coming between them.

Guy steps back.

"She's had enough, all right? I'm not sure what you think you're playing at here, but—"

"Oh, I'm not playing," says Guy. "I'm deadly serious."

"Wise guy, are you?" Tim sneers.

"Just Guy, actually."

Guy offers a handshake, but it has the air of a windup. Tim puffs out his chest, plays for dignity, but refuses the shake. After a moment, Guy retracts, turns it into waggle-fingered raspberry.

"How very mature," says Tim, then he looks to Jess. "Are you okay? Do you need me to get someone to escort this...desperado out of the pub?"

"Desperado?" says Guy. "What...you can't take a bit of healthy competition, my quote-unquote 'mate'?"

Tim inhales, eyes bulging.

"You're hardly competition," he growls. "She's with me. She isn't interested. You've teased her with her grandmother's necklace for weeks, and now you've got the cheek to barge into her family wake and act like you're some kind of jumped-up heroic Romeo. But my instinct is that you're merely a freeloader. Always were, always will be. Leopards don't change."

At this, a veil of anger shadows Guy's face. His whole body tenses. Tim stares him down.

Don't fight, Jess wills them. *Anything but that.*

Too late. Guy attempts to put Tim in his place with a dismissive flick of the hand. Tim flies back at him, dignity over, fists in the air. But being of otherwise gentle character, unaccustomed to pub brawls, he misses and stumbles into a stack of chairs. He gets up, wipes his brow, has a second go. On both sides, there is some shoving, scrapping, a definite attempt to tug hair. Then they stumble apart, breathless and messy. And then, just in time, Jess's dad returns with a tray of frothing amber pints.

"So." He grins, oblivious. "How are we getting on? Here you go, Tim. Get this down you and—"

Suddenly he spies the necklace in Jess's hands. The color drains out of his face and he drops the entire tray of drinks to the floor. Beer and foam and shards of glass fly everywhere, the sound reverberating around the pub. If they weren't watching the unfolding drama before, they will be now.

"Where…where did you get that?"

"From Nancy," says Jess sullenly. "She made me find it before she died."

"How?" He looks aghast. "How could she have? I made sure—"

Jess cocks her head.

"You knew about it?"

"Of course I bloody knew about it!" he yells, and then without a goodbye, he storms out of the pub.

⸙

"Well," says Aggie, smarting in the corner, her red lips pursed, "*this* has all gone how I hoped it would."

Meanwhile, regardless of what Tim would like to do to Guy, the bar staff save him the pleasure. They pick Guy up by the scruff of his shirt and walk him toward the door.

"You need some fresh air, mate."

"I'm not *your* mate either," Guy protests, but the staff are unmoved.

As he's carried away, he calls to Jess: "Let's have an adventure, you and me!"

Just make it stop, she wishes. It's too much. Too, too much. She drops her head, shuts her eyes.

"Join me!" he cries as he is dragged out of the door, the last of his dignity trailing after his feet. "Arms wide open!"

And then he is gone. And the pub is silent. And Jess feels like crawling into the biggest hole she can find and never coming out.

But first she has to face Aggie, whose big-sister scowl says: *Jessica Taylor, you've got some explaining to do.* And Ed, who has leaped into brotherhood mode, ushering Tim back to the family table, smoothing his shirt, telling him to stay cool. And Marcus who is giggling uncontrollably into his games console—who'd blame him? And then of course Steph, dearest Steph, her eyes on stalks, unlikely to ever take her aunt's romantic advice seriously again.

Within all of the noise, however, Jess also has her father's appearance and sudden disappearance to cogitate on. His reaction to the necklace, what was that about? Oh god. The necklace, she hugs it. A bolt of emotion strikes her—the realization that Guy brought it back for her. All this drama, just so he could give her the necklace. And now she has them both, Tim's charm chain and the Taylor butterfly. Their twin presence is almost suffocating.

She looks across at Tim, the Taylor-Hoppit clan rallying around him, patting his back. Their eyes meet. He gives her a withering look and mouths *I love you*. He'll be apologetic later, mortally embarrassed. He'll have the good sense to admit he acted rashly, that he was an idiot, but he'll also tell her he'd do the same again, if it means protecting their relationship. He'll always be loyal.

Yet her heart screams to check on Guy. She owes him that at least.

She finds him in the street. He is pacing, looking out for a cab. His lip is bloody.

"Wait!" she cries. "Oh god! Is your mouth okay?"

He turns to her.

"Bah, it's nothing," he says with dented pride.

"I'm sorry," she whispers. "Tim was just…really… He isn't normally like that…although, to be fair, you did kind of piss on his patch."

"Maybe," says Guy, half-smiling, running a hand through his curls. "But to be honest, Jess, I'd do it again. I've got an idea for us, you see. I was thinking—"

Jess sighs. Here he goes again. He is torturing *himself*, never mind her.

"One last shot," he says. "Just listen. I'm going away—and I know it's a whirlwind—but I think you should come with me. That tip-off I got at the Capital Gala was about an antique ruby brooch in Cape Verde. For a good old boy who wants it for his sick wife. Decent commission. I'm taking the 19:20 ship from Southampton two weeks from Saturday. I thought you might prefer a ship to a plane. Who doesn't like to cruise? We'll travel in style. Old school. Treasure hunter's way."

Jess shuts her eyes. Somewhere in her mind there is space for this, a space that says YES! But it's not a space she can venture to right now. All she needs now…is grounding. Guy nods, as though the action will persuade her.

"I know there's Education Tim to think of," he continues, "but what can I say? He's an arsehole, leave him. Except…he's not, is he? He's obviously a nice person—despite calling me a desperado and trying to punch me—and he gets the backing of your sister and he's got one of those really big Fitbits, which only super-reliable, sporty dudes wear, but"—he gives her wink—"he's not the guy for you. *I'm* the Guy. Hey, did you hear what I did there?"

"Everything's a joke to you," says Jess, exasperated.

"But you like a joke."

"Guy, you have to leave me alone."

"But—"

"I feel secure with Tim, secure and happy. We have plans. We have a future. Meeting you, all the chemistry between us, I kind of think it's been a test, just a test to see whether Tim and I really are meant to work out—"

"A test? Jess, I think about you all the time. Honestly, it's like I'm *addicted* to you. And yet…you're trying to tell me you think it's just a test. Are you kidding?"

Jess tenses, looks down.

"And we passed," she says solemnly. "I know what I need in life, and I'm sorry, Guy, but it's not you."

He frowns, the hurt etched into his face.

"What, Jess, what is it about me that you're so afraid of?"

She shrugs, holds up her walking cane.

"*This*," she says, suddenly teary. "Going through all this again."

"I promise I will *never* pack you a parachute—"

"Not literally. Just…the hurt of being let down by someone I thought adored me." She backs away. "You said it yourself. You're not able to give me guarantees. But Tim is. It's his way. So if you really care about me, if you really care, then you'll leave me alone."

A cab pulls up. Guy opens the door, hopeful that in the final moment she'll change her mind. But Jess stands resolute, emotions in lockdown. Eventually he climbs in, briefly dipping his head to acknowledge the butterfly necklace at her hands, then slams the door and looks ahead. The cab moves away. And this time Jess doesn't attempt to chase after it.

Chapter Nineteen

Jess puts the necklace in its purple box and tucks it away in a drawer. The next day, she adds the boat ticket Guy has sent her, promised passage to Cape Verde, along with a photograph of the prize ruby brooch. His presumptuousness, among several other attributes, is both his allure and his downfall, she thinks. He sends her a message asking if she received the ticket. Has she possibly come to her senses? She doesn't respond, and whether respecting her request for space or having moved onto the next, he doesn't message again.

Tim takes over and Jess lets him. He soothes the frustration she holds, not just toward Guy, but toward all the exes who'd promised her the earth, then only delivered the topsoil. His even temperament wraps her in comfort, and they get on with the business of selecting the kitchen countertop and appliances. He takes her on a cheer-up spa day, even though saunas make her break out in hives. He cooks for her. Lets her watch what she likes on Netflix. And in the moments he's not with her, he bombards her with photos of Persian cats.

"We should definitely get a pet," he says. "Our first shared love. I've heard it's good practice for parenthood—and good for the nerves."

In anticipation of the move, Jess starts packing up her things. With every filled box and suitcase, she feels a step closer to the rest of her life and it feels…good. She even boxes up her jewelry, contemplates the possibility of that teaching post. Aggie is all for it.

"Very wise to maximize your salary before maternity leave comes around. And think of the pension. Obviously you need your pension sorted out, Jessica."

Any lingering enthusiasm for the "charming thrills" end of the boyfriend spectrum is quashed completely when Steph comes home early one afternoon in a flood of tears. At first, fearing a tragedy, Jess suggests she call Aggie—a mother needs to be the first port of call in such circumstances—until Steph begs her not to, then finally explains, between deep, racking sobs, the reason for her anguish.

"He's dumped me and gone off with Lina Bird, just because it says on her Twitter that she volunteers for Greenpeace, and he thinks it'll make him look cool—"

"Jared?"

"Yes."

More wailing. What should Jess say? There, there. Plenty more fish. It'll all be okay.

"What a fucking rat! He doesn't deserve you, Stephanie Hoppit!"

"But I'm soooooo in love with him. He's my one. Always. I'll *never* stop loving him."

"You will," says Jess softly. "One day, really soon. You'll meet someone else, and they'll show you a different kind of love. And it'll be a better love. Or maybe it will be worse. But either way, it will teach what you *do* want in life and what you don't."

Steph wipes her tears with her sleeve.

"Promise?"

"Absolutely."

"Thanks," sniffs Steph. "But don't tell my mum, will you? She'll only say 'told you so.'"

"I won't. But I think *you* should. Your mum can actually be great in a heartache. Lord knows, she's nursed me through a few and never once has she said 'I told you so.' Well, once or twice, maybe, but—"

"What about that man at Nancy's funeral?"

Jess winces.

"You know the one I'm talking about, the one you kissed in front of everyone."

"I didn't kiss him, Steph. He kissed me. There's a difference."

"Yeah, whatever. Mum told me I wasn't allowed to ask you about it, but—"

"You will anyway."

"Were you having an affair?"

"*No*. It was… I was… We had a bit of chemistry between us…a lot of chemistry, in fact…but…in the end, it wasn't to be."

"But you got the feels?"

"Yes. No. Look, if you must know, a few years ago, yes, I would have totally 'got the feels' for someone like that, because I used to love freedom and spontaneity and doing crazy shit at 4:00 a.m. But now I want something different. I want to feel grounded."

Suddenly she feels it, the sense of herself falling through the air, the parachute above her, the rush of the clouds.

"I'm happy with Tim."

"Oh."

Steph looks disappointed.

"You'll get it one day," says Jess. "When you've been around the block and learned that shiny exteriors can be quick to tarnish."

"It's just… That kiss, Aunty, it was…proper."

Jess stalls.

"No," she says with a sigh. "It was a show. Some men like to put on a show. That doesn't mean we should applaud."

Later that afternoon, when she's packing jewelry, her heart a little weary, Jess's father calls. His name and number appearing on her phone is an eerie sight. She resists the urge to answer, having felt the wound of him abandoning her too many times, but then he calls a second time and then a third. Finally, her curiosity caves.

"Hello?"

"Jess, oh Jess, you answered. I didn't know if you—"

"What do you want?"

"I realize I may have some explaining to do. I'm sorry I left the wake like that. It wasn't my plan to. Could…could we meet?"

Jess exhales, stares at the wall clock.

"When?"

"I'm your way this afternoon. I thought, maybe, we could lay some flowers on Nancy's grave, if…if you're up for it?"

"Yes," says Jess, too tired to battle. "Yes, okay."

They meet at the entrance gates of Abney Park Cemetery, both with bunches of flowers. Jess has assembled some wildflowers and bracken, knowing they were Nancy's favorites. Her dad clutches some sad petrol-station affair. At least he has made an effort with his jacket and hair, a little less shambolic than before. He smiles at her, then his attention catches on the necklace, which she has worn deliberately, provocatively perhaps.

"Looks nice on you, Jessy," he forces himself to say. "Do you wear it a lot?"

"Yes. It makes me feel close to Nancy."

"So where exactly did you find it?" he says, eyeing her.

"At auction. I'd been spending a lot of time searching auction sites. Nancy described this necklace to me in painstaking detail. She was passionate about it. So for months I kept my eye out, and then one day it popped up on my screen and I kind of knew straightaway, it was the one. Coming home to us. Like it was meant to."

"Because I have to tell you, Jess, when I sold it, I never for a second thought I'd see it again. Honestly, I took it to the most obscure backstreet dealer I could find."

Jess narrows her eyes.

"So it was you? You got rid of it? You're the reason it came out of our family—"

"Yes."

"But it was my mother's heirloom," she quarrels. "All that history...it was never yours to sell."

"No," he says limply. "You're right. It wasn't."

They walk together through the graves, row after row of mossy gray headstones, some elaborate, some simple.

"So why *did* you sell it?" she asks, after a moment.

Her dad sighs.

"You know your mother believed it was charmed," he says, "that it had mystical power. She had some daft idea that it lured me to her. Some French nonsense. There's a word on the back, right?"

"Yes," says Jess. "It just says '*OUI.*'"

"That's right. She used to say she finally understood the meaning of the word the day she met me, that I made her come out of herself. Carmen was a shy one, you see. Shy and thoughtful. But I gave her confidence. Believe it or not, Jess, I was once a social dynamo."

"Hmm."

"The thing is she'd had a funny old upbringing, Carmen, after her dad died—"

"Paul?"

"Yes, that's right. He died when she was young, and soon after, Nancy went off to do her own thing, so Carmen was left in the care of her grandmother."

"You mean Anna?"

"Oh. Yes. You know all this?"

"It's been of interest, yes."

They walk on, the birdsong following them.

"The thing is, Anna, she had a lot of opinions about how Carmen should be. She was overbearing. Quite a snob, hell-bent on marrying Carmen off to the nearest available banker. 'Look for cuff links,' she used to say, as if that meant anything. But two days after

Carmen's fifteenth birthday, Nancy came back into her life, tanned and wrinkled and very different from how Carmen said she remembered her. Apparently her hair was spiked and dyed purple. She'd lost a front tooth, gained an ear piercing. You can imagine what Anna had to say. I mean, how's that for a mother figure?"

That's Nancy, thinks Jess.

"One thing that hadn't changed, however, was that Nancy was still wearing the necklace. Turns out it had traveled around the world with her."

At this, Jess tingles, feels the beat of the butterfly's energy.

"Then that night," says Richard, "she gave the necklace to Carmen, said it was *her* turn, made her promise to wear it."

"And did she?"

"Not straightaway. Under Anna's influence she was busy with a secretarial course. Then the following summer she enrolled in art college, much more her thing, where she befriended two punks with shaved hair and safety pins on their jackets. They took her to a music festival, told her to dress wild. Since the butterfly necklace was the wildest thing Carmen owned, with a pair of jeans and a cardigan, that's what she wore."

"What festival?"

"Glastonbury, 1982."

Jess blinks. "Glastonbury?"

"The mud was biblical, Jess. I don't think Carmen had seen anything like it. Within an hour, she'd lost track of her college friends, so she forced herself through her shyness, bought a pint of cider, and trudged across the mudscape. She came to the main stage, where

Jackson Browne was performing—someone she remembered her father talking about, one of the last musicians he'd photographed before he died. She made her way to the front and stared at the stage.

"She had little more than a trash bag to protect her from the rain, but as the crowds danced and cheered, she was happy. It didn't matter that she was freezing, soaked, and *way* out of her depth. She was just so happy. Then someone fell into her, caked from head to toe in gray sludge, as though he'd been bodysurfing in the mud. He looked like one of *those*, Jess, the class fool who wants everyone's attention and plays it for laughs. Carmen gasped and backed away, then through the filth, she saw the shine of his piercing green eyes, which then fell to the wings of the necklace poking through her bin-liner cloak. 'I'm Richard,' he said and their faces lit up with smiles."

"You?" says Jess, amazed. "You met at Glastonbury?"

She can't help but smile, the thought of her frumpy, fusty father in a field full of rock music and chai tents.

"Oh yeah. We were right in the thick of it. Me with my mud suit on, dancing like a maniac, and your mum with her necklace. And that was it for me. In all that rain and mud, there she was, my Carmen, a jewel in the dirt."

"But if the necklace brought you together," Jess presses, her bitterness resurfacing, "why get rid of it the minute she's dead?"

Richard bows his head, folds his arms.

"Perhaps the magic of it wore off," he says, shoving his hands in his pockets. "Because it didn't remind me of our union in the end. It reminded me of what went wrong. I loved her, Jess. I adored her, but—"

"Don't tell me. She met someone else. The necklace somehow led her to her true love, her soul mate…and all the rest."

He glares at her.

"Why do you say that?"

"Because I get the feeling that's what the necklace does. Because that's what all the women in my family have done when in possession of it. They've run off and found happiness with some random other man."

"No, Jess. It wasn't your mother who met someone else. It was *me*. With Eileen. You have to understand… Your mother and I, we were in love, insanely in love, but we grew apart. Having you girls changed me. Suddenly it was all on my shoulders. I stopped being the person she'd first fallen for, the fun, zany guy. I got serious, working all the time, worrying about money, taking it out on her, yelling and sulking."

"That still doesn't explain why you sold off her necklace—"

He stops again, breathes slowly. He looks beaten, she thinks. All this has beaten him.

"After her death," he says, "I felt so angry. Angry at the world. Angry at myself. Angry at Nancy who was on at me constantly, clearly blaming me, not for your mother's stroke, but… Her final year, it wasn't a happy one. We were arguing a lot. I'd started my thing with Eileen. The marriage became toxic. Honestly, given everything that was going on, it's a miracle you girls turned out so well—"

"That's debatable," says Jess solemnly.

"Nancy believed it was my fault that her daughter's last months were a misery. Of course, I wasn't to know they were her last months

at the time. Oh, Jess, it was all so sudden. One minute she was standing at the sink, washing mugs. The next…" He sighs. "Hindsight,
eh? How differently I'd do it if I could go back. Anyway, after she
died, that necklace sat in the house, and it was as if it were glaring
at me, some kind of cruel souvenir of what we'd had, what we—
what *I*—had thrown away. Eventually I couldn't take it anymore, so I
wrapped it in a carrier bag and took it to a dealer on the Commercial
Road. Got twenty quid for it, which I drank away in a weekend."

"Jesus, Dad! Do you know how much it's now worth?"

He shrugs.

"When Nancy discovered I'd sold it, we had a crazy, crazy argument. Your sister might remember. It all happened in front of her.
Nancy called me a coward and a shit, and I told her she was a cold-
hearted madwoman who'd failed her own daughter. And that was it,
the fault line in our relationship. We worked together to do what we
could for you girls, but we were never friendly again."

"No," says Jess. "I saw that."

"She really resented Eileen and the twins, but maybe one day
you'll understand… For me, that was my chance to put the mistakes
behind me, get things right, even if it meant"—he looks down—
"failing you girls."

As he says this, he steps back, stalled by regret. A storm of emotions whips through Jess's soul, and she has no idea what one will fly
out first. She breathes hard, then she leans forward on the tips of her
toes and kisses him once, on the cheek—because in spite of it all, he
was, is, and always will be her father. And he has a tear in his eye.
And she now knows that he is sorry, truly, deeply sorry.

A few steps on, they find Nancy in the sun. The earth is still fresh. Jess kneels down and places her flowers at the stone, while her father places his hand on her shoulder.

"In spite of everything," he says, "there was something about the old girl I admired. I mean…she was a one."

"Yes," says Jess, "she really was."

They walk on together, take the long path around to the exit.

"Oh, look," says Richard as they pass the final row of graves. "Talking of the past, that there is your great-grandmother's headstone."

"It is?"

"Anna Elizabeth Taylor. Like the film actress."

Jess blinks.

"That's *her*? That's Anna?"

"What? You mean, you didn't know? I thought that's why you chose Abney Park Cemetery—"

"We didn't," says Jess. "It was stipulated in Nancy's will. We didn't know there was a family connection. You know what Nancy was like. She didn't talk about the past. So…do you really think that's our Anna?"

"Oh yes, your mother brought me here when we were dating. She said it gave her peace to be here. I only knew Anna briefly, but as I said, she was quite a force. Once engaged to a movie producer. And did you know Nancy was—"

"Born in Hollywood," they both say together, smiling as they catch each other's eye.

Before they move on, Jess kneels beside Anna's grave, wishes she had more flowers.

"Anna Elizabeth Taylor," she reads, "1913–1982."

Then her gaze catches on the headstone beside it.

"Archie Marshall Jossop. 1914–1983. Beloved to Anna."

She gasps. Her eyes well up as the resonance sinks in: Anna and Archie, so they *were* reunited.

"Oh my," she says. "Right here. There's a love story right here."

"There certainly is," says her dad. "Archie was an old boy Anna knew from her Hollywood days. Your mum was rather fond, said he made Anna happy."

"Tell me," says Jess.

"From what I gather, it happened out of nowhere. Still early days for Carmen and me, so I was on my best behavior, trying to impress. Carmen had been out, back to Denmark Street to sign paperwork for her late father's business premises. That afternoon she returned to the house with a guest. I remember the moment…the way he walked in beside her. 'Well, I'll be damned!' he said, with his GI Joe accent. 'If it isn't Anna Taylor!' An old boy, he was, face lined, salt-and-pepper gray, eyes near disappeared into wrinkles when he smiled. But how he smiled—and how he talked! 'Oh, Anna,' he said, 'you're not gonna believe this, but there I was, making my way down Denmark Street!'

"He claimed he was musically inclined, in the market for a new guitar, that he'd been browsing the shops when he bumped into Carmen. He'd had to look twice because he recognized her face, but couldn't get the age right in his head. Then he spotted the necklace around her neck. He ran straight after her, asked outright: 'You're not related to an Anna Taylor, are you?' 'Well, sure,' said Carmen. 'She's my grandmother!'"

Jess smiles, delighted. "So what happened then?"

"He came back with Carmen and joined us for tea. 'Oh, Anna,' he said, 'have I had a life!' He told us all about how he'd taken off from his family farm when the war needed Americans, that he thought he'd be fighting for glory, then found himself running for his life. He said it had messed with his head, and for a while he'd lost his way. When all that nonsense was over, he decided to stay in England, try his luck in the music industry."

"So?" says Jess.

"He was tone deaf. Anyway, he got on with life, got himself a little business, wholesale belts and handbags. Did all right in the end, five warehouses and a nice place in Holland Park. 'It's not corn farming, anyhow,' he told us. Do you know, he'd lived in London for twenty-two years before bumping into Carmen. Married once. Divorced once. Three grown kids. But the way he looked at Anna… even I felt it. He talked to her about brisket, had a lot to say about brisket. But all I could see was Anna smiling from the depths of her soul, flinging her bony, seventy-year-old arms around his shoulders and saying: 'Archie Jossop, I've been waiting for you!'"

"Oh wow!" Jess sniffs, wipes her tears—happy tears. "So the necklace finally brought them back together!"

"Yes, I suppose it did," says her dad. "He certainly became a fixture after that. He and Anna were inseparable."

"Do you have more stories?"

"Plenty."

"Then maybe we should talk more," she says.

"Yes," says her dad kindly, "maybe we should."

"I'd like that."

"Me too. Perhaps…in a few weeks you could come over, you and Aggie, come for lunch. See the twins. And Eileen, she'd love to see you. She's always asking."

"Yes," says Jess.

"And bring…Whatshisname?"

"Tim."

"That's it, Tim."

"Did you like him? You know we're moving in together—"

"Yeah. He told me. Yeah, he was…really pleasant. But I kind of liked that other fellow, the bounder with the kiss. Now *that* one had something about him."

Jess sighs, throws her face to the sky.

"Oh, please. Not you as well."

"The thing is, Jessy, I learned the hard way. I ignored my heart and followed my head. And in doing that, I messed up the thing that mattered most. Your mother was the love of my life. Eileen, she's a worthy second, but your mum was the one. And I blew it with her because I was so fussed about saving money and being sensible and keeping control. Don't make the same mistake I did. Listen to your heart, girl. Go and have fun while you can. Life's too short." He pauses, then adds, "Do you know what your mum would have said?"

"What?"

"Trust the necklace."

Chapter Twenty

TIM IS ALONE IN HIS CLASSROOM, SURROUNDED BY TEXTBOOKS AND papers, timetabling staff for the forthcoming school year. He sees Jess approach and smiles.

"A lunchtime surprise! To what do I owe this pleasure?"

But immediately he senses something's different.

There is apprehension in her face, a tightness in her brow. She is wearing that old-fashioned butterfly necklace again and, somehow, the fact of this feels significant. He clicks the lid on his pen, lays it in front of him. The corridors echo. The late August sun shines through the skylights, casting shadows on the freshly polished rubber floor. In a week it will be covered in scuffs as the pupils of Baxter Academy return to drag their chairs and trample each other's rucksacks. There is something about a school when it's empty, he thinks, that feels so…expectant. He smiles again, and it wallops him in the chest, the sense of what's coming, what he has known would come all along.

"Hmm," he says, rocking back on his chair. "Something's up?"

Jess smiles, but there are telltale signs of old tears in her eyes. He can at least take gratitude from the fact that this is difficult for her.

"I've been doing some thinking," she says.

"Sounds ominous."

She clutches her hands in front of her. The folds of her tea dress—the kind he loves her wearing—ripple against her body. She looks so delicate and he wants to put his arms around her, to protect her, but…this is not what she wants. He understands that now.

"I get the feeling I know what you've come here to say," he says as gently as he can. He isn't, never was, and never will be an arsehole. It's hurting her to do this, and so it should, but he'll make it easy. In a few hours' time, he'll meet Duff in the Star. He'll drink too many pints, have a cry, get a kebab, punch a wall on the way home. But to her, he'll be a gentleman.

"Come here," he says, taking her hand, pulling her close, pushing his own hurt aside.

A tear trickles down her cheek. He wipes it with the tip of his finger.

"I think the world of you," she whispers. "You've given me so much. You've restored my confidence. You've made me feel loved when I was lost. You've offered me a home. Even a job! But, above all, you've showed me that there really are smart, kind, mature men who can cope with conversations about babies and house buying and plans for the future. But"—the tears flow freely now—"as much as I'd like to share all of that with you, in my heart, I know I can't. I'm not ready. I might never be ready. I'm not…*wired* that way."

"It's okay," he says, squeezing her hand. "It's okay. I knew. I *knew* it was coming. I've denied it for ages. I've been trying, *trying* to grasp on to you, but I could tell you were always edging away. And that's what you have to do. I get it."

She sniffs, reaches into her bag, takes out the key to the Stratford apartment.

"This is yours," she says, pressing it into his hand.

It's a sting to the soul, but he braces himself, smiles through it.

"Thanks," he says, closing his fingers around the key, making a fist. "So what now?"

"I'm thinking of going on a trip," she says.

"With *him*?"

"Maybe," she says after a pause. "I'm really sorry."

"Oh god—"

He tips his head back and groans, the leaden truth hammering into him.

"The fact is, Jess, that day at your grandmother's wake, when he stormed in and kissed you and behaved like a nob and…as mad as I was, and how insane it all was, deep down, I *knew*. I could never kiss you like that, with so much *pizzazz*. It's not my way. But it's *your* way. So…I understand."

Now she sobs.

"Oh Jesus! You're *so* good! And you know what? One day really soon you'll meet someone who's perfect for you and you'll blow them away." She gives a wry little laugh. "Is it right that I already feel jealous of them?"

"No, it's not," says Tim, a little more bitterly than intended, "because you've made your choice, but…thanks for the compliment."

She sighs, frowns, then kisses him lightly and walks away.

For a moment he feels proud that he's been so magnanimous, then the numbness engulfs him, then the sadness. Because in his mind's eye, he sees his dreams—a home and a family with Jessica Taylor—now ghosts on the breeze. And through the silence, the tick-tock of the wall clock creeps into his consciousness. The sound makes him panic.

Jess hastens to the exit, sorrow like a rock in her throat. He took it so well, which says everything about his temperament. He was, *is* a lovely human. In her wretchedness, she can only question her judgment. Has she just taken a pass on the best option she might ever have? Thrown away serious potential…for *what*? Her head and heart do battle again.

But as she reaches the door, she catches sight of the "who's who" staff photographs in the lobby, spots three new starters beaming out. One of them is an attractive fortysomething woman with auburn waves and an open smile. She is wearing a shiny charm necklace, not dissimilar from the one that Tim bought Jess; and beneath her photo, her interests are listed as history, cricket, and cycling. Jess smiles, feels the bud of hope returning. There is someone for everyone. As she exits, a second wave of emotion washes over her, and this one is elation. Elation mixed with clarity.

She finds the ticket in the drawer where she hid it, trying to forget its presence. She checks the time and, with a rush of adrenaline, realizes there are only four hours until the boat leaves. She messages Guy.

Are you still sailing? Doughnuts x

No reply. He really has taken her hint and left her alone. But if she's to take the chance, she can't afford to wait for his acknowledgment. In haste, she throws her favorite dresses and jewels into her traveler's backpack. A toothbrush. Medication. Face wipes. Sandals. Trainers. Swimsuit. Notebook. What else? What, really, is this trip all about? How long will it last? Where will it lead? All these questions—and she doesn't want the answers. The not knowing is the thrill, a vibrant reminder of what it is to go chasing into the unknown, following an urge, hunting for treasure, whatever that may be.

As she drags her backpack down the stairs, clattering her cane against the banisters, she hears the front door click. Aggie flusters through, takes one look at Jess's baggage, and balks.

"What? You're not moving already, are you? I thought the flat wasn't finished until October?"

Jess sighs, braces herself.

"Actually, I'm not moving into the flat."

"Oh—?"

"Actually, I broke up with Tim."

"You...*broke up*?"

Aggie's mouth drops open.

"Oh, come on, Aggie. Surely you twigged. You know me better than anyone."

"But...*Tim!* Perfect Tim. Lovely Tim, with his really good job." She blinks, the horror building as she processes. "You can't. You... *can't.* What are you going to do? How are you going to live?"

Jess sighs.

"Actually, I'm going away for a while."

"Where?"

"Guy bought me a boat ticket. To Cape Verde. To find a long-lost ruby for an old general."

Now Aggie is incredulous.

"You cannot be serious, Jess? I *urge* you. This is madness. Utter, reckless madness. Besides, I thought…I thought we were *done* with all of that—"

"No, Aggie, *you* were done. I was always…confused. I've listened to you enough, too much probably. I value your opinion and I love you to the ends of the earth, but you need to understand that I'm different than you. I want different things from life, and that doesn't make me better off or worse off. Just different."

"Oh, Jessy—"

Her ire now turns to tears. Jess softens, takes her hands.

"Aggie, this is about me. Not what you want for me. But what *I* want for me."

"But can you trust that man? He has traits—and you *know* what I'm talking about. This isn't the first time you've chased after a charming rake. You hardly know him. What risk are you willing to take, after everything?"

"I realize it's nuts, but it's making me feel *alive* again. I don't think I want a settled life. I don't even know if I want children. I adore yours, but nothing in me seems to want my own. Although I tell myself I do because…that's what's expected. But I can't funnel myself into the wrong-shaped life, just because the world assumes it of me. I'm saying no. Not now. Maybe in the future, but not now. Please, you have to understand—"

"Oh god," Aggie sobs, "why do I feel like my nexus of control is collapsing?"

She squeezes her sister super tight.

"I love you to the ends of the earth too," Aggie whispers. "And I'm proud of you. And…maybe, deep down, maybe I wish I was more like you. So okay, you have my permission to go with Guy. Because, believe it or not, sometimes…sometimes *I* wish I could let go and do something out there too."

Jess brushes the teary waves of hair from her sister's face.

"Aggie," she says, smiling, "you can do whatever you want to do. You're a Taylor."

She catches sight of the time.

"Oh shit. If I don't leave now, I won't make it. Oh—" .

She dithers. She hasn't thought this through.

"Where are you headed?"

"Southampton dock."

"That's miles away. Jesus, Jess, how were you planning to get there?"

"I was thinking train, but—"

"Give me your bag," says Aggie. "I'll drive you."

"Really?"

Jess beams at her sister.

"I've been looking for an excuse to go flat out in the Merc. Ed doesn't allow me to go over sixty."

"Roof down?"

"Obviously."

And with matching grins, they exit the house, jump into the

car, and take off, almost literally, leaving Ed, who is just wheeling his bike up the street, to blink and wonder, oblivious to the unfolding Thelma and Louise excitement in the air.

"There. It's *there*," says Jess, pointing at the sign for the passenger terminal.

Aggie swings the car right.

"Shall I drop you? Shall I park? Is there time?"

Jess checks her phone. Half an hour to spare. But Guy still hasn't replied to her message. The thought dawns on her that all this go-get-your-man exhilaration might be for nothing. Maybe he has found a better prospect, started chasing that instead. Or worse, has slunk back to the kept-soul convenience of Stella Weston.

"I don't know, Aggie. I think, drop me. I'll figure it out."

If she's about to be stood up, Jess would rather be stood up alone, away from an audience.

"Okay," says Aggie, "but if you need me… I won't drive home just yet. And you'll call when you get there? And you'll send us lots of pictures? And when you get back—"

"We'll come for Hoppit Sunday lunch."

"Promise."

"Of course," says Jess. "And…one more thing…I had a chat with Steph last week. I think she and Jared have had a wobble—"

"Hooray!" cries Aggie.

"Just go gently with her, won't you?"

Aggie growls.

"The sooner that pleb is out of her life—"

"Aggie, perspective! When we were young, our dad had to worry about whether our boyfriends were sneaking us into illegal all-night raves and plying us with fake ecstasy. If all you've got to worry about is whether Jared is going to lecture you that eggs Benedict is a sin or that carbon neutral is the only way forward, then count yourself lucky. He sounds like one of the good guys."

"But I want her to have options—"

"She's sixteen."

"Meet someone who'll give her what she needs—"

"Sixteen."

"Someone who's got their act together—"

"Aggie! Steph is only *sixteen*. Let her go on her journey."

Jess smiles at her sister, then kisses her cheek.

"Thank you," she says.

"Thank *you*," says Aggie.

And with that, the Taylor sisters part.

With her backpack and her cane and a pair of sturdy walking boots, Jess marches through the terminal. Her legs feel good. The discomfort in her hip is distinctly diminished. Perhaps, she thinks, the pain is starting to become a lesser feature of her daily life. Through the glass walls she can see huge six-decker cruisers jostling for dock space, rich with the promise of exotic destinations and glamorous captain's table dinners. At the kiosk, she hands over her ticket and her passport, all the while furtively looking around her, looking for *him*. It was a simple question she'd messaged, requiring a simple answer. She breathes slowly, tries to still her nerves. Now that she has said goodbye to Aggie, it all feels very final. Sudden limbo, anchors raised.

"Oh boy," she reassures herself. "It'll be fine. Whatever happens in the next ten minutes, it will be *fine!*"

"You all right?" says the man in the ticket office.

"Oh yes," she says, hands on hips, grinning to mask her spiraling apprehension.

"You've only got twenty minutes. If you hurry down there, you'll find the foot passenger entrance. That'll get you straight on deck, then someone will show you to your cabin."

"Thank you," she says.

But then a thought catches. Jess raises her hand to her neck, feels the pulse of the necklace, its butterfly wings beating the rhythm of her heart.

"Excuse me," she asks, "how do I get back to the visitor parking?"

The man shrugs. "At the other end of the terminal, but…you'll struggle to make it there and back before—"

"I'll chance it," says Jess, staggering away as fast as her crooked hip will allow.

She pulls out her phone, calls Aggie, who answers immediately.

"What? Is everything okay?"

"There's something I forgot," says Jess. "Where are you parked?"

"Next to a yellow bollard… Wait…I can see you… I'm waving—"

Jess spots Aggie in the distance and, pulling on the straps of her backpack, works up to a run—the first since the accident. She arrives panting, flustered, a little overawed, then hastily removes the necklace and hands it to Aggie.

Aggie blinks. "No offense," she says, "but I don't want this. It's really not my style."

"Not you, Aggie. It's for Steph. Give it to Steph. Tell her…when the time is right… It just might help."

Jess smiles, gives her bewildered sister a final hug, then runs/hobbles back to the terminal. She reaches the boarding gate, shoves through it just in time, a sense of joy blooming within her, freedom taking over. She looks around the deck, but he isn't anywhere. A crew member offers to show her to her cabin. Perhaps he'll be waiting inside or has left some hint of his presence—an item of clothing or a note telling her where and what time they should meet…

But the cabin is undisturbed, pristine. Ah well.

Jess flops back on the bed and stares at the ceiling. Her mind swirls. What was it Bevan Floyd told her about soul mates…that they fly into your life for a reason, then they leave. Certainly, it happened to Minnie and Emery. Then Anna had a long time without her Archie. Nancy lost Paul. Carmen lost herself. And now…Jess is here and Guy is not. Could it be that he brought her to this point, then fluttered away?

She gets up again, goes to the outdoor deck, walks the length of it. The sun is just starting to set, a smear of peach and pink. As the ship moves way, its huge hulk heaving from the land, the thought that she is on this journey alone is immense all around her. She leans over the balustrade, faces the breeze, the great ocean ahead. She feels both elated and sad, but it will be okay, she tells herself. She is a Taylor and it will be okay. Guy played his part—a soul mate's way—challenging her, helping her move forward in her life. Maybe that's enough?

She grips the balustrade, blinks back her tears, takes a bolstering breath.

But then, just as she's about to return alone to her cabin, she feels a hand slide beside hers. She looks down, sees two emerald leopard eyes gazing up at her.

"You're here!" she gasps.

"So are you," says Guy.

"*Oui*," she says with an enormous smile.

He takes hold of her shoulders, then pauses and scans her neck, a glimmer of concern on his face. "But…you're not wearing your butterfly?"

"I passed it on," she says. "I think…I think it served its purpose for me."

And, sure enough, as she takes in the glow of Guy's face, she realizes the vibrancy between them is there regardless, necklace or otherwise. Her heart beats so fast, it's as if a billion plique-à-jour butterflies have taken it over. And they are all with her, she thinks, agreeing with her: Minnie, Anna, Nancy. And Carmen.

The boat sounds its horn. The fresh sea air whips up.

"So," says Guy, "are you ready for an adventure, Doughnuts?"

Her eyes flash with the thrill.

"I couldn't be more ready," she replies.

Then they curve together, laughing and kissing, the entire world ahead of them, the sunset in their eyes—and the love between them now ready to fly.

Reading Group Guide

1. Aggie accuses Jess of being too nostalgic. What are the benefits and drawbacks of nostalgia? How do you see that throughout the book?

2. What did you think of Steph's rebellions? Why is she acting out?

3. Jess and Guy agree that jewelry is a window into a person's personality. What does Guy's leopard ring say about him? Jess's True Love Necklace? What messages are you sending with your own jewelry?

4. When Tim tries to be supportive of Jess, he comes across as smothering and undermines her independence. Discuss the ways that Jess balances her need for self-sufficiency with her chronic pain. Does her pride ever get in the way of help she genuinely needs?

5. Early in the book, Jess is determined to accept a grounded life and predictability. What do you think of her approach? If you were in her place, how would you have reacted to Nancy's accusation that Jess has lost her spirit?

6. What did you think of Tim? Were he and Jess a good match? How does he compare to Guy?

7. Bevan Floyd claims that a soul mate's job is to move us forward in some way, not to be a long-term companion. Do you agree? Which characters would you consider soul mates under Bevan's definition?

8. Do you think the True Love Necklace is actually magical, or does it just remind its wearers to be open-minded?

9. What effect do you think Anna's pining had on Nancy's upbringing?

10. Jess rankles at the idea of Aggie and Ed steering her life for her, even though she knows they mean well. Why does their meddling bother her so much? Why does Aggie feel like she has to take care of Jess?

11. Describe Jess's relationship with her father. What other work do you think they'll need to do to truly reconcile?

12. Do you think Jess made the right choice? What's next for her?

A Conversation
with the Author

Aggie meddles a great deal in Jess's life. Do you have nosy siblings?

I have an older sister and a younger brother. We're very close. My family are, in fact, my favorite people to hang out with, mainly because we laugh so much when we're together. I feel lucky. Over the years, I've learned this isn't something to take for granted. Also, it's taken some work. We were rotten to one another when we were teens, and when we were little, our parents had to be scrupulous about dividing everything equally between us. But now that we're grown with families of our own, we understand one another's differences and want the best for one another. Basically, we've found the sibling sweet spot. I believe Jess and Aggie are destined for it too. Even though their relationship is fairly fraught at times, it's driven by love, and as they grow through the story, their bond proves stronger than their differences.

Jess believes that jewelry expresses personality more than anything else. What kind of jewelry do you wear, and what message would Jess get from it?

I'm crazy about earrings. My mum recently gave me a box of her old earrings, and there are so many, I think I'll have a pair for every day of the year. I occasionally wear necklaces and bracelets, but I haven't the patience for rings. They get in the way when I'm typing or wrangling my children. I'm not bothered by value, status symbols, or designer labels. I like unusual, dramatic pieces, random vintage finds, hand-me-downs, costume rather than fine. Jess would no doubt think I'm arty, playful, and a little bit hippyish. I'm fascinated by the geology of precious and semiprecious stones, how they're formed from the earth. I own one diamond, on my engagement ring, which is black. My husband chose it. He did well—better than poor old Tim!—realizing I'd want something unconventional and expressive.

Do you share Bevan Floyd's definition of soul mates, that they incite change in us but are not meant to be our lifelong companions? Who would you call your soul mate with that definition?

Like many, I had the misconception that a soul mate is a person you fall most in love with or feel destined to be with. When I researched the concept, I was surprised to learn that one of the more traditional definitions is the idea of someone who comes into your life to incite meaningful change but doesn't stay. I've got to give it to my husband; he really feels like my soul mate. But if I'm going to go with Bevan's definition, then it's the boyfriend I had *before* I met my husband. We met through mutual friends and were instantly drawn to each other. He moved in with me within a few weeks. We went traveling together. We supported each other emotionally. We were good for each other. And then a few years later, we both reached a point where we had to start making decisions that would affect the rest of our lives—where we were going to live, careers, family, etc. Our good relationship had helped us become wiser and stronger, but it suddenly felt like we'd outgrown each other. We separated, and within months, we both met the people who would then become our lifelong companions.

The love triangle in this book feels more like a choice between two lifestyles for Jess. Did you ever hesitate when deciding which path she would take? Would you have chosen the same way?

I felt very aware that there would be readers who would want Jess to stick with reliable Tim—and for perfectly valid reasons. But the story I wanted to tell was one about taking risks, about breaking away from safety to find your own version of happy. It's a broader impulse than simply picking a lover—it's about identity, about learning not to be swayed by the judgment and influences of other people or conventional viewpoints about how women's lives should be. Jess has always had an appetite for adventure but is being pummelled by the popular opinion that she should be settling down and thinking about starting a family. The trauma of her accident is also adding pressure, the shame and regret of it making her question her choices. In the end, Guy wins because he offers her challenge, excitement, and liberation from her fears. Tim is not a bad option, but he's like a comfort blanket. I couldn't help thinking that if Jess were to stick with him, years later, it would all unravel. Would I make the same choice? Of course. I subscribe to the life's-too-short-not-to philosophy. I love traveling, and I'm a dreamer whose motto is *Seek and you shall discover!*

Throughout *The Lost and Found Necklace*, you draw a pretty firm line between comfort and passion. How do you strike the right balance between passion, spontaneity, and stability?

I think the key word is *balance*. Never too much of one thing, never too little of another. I pay attention to different aspects of my life—health, work, family, finances, fun—and I constantly aim to balance the scales. For instance, I run and do yoga, but I also eat chocolate like it's going out of fashion. I've followed my passion, building a career as a writer, but I also have a teaching qualification if finances ever get tight. A few years ago, I had a life-threatening health complication, perhaps echoed in Jess's accident, and this experience changed my outlook on life. It made me realize the precariousness of it all, the need to enjoy things while you can. So basically, I say go on that trip, buy that great pair of red shoes, eat that triple-scoop ice-cream cone. Then do what you need to do to balance the scales: buy travel insurance, save some money next month, and go on a five-mile hike. All of it! Do all of it!

The plot hinges on several characters who are devoted to preserving their history. Do you think of yourself as sentimental? How do you fulfill the duty of passing on history?

I'm ridiculously sentimental! I'm intrigued by historical objects, particularly everyday ones like clothing and furniture. One of my favorite aspects of writing about the True Love Necklace was

contemplating the possible histories of different pieces of jewelry—
the idea that a brooch or bracelet could have been worn to a first
date or anniversary dinner, chosen for the significant moments in
a person's life. I then caught on to the idea that an older piece of
jewelry could have several different owners, be witness to several
eras, and was tremendously excited at the thought. All that history
encapsulated in one tiny item. I guess it's no surprise that my house
is full of random antiques and hand-me-downs. I don't do minimal-
ism. One of my favorites is a mid-century Ercol table passed on to
me by a friend's mother. When I came to collect it from her, she
was worried about a scorch mark on the surface that had been made
when her children's gaming computer overheated way back in the
early eighties. She hoped I'd be able to sand it down and erase it, but
I never did because I love that scorch mark. It's part of the table's
story, like the rings of a tree. Now my children are inflicting their
own dents and scratches on this timeworn piece of furniture, but
somehow it survives. That's the other wonder of old things. They
were built to last!

**In your previous book, *The Second Chance Boutique*, you dis-
cussed your work for the Victoria and Albert Museum, writing
about archival wedding gowns. Did your work for the museum
influence this book as well? How did you research jewelry history?**

After writing about the Victoria and Albert Museum's wedding
dress collection, I had the privilege of writing about their collection
of art deco artifacts. This led me to their jewelry galleries, where
they had some stunning art deco belt clips and brooches, but my

eye was constantly drawn to the more ornate art nouveau designs that preceded them. So yes, I think this was the seed of *The Lost and Found Necklace*. When I finally started working on the book, the jewelry galleries had closed for refurbishment. It was painful, waiting months to get back in and ogle at all the lovely things. But I had fun going to auctions, browsing the antique markets on Portobello Road, reading up about jewelry design, and creating lavish Pinterest boards. I also enjoyed researching the locations and eras of history represented in the book, such as the nineteenth-century world fairs, where influential designers like Lalique would have showcased their work. One of my favorite research trips was to the site of the Crystal Palace in London. It's now a ruin, but it was tantalizing to imagine how it would have been. Thankfully, the internet helped bring it to life. There are many paintings and photographs of the original building online. And there is some wonderful footage of the 1889 Paris World Fair on YouTube, featuring the Eiffel Tower. I couldn't stop watching it. I also became mildly obsessed with photographs of faded Hollywood mansions. The research is fun and can get *very* distracting.

Did you have a favorite character to write? How do the characters you enjoy writing compare to the ones you enjoy reading?

I loved writing Jess, as she goes on such a journey and ultimately finds the courage to go against the grain of expectation. At the same time, I had fun writing Aggie, with her high-maintenance, control-freak ways. The love-hate tension that unfolds between the two of them was interesting to write, that the people you're closest to can be the ones who infuriate you most. I also loved writing about the different generations of Taylor women. I have lots of affection for poor old Anna, with her dashed dreams of Hollywood glory. I could write much more of her story! And then, of course, there's Guy, whose playfulness was fun to explore. Basically, it's hard to choose, because I enjoyed writing them all. In the characters I both write and read, I want that enjoyment. I don't want perfect heroes. I don't want super nice or vanilla bland. I want interesting energy and I want flaws: characters with commitment issues, insecurities, hot-headedness, impulsiveness, irrational jealousy, paranoia—all the stuff that makes people complicated and real. Then I want to see them grow, figure it out, do incredible things. And ultimately, I want to find myself rooting for them, punching the air with joy when they get what they need/want in the end.

Do you have a plan for your next project?

Absolutely. I get twitchy when I don't have at least one writing project on the go. I'm in the first draft stage of my latest project. It's nearly there, but I'm looking forward to a time when the foundations of the story are established and I can enjoy revising, editing, and polishing it into a final draft—my favorite part of the process. This time, I'm going for something bigger and a little darker, with a family saga at its heart.

What are you reading these days?

I always have several books on the go. I'm nearly finished with Donna Tartt's *The Goldfinch*, late to the party (I think I was intimidated by its length, because I'm a painfully slow reader), but I'm adoring it. I've also just read a UK book called *The Flatshare* by Beth O'Leary and *Where the Crawdads Sing* by Delia Owens. I thought it was wonderful. I loved the evocative setting and the underdog charisma of the main character, although I must admit I had to look up what a crawdad was! With my children, I read a lot of picture books and middle-grade fiction. Now that my daughter is older, I'm getting more into young adult fiction. I like to read the books she chooses, then we can discuss them. She's a horror enthusiast, so it's pushing me toward books I wouldn't normally pick up!

Acknowledgments

A huge thank-you to my editor, Shana Drehs, and the team at Sourcebooks for understanding the spirit of my writing so brilliantly, for making the books look beautiful, and for helping me remember my dumpsters from my skips. Another huge thanks to my agent, Sarah Such, for her style, her smart mind, and her ongoing support. As this is very much a story about inheritance, a thanks is certainly due to my maternal family—my cousins, aunts, uncles, and grandparents—the "Greens," whose heirlooms I grew up with and was fascinated by. And, of course, my mum, for her strength and pragmatism, for letting me rummage through her jewelry box when I was a kid, for handing down so many earrings I almost have a different pair for every day of the year! A thanks also to Mary and Sophie for humor, supper club, and wry conversations about Wanstead kitchens. To the V&A Museum for being a constant source of visual joy. Endless, unquantifiable thanks to Julian, Tove, Harper, and Emil, my Team Guido, especially when I have a deadline and "magic hour" becomes "magic fortnight." And lastly, a lifetime of gratitude to my incredible dad, who passed away during the writing of this book, whose influence is woven into every word and whose own backstory was more extraordinary than fiction.

About the Author

Louisa Leaman was born, was raised, and lives in Epping Forest near London. She writes contemporary romantic fiction. Her debut novel was *The Second Chance Boutique*. She studied art history at Leeds University, became a teacher working with children with special needs, then turned to writing after winning the *Times Educational Supplement*'s New Writer's Award. She has written a number of teaching guides and children's books for Hachette. She is currently working on her next book and also writes for the Victoria and Albert Museum, the world's leading museum of art and design. When she isn't busy writing or rearing three lively children, she paints portraits, goes running, and spends far too long browsing in vintage clothing shops.

The Second Chance Boutique

A heartwarming story about the power of the perfect dress—and the perfect love—to change your life.

Francesca Delaney has a knack for matching a bride-to-be with the wedding dress of her dreams. Her shop, The Whispering Dress, is no ordinary bridal boutique. Every gown is vintage, and the wedding dresses seem to share their stories with Francesca, pointing to which woman needs them next.

Fran credits her success to two rules: never covet a dress and never sell a dress that led to a doomed marriage. But then she finds a beautiful 1950s couture floor-length gown, and her obsession threatens to win out. The owner, however, would quite like the dark past of the dress to remain hidden forever…

"Utterly charming and sigh-worthy."
—Josie Silver, #1 *New York Times* bestselling author of *One Day in December*

For more Louisa Leaman, visit:
sourcebooks.com